D0436092

PATRICK CARMAN

RIVERS OF FIRE

THE SECOND BOOK OF

LITTLE, BROWN AND COMPANY
Books for Young Readers
New York Boston

Little, Brown and Company

Hachette Book Group USA
237 Park Avenue, New York, NY 10017
Visit our Web site at www.lb-kids.com

First Edition: May 2008

ISBN 978-0-316-16672-0

10 9 8 7 6 5 4 3 2 1

RRD-IN

Printed in the United States of America

For David Carlson at AGROS.ORG

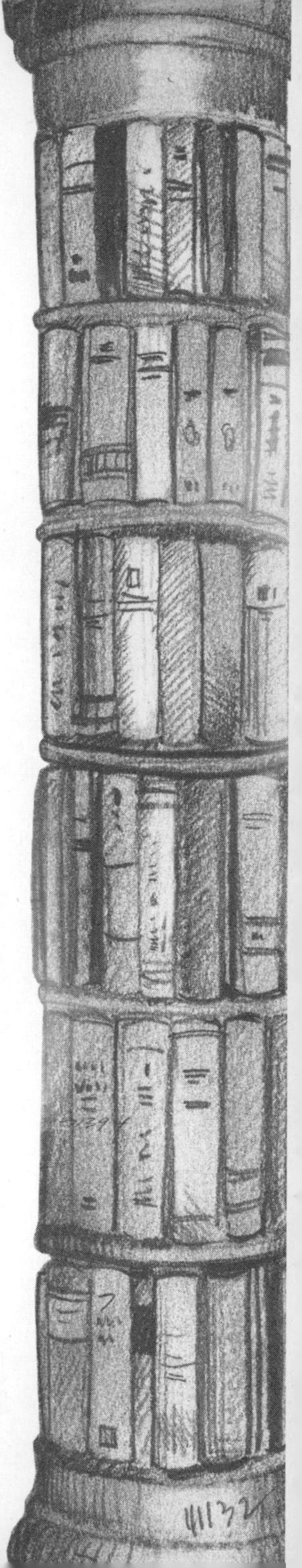

MEAD

TABLE OF
CONTENTS

THE WORLD OF ATHERTON viii

THE KEY CHARACTERS ON ATHERTON............xi

PART 1: EXODUS

CHAPTER 1: Edgar Returns Home 5

CHAPTER 2: Intruders 10

CHAPTER 3: Mysterious Companions 21

CHAPTER 4: Unseen Ladders.......................27

CHAPTER 5: A House Divided......................35

CHAPTER 6: Into the Hollow 41

CHAPTER 7: Dawn Breaks on a Changed World........50

CHAPTER 8: The Falling Rope......................59

CHAPTER 9: An Unnatural Quiet....................70

CHAPTER 10: Flying Rocks 78

CHAPTER 11: A Plan Set in Motion..................85

PART 2: MULCIBER

CHAPTER 12: Two Parties Unite 99

CHAPTER 13: The Secret at the Source 112

CHAPTER 14: The Yellow Line 122

CHAPTER 15: One Village Remains 131

CHAPTER 16: Mulciber 137

CHAPTER 17: Dr. Harding's Laboratory 147

CHAPTER 18: Unlocking Dr. Harding's Brain 153

CHAPTER 19: A Cleaner in the Grove 166

CHAPTER 20: A Motherless World 176

CHAPTER 21: The Cavern 185

CHAPTER 22: Inside Atherton 195

CHAPTER 23: Night in the Grove 199

CHAPTER 24: The Keeper of Atherton 206

PART 3: INVERSION

CHAPTER 25: A Storm in the Highlands 217

CHAPTER 26: The Nubian..........................224

CHAPTER 27: Across the Valley Floor................232

CHAPTER 28: Flight from the Grove..................241

CHAPTER 29: The Inferno...........................248

CHAPTER 30: A Thousand Cleaners..................261

CHAPTER 31: The Flood............................269

CHAPTER 32: Edgar's Departure.....................282

CHAPTER 33: Reunited.............................289

CHAPTER 34: One Year Later........................294

THE WORLD OF ATHERTON

A NOTE FROM THE AUTHOR

If you read The House of Power *but it's been a while since you turned the last page, you might benefit from this brief reintroduction to the story and the characters of Atherton. If, on the other hand, you know nothing of the climbing boy Edgar, the disappearance of Dr. Maximus Harding, or the collapse of the three levels of Atherton, then this introduction is essential reading. See you on the inside!*

Atherton is a made world, forged by the mind of a madman. It is inhabited by volunteers from the Dark Planet, a future Earth ravaged by pollution and overpopulation. Every inhabitant of Atherton has undergone a kind of memory retraining, leaving them under the assumption that Atherton is the only world that's ever been, the only place they've ever known.

Atherton was originally created on three circular levels, each one smaller than the level below it. The lowest level—the Flatlands—was a vast, barren, and largely unknown place. The middle level was known as Tabletop and contained most of Atherton's people, all of whom were poor laborers charged with maintaining the groves of trees or herds of livestock that provided all means of sustenance. At the top were the lush and beautiful Highlands, inhabited by the ruling class who controlled the sole source of water. These levels—the Flatlands, Tabletop, and the Highlands—were all separated by treacherous cliffs that established almost complete separation between the lands. But that distance exists no more.

I refer to these places in the past tense because when the second book of Atherton begins, the world of Atherton is not at all like it is described above. Throughout *The House of Power,* Atherton experiences catastrophic changes that alter everything about the world the characters live in. The Highlands descended until no cliffs remained and the ruling class was forced to come face-to-face with the people of Tabletop. The two lands were made one. Soon after, the joined lands of Tabletop and the Highlands moved down as well, until they came even with the Flatlands. When *Inversion* starts, the world of Atherton is, quite literally, flat. The images below, drawn by Dr. Maximus Harding, will help you better understand what happened to Atherton in *The House of Power.*

As Atherton changed, people from all three levels were

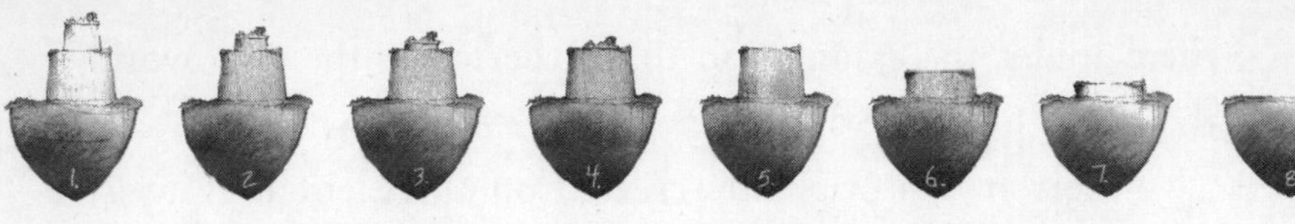

forced to confront one another, choose sides, and ultimately decide whether they would stand together or apart against a mounting threat that rose up from the Flatlands—a threat that draws near as *Rivers of Fire* begins.

Atherton is changing once more, in ways that even those who were involved in making this world could not have predicted. For there is only one who knows the whole truth—Dr. Maximus Harding—and he has been missing for a very long time. It is in this book that we shall discover the whole truth of the matter.

Patrick Carman

THE KEY CHARACTERS ON ATHERTON

Edgar

A young orphan who lived in the fig grove on Tabletop, climbing the cliffs of Atherton in secret. In his search for answers to Atherton's destiny, he became the only person on Atherton to have climbed above to the Highlands or below to the Flatlands. He is now allied with Dr. Kincaid and Vincent, mysterious dwellers of the Flatlands.

Samuel

A boy of the Highlands who is caught between two worlds by his relationship with Edgar and Isabel, two children of the grove on Tabletop. He is a smart boy, not physically strong, and his father has been missing and presumed dead for over a year. He lived within the House of Power until he escaped in search of Edgar.

Isabel

A wily and bright girl of the grove, she is thrust into a clash with the Highlands when it is discovered that she can use a sling with great skill. She passes on her knowledge and strikes a near lethal blow to Lord Phineus, the leader of the Highlands. When Inversion begins, Samuel and Isabel are secretly making their way back to the House of Power. They are searching for the only source of water on Atherton, its flow ceased by the evil hand of Lord Phineus.

Vincent

A protector of people on Atherton, he is charged with watching over Dr. Kincaid, a scientist trapped in the Flatlands. But when the three worlds of Atherton collide, Vincent's true mission is revealed: to help his companions find Dr. Harding and uncover the real nature of the world he created.

Dr. Maximus Harding

The creator of Atherton, a mysterious man of science who has been missing for years. Gone mad during the making of Atherton, Dr. Harding is thought to be alive but lost, both physically and mentally.

Dr. Luther Mead Kincaid

An old man of science, presumed at one time to be Edgar's father but later discovered to be a mentoring figure to Dr. Maximus Harding, Dr. Kincaid has lost control of the world he helped build. When *Rivers of Fire* begins, he is traveling with Vincent and Edgar in search of answers about the maker of Atherton.

Lord Phineus

The cruel ruler of the Highlands and all of Atherton. When *Rivers of Fire* begins, he has crept beneath the House of Power by a secret way known only to a few.

Sir Emerik

Lord Phineus's longtime ally, he is also a conniving and wicked man with secret aspirations to rule all of Atherton.

Horace

The lead guard in the House of Power, he has turned against Lord Phineus and is mounting a plan of his own to unify the people of Atherton against the coming threat: violent, monstrous creatures from the Flatlands known as Cleaners, once trapped in the Flatlands, now free to roam all of Atherton in search of food.

Wallace

The leader of the people of the Village of Sheep, one of the three villages on Tabletop. Wallace is the wisest and most peaceful of all the leaders.

Maude

A feisty woman from the Village of Rabbits, one of the three villages on Tabletop. She previously helped Edgar escape Sir Emerik and becomes one of a handful of leaders of the free world along with Horace and Wallace.

PART

ONE

EXODUS

There are some who can live without wild things, and some who cannot.

A Sand County Almanac
Aldo Leopold

CHAPTER 1

EDGAR RETURNS HOME

It was the middle of the night when Edgar entered the fig grove alone. A heavy quiet filled the air, and he wondered if everyone was sleeping, unaware of the approaching danger. He touched the trunks of the trees as he went, and this helped him find his way through the darkness. Though he'd only been gone a few days, he had a deep feeling of having come home after a long time away.

His first few steps into the grove reminded Edgar of what it had felt like to sneak home after a night of secret climbing. How long had it been since the Highlands were looming far above on a pillar of stone? He couldn't remember for sure. And when was the last time he'd climbed, *really* climbed, high into the grey evening sky against a forbidden wall? He couldn't remember that, either. Time seemed to have lost its meaning.

"Don't move another step!"

Edgar froze. Someone dropped out of a tree directly in front of him. He had let himself drift aimlessly into a tangled web of thoughts and emotions, and now he'd been caught.

There was hardly any light at all, only a dim whisper of dark grey, but Edgar could see a man carrying a club in one hand and a rock in the other. But it occurred to him that he knew the grove better than anyone and could make a quick escape if he wanted, especially at night.

"Edgar?" asked the man. He bobbed up and down like a rabbit, trying to catch an angle of light in the trees as he sized up the boy before him.

"Yes. It's me," said Edgar. The two did not know each other so much as know *of* each other.

"I've been gone awhile, but I'm back. There are some things I need to tell the people in the village. Can you let me pass?"

The man let the club he was holding hang down at the side of his leg and peered through the low branches of the trees, then his eyes settled back on the boy.

"Don't expect things to be the same as when you left," said the man. He was tired and unwilling to tell a young boy bad news. "Go that way." He pointed with the club toward the village.

Edgar watched the man pocket the rock he'd held and clumsily make his way back up into the limbs of the tree. As Edgar walked past, the man spoke.

"Is it true you climbed all the way to the top of the cliffs and back again?"

Edgar nodded in the darkness. "I did."

"And to the very bottom—to the Flatlands—you climbed down there as well?"

"I did," answered Edgar. It seemed that word of his adventures had spread.

"I don't believe you," grumbled the man. And he didn't. It had been so far to the bottom, and so difficult a stone surface to climb. It didn't seem possible that *anyone*—let alone a boy of eleven or twelve—could climb down.

Edgar walked on, feeling suddenly in a rush to finish his task and get back to Dr. Kincaid and Vincent. He had two similar encounters along the way, in which men dropped from trees, asked him questions, and let him pass. Each of them knew Edgar by sight if not by name. He had been a quiet orphan boy from the grove, a good worker, a familiar face. There were stories circulating concerning his recent whereabouts that were hard to believe.

When Edgar reached the clearing before the village, he spotted a surprising number of wakeful men and women moving in the shadows of open fires. He did not see Mr. Ratikan among them and began to wonder where the master of the grove was hiding.

Edgar stepped out into the open of the clearing and shouted toward the villagers. "It's me, Edgar!"

A small group approached, a single lit torch among them, and soon the two parties were shouting back and forth as the gap closed between them.

"Edgar?"

"Yes, it's me!"

"Where have you been hiding?"

When Edgar didn't answer, another question filled the air.

"Have you seen Isabel?"

This question scared Edgar. As he met the group in the middle of the clearing, he saw that the man holding the torch was Charles, Isabel's father.

"Have you seen her, Edgar?" he asked, bending down on one knee. Charles knew his daughter liked the boy and had been hoping the two were together.

"I haven't seen her in days," said Edgar. "Where is she?"

Charles had the look of a man whose last hope had been dashed.

"She's gone," he said. The voice was cracked and dry, full with emotion.

"What do you mean, *gone?*"

Charles shrugged and Edgar thought the man's shoulders looked unbearably heavy. A dead silence enveloped the clearing. Edgar's mind raced to all the places Isabel could be, for he couldn't bring himself to believe Isabel was lost. Charles put his arm around the boy and the group began walking back to the village.

"Where have you been?" asked Charles, stopping short and looking down at Edgar. "There are rumors of a climbing boy . . ."

Edgar took a moment to breathe deeply the smell of the grove before answering. The place smelled dry and dusty, like it was gasping for relief from a waterless world it couldn't escape.

And there was something more. Though it was dark, Edger felt a sense of discomfort at the thought of looking up and finding the Highlands were no longer there. Without the cliffs, danger lurked from in front and behind the grove in ways that it never had before, because the world of Atherton was flat.

"I've been to the top, before the Highlands fell," said Edgar. "And I've been to the bottom, before the Flatlands rose up." Edgar looked up to where the Highlands had once been. "But I suppose that's little more than a legend now, because all the cliffs are gone." Somehow, Edgar got the distinct feeling that Charles *wanted* to believe him.

They continued on beneath the canopy of trees and when they arrived at the shattered remains of the village, a small group gathered near a fire—Charles, Edgar, and a few others. Edgar told them everything he was meant to, leaving nothing out. He was surprised to find they already had knowledge of the Cleaners, though Edgar's description of their size and viciousness startled them. For his part, Edgar heard of Mr. Ratikan's demise and the battle with the Highlands, all new information he could barely bring himself to believe.

But even the knowledge of Mr. Ratikan's death paled by comparison to the news of Isabel's disappearance. Edgar asked over and over again about her—where she had been seen last, to whom she had spoken, whatever was known. The more he learned, the more he had a sense that she was not only alive, but that she may not be alone. He suspected that Isabel had found Samuel, his friend from the Highlands—and that they had gone somewhere they should not have.

CHAPTER 2

INTRUDERS

"I think we fell asleep."

"I believe you're right."

Samuel and Isabel were hiding in an abandoned drain carved into the earth near the wall that surrounded the House of Power. They had been lying in the narrow space for several hours, like a long snake that began with Samuel's head and ended with Isabel's feet. With the absence of water on Atherton, a profound thirst had settled on them both.

"It's still dark outside," said Samuel, his dry voice only a whisper. "We should keep moving before light begins to creep back into the courtyard. We just need to be quiet and careful."

"If you say so," said Isabel, but she was unsure. She wished Edgar were there with them. Isabel had always felt safe in the grove when he was near, and she missed his presence. As Samuel

started moving slowly forward through the drain, she began to wonder if their search for water would come to a bad end.

"Where are you going?" asked Isabel. She could hear him shifting back and forth and moving away from her.

"Come on," answered Samuel. "It's late and the courtyard will be empty."

Samuel felt a surprising confidence about his plans to find the hidden source of water within the House of Power. He had spent his entire childhood sneaking around this place and he knew its secrets. And more than that, in recent days he'd finally broken free of a long-endured fear of failure that he'd experienced since the loss of his father. He felt a new and unexpected boldness as the night grew deeper.

Isabel had no idea where they were going, but the two went on in silence, dirt falling all around them as they proceeded. The drain rose slowly before them in the dark until Samuel came to a place surrounded by something much harder than dirt.

"This will be a tight squeeze," whispered Samuel. "Try not to make any more noise than you must."

They had come to where the drain cut through the wall around the House of Power. Samuel reached out with his arms and gently shimmied back and forth, making slow progress until his fingers touched the hard edge of stone on the other side. He pulled as hard as he could, feeling bits of falling rock stinging his eyes, until he made it to the other side of the wall, where the drain widened to a space big enough for both of them.

Isabel's smaller build allowed her to move quickly, and soon she was standing next to Samuel in the dark, where they faced each other in the small space. They were uncomfortably close.

"This is the end," Samuel said in a quiet voice Isabel could barely hear. "Follow me and don't make a sound." The two stood silent for another moment as Samuel listened for the echo of footsteps overhead.

Then Isabel heard a grating sound as crumbs of dirt filled the air. Samuel held a square stepping stone from within the House of Power. He pushed it aside carefully, put his hands over the ledge, and pulled himself up with great effort.

The top of Samuel's head poked out into the courtyard of the House of Power and he scanned the area. There were dots of light here and there where torches had been left glowing.

"Are you sure this is a good idea?" whispered Isabel. The moment of entering the House of Power, where Lord Phineus ruled, had come. Isabel had always enjoyed a sense of bravado in the shelter of the grove, but this was different. She wasn't sure she wanted to get so close to something that felt of darkness and evil.

"Take my feet and push me up," said Samuel. He was holding steady above her, but in past adventures of his own he'd only gone down the drain, not up it, then he'd snuck back into the House of Power through the gate.

Isabel hesitated. She was farther away from home than she'd ever been, doing something that could get her into real trouble. What was she doing with this boy from the Highlands?

"We've got to go now, Isabel—I mean *right* now."

Isabel took Samuel's feet in her hands without thought or emotion, almost as if someone else was doing it and she was only watching it happen, and pushed until Samuel was halfway out and only his legs and rear end dangled wildly at the top of the hole. A moment later he had scurried out entirely.

Just then something happened that made Isabel think she'd done the wrong thing. Samuel looked down at her for a split second with panic in his eyes, and then he placed the square stone back over the hole. Isabel was all alone in the darkness of the drain.

Sir Emerik was sure he'd heard something. There had been a lot on his mind and he hadn't slept but a few hours before waking in the middle of the night, and yet he felt certain he wasn't imagining the noise. It had sounded like a piece of stone falling into a slot from a corner of the courtyard. What could it be at such a late hour but the sound of someone sneaking around?

He stood calm and unmoving, listening for the sound to repeat. Though it didn't come again, Sir Emerik was a highly suspicious sort of man, and once his senses were alerted it was hard for him to turn them off. *Something's not right. I must go and see for myself.*

As he moved ever so quietly along the winding path of the courtyard, Sir Emerik pondered his own grim circumstances.

His home, the Highlands, had come crashing down and now sat even with Tabletop. Control over the House of Power, which sat alone at the center of the Highlands, seemed precarious. It was at once a time of great danger and a moment of opportunity. But first he would have to deal with Lord Phineus. And there was also the boy Samuel, who had escaped unexpectedly from his grasp. *Samuel might cause me trouble. He knows far too much.*

He would need a torch in order to search the courtyard properly, and this was a bit of a problem for Sir Emerik. He touched the scabs on his head and his eye began to twitch. Lately it happened involuntarily whenever he came within a few feet of a flame. He cursed the boy Edgar in his mind, remembering how Edgar had burned all the hair off his head. It was a memory he couldn't shake. Sir Emerik took the torch with a shaky hand, holding it as far away from his face as he could. The flickering firelight made all the colors in the courtyard turn a bleary shade of orange.

Before long, he was standing near the stone that Samuel had moved to enter the House of Power. Isabel could hear him standing directly overhead on the stone. She had a terrible thought that whoever it was might break through and fall on top of her. Or maybe the person standing above her knew of the old hidden drain cover and was getting ready to slide it off. She kept very still, barely breathing as she waited for the person to leave.

From his hiding place, Samuel could see Sir Emerik as his

boots clicked back and forth on the floor of the courtyard. The landscape within the courtyard was full with deep green rows of hedges and bushes trimmed into curious shapes, and it was easy for a small person like Samuel to encase himself within the grasp of branches or vines, completely hidden from view. Samuel's anxiety rose as he watched Sir Emerik pause as if he'd found something. He had heard one stone sound different than the rest, as if it were covering a hollow space.

Sir Emerik lowered himself to the ground, carefully whipping his red robe behind him, and then with one hand he ran his fingers around the edge of the stone, feeling for a way to remove it. As he looked at the dancing flames of the torch in his other hand, his eye twitched, moving him to set the torch down next to him where it burned dimly on the cold floor.

Samuel didn't know what to do when Sir Emerik took hold of the square stone by its corners. It crossed his mind to bolt from within the hedge and run through the courtyard to distract Sir Emerik, but he couldn't risk anyone knowing of his presence in the House of Power. This thought froze him where he hid until Sir Emerik had removed the stone and was peering down into the drain.

Sir Emerik held the torch down into the hole, but he didn't see anything, at least not anything he didn't expect to see. He sniffed the air and touched the dirt with his hands, then pushed the stone back where it had been. This time he noticed small dirty fingerprints on the square slab. Sir Emerik looked up, suddenly sure. *Samuel has returned by this secret way. He must be found and gotten rid of.*

Sir Emerik rose to his feet, waving the flame over the hedge as he searched the courtyard. "I know you're in here, Samuel," he said softly in a raspy voice. "You can't hide from me. You should know that by now." He remembered how he'd found Samuel only a few days before with a secret book, how the book had foretold the Highlands's descent into Tabletop, and how he'd captured the boy and locked him away in the House of Power. "Come out and we'll go to see your mother in the kitchen. She'll be very glad to see you."

The idea of finding his mother seized Samuel and he nearly burst out of his hiding place. Samuel could hear and feel Sir Emerik getting closer. A few more seconds and he would be caught. He was ready to spring out of the hedge, to run into the twisting array of creeping plants. But just as Samuel was about to move there came another voice, much louder and meaner than Sir Emerik's.

"Emerik!"

The booming sound of Lord Phineus calling for Sir Emerik filled the air as he shouted from the window of the main chamber. Hidden in a part of the courtyard that lay beneath a thick canopy of vine-covered trellises, Sir Emerik was momentarily torn. Though he felt sure he was close to finding the concealed boy, he knew he should not keep his master waiting.

"You can't hide from me for long, Samuel," said Sir Emerik. His eye twitched once more at the sight of the flaming torch in his hand. "You should come out now and save me the trouble of having to find you."

"Emerik!"

The howling voice roared again, and this time Sir Emerik didn't hesitate. The anger was growing in the lord of the House of Power, and it would not do to keep him waiting a second longer than he had to. He took one more look at the hedge, cursed the boy who hid there, and moved off toward the main chamber.

When Samuel felt sure he was alone, he crept out and removed the square slab of rock that covered the drain. He couldn't see very far down, so he whispered Isabel's name and waited. Nothing.

The House of Power was stirring from the sound of Lord Phineus's voice, and soon people would be everywhere. Just when Samuel felt ready to jump into the hole and search for Isabel, he heard her moving around. Once his eyes adjusted to the dim light, he could see her head poking out from farther back in the drain where it curved and narrowed.

"I am *so* ready to get out of here," said Isabel. Her face was smeared with dirt and dead leaves hung in her tangled black hair. Her dark, thick brows lay heavy over her eyes as she looked up at Samuel.

"Better hurry," whispered Samuel, glancing between the drain and the courtyard. "We've almost missed our chance."

Either Isabel was heavier than he'd expected or he was weaker than he'd hoped; regardless, it was a mighty struggle pulling Isabel out of the drain and into the courtyard. She slid back down more than once before she was finally able to get her elbows over the edge and hoist herself the rest of the way out.

Samuel quickly moved the stepping stone back over the passage and grabbed Isabel's hand. "He knows we're here," he said, pulling her along the vine-covered wall. "But he'll be gone awhile."

"I hope he didn't send a guard to do his looking for him," said Isabel.

"He wouldn't do that," said Samuel. "Sir Emerik wants me dead, and none of the guards would kill me if they found me. They'd take me straight to Lord Phineus, which is just what Sir Emerik is afraid of."

Isabel started to ask him why Sir Emerik wanted him dead, but Samuel silenced her with a raised hand. Then he was running, waving to Isabel to follow. They swished past winding hedges, slithered under vines, and crawled beneath low, rounded walls until they reached the other side of the courtyard. Samuel heard the sound of boots on stone coming near and seized Isabel's hand once more, pulling her down into a sea of thick ivy that lay before a bone white wall dancing with shadows.

When the guard had passed, they made their way up a set of darkened stairs to a narrow hall with a rail of grey stone that ran the length of one wall. At the very end of the hall was one of Samuel's favorite hiding places, an alcove buried in thick ivy. The ivy crept down the side of the wall like dark green water, filling the space as high as their heads with waves of tiny leaves. It felt to Isabel as if a thousand tiny green hands were pulling her inside as she crept forward into the alcove.

"I wish Edgar was here," said Isabel, feeling the itchy touch of leaves against her face.

Samuel peered out from their hiding place, which had a commanding view of the whole courtyard and the guard towers at the gate. He was thinking of the place they would soon be going, to a set of stairs leading up to the main chamber, in which Mead's Head could be found.

CHAPTER 3

MYSTERIOUS COMPANIONS

Edgar walked quietly along the unlit path that snaked between the houses of the village. The hour had turned very late but only a few from the grove had settled in for a fragment of much-needed sleep before dawn. Some were scattered through the trees trying their best to keep a watchful eye on the sprawling grove, a nearly impossible task since it offered a thousand points of entry. The rest were hastily making plans, fashioning weapons, or piecing together places to hide.

Edgar did none of these things. He had said all that he'd been instructed to about how Tabletop had collapsed into the Flatlands. He'd told them about the approaching threat of the monsters known as Cleaners and the need to get ready by making spears and barricades, and now they were preoccupied with the preparations. It was time for him to go, for he was expected elsewhere. Edgar slipped away unnoticed, taking great care not to be seen or followed. Soon he had made his way to an outer line of trees where no guards were posted.

Edgar rubbed the bandaged nub where his pinky finger had once been and it stung sharply; then he made a fist with the hand and squeezed with the fingers he had left. It hurt, but not that much. His shoulder was still sore from the catastrophic fall he'd taken when he'd climbed down into the Flatlands, but it felt remarkably healed. His body wanted to climb if only a cliff could be found.

After a time Edgar spotted a dim figure approaching cautiously from the direction of the Village of Rabbits. The person carried no light to speak of and would have been visible only to those looking for him.

"Is that you, Vincent?" whispered Edgar. He was aware of the dryness of his throat when he spoke and of how thirsty he was. The advancing shape stopped short of the grove and Edgar heard the muffled sound of one man bumping into another in the night. It had looked like one man, but there were two, walking single file toward the line of trees.

"It's me, Edgar," said Edgar, sure that he'd found his two friends once more.

"It's just the boy," said Dr. Kincaid. "There's no need to panic."

"I didn't panic," said Vincent, who stood in front and had stopped short. "You shouldn't follow so closely behind."

"Come away from the clearing," said Edgar. "This is a good spot, as I'd hoped."

Soon the three were sitting beneath a tree whispering about their errands. Dr. Kincaid and Vincent, Edgar's two mysterious companions from the Flatlands, had gone in different directions as they'd approached the grove—each to warn one of the other two distant villages about the coming Cleaners—while Edgar stayed to inform those in the grove.

"How did it go?" asked Dr. Kincaid, holding out a leather bag full of water. Edgar gratefully took it and eagerly began drinking. "Not too much, Edgar. It's all we have."

Edgar returned the bag of water and watched as Dr. Kincaid took a small sip. He was surprisingly alert for such an old man at so late an hour. He'd walked all the way to the Village of Sheep and back again in the night, which would have been several hours on foot, and yet Dr. Kincaid seemed reasonably well rested.

"They're not used to seeing me as someone with information they could use," said Edgar. "It takes awhile to convince people of certain things that are hard to believe."

"Like monsters coming from the Flatlands into the grove?" asked Dr. Kincaid.

Edgar nodded, stretching his arms up over his head and feeling the dull roar of pain in his shoulder. He had the peculiar feeling of being exhausted and full of energy at the same time. He had only managed a couple hours of rest in the village, but he felt oddly alive. Maybe it was all the food he'd eaten or the unexpected time of rest at Dr. Kincaid's home.

"That man Wallace in the Village of Sheep is a good shepherd," said Dr. Kincaid. "They're lucky to have him, though it's hard to imagine they'll be able to stay in their village when the Cleaners find it."

"And you were right about Maude," added Vincent. Edgar had pointed Vincent in the direction of the inn and the strong-willed woman he would find there. "She was quick to take the lead in the Village of Rabbits."

Dr. Kincaid handed Edgar a chunk of Cleaner from his bag. The outside of the meat had dried in the night, but it burst with squishy liquid once Edgar broke the surface with his teeth.

"How long do you think it will take for the Cleaners to find this place?" asked Edgar. He had already gobbled up half the food and was wiping one of his hands in the dying grass at his feet.

Vincent looked off toward his old home. "I think they'll go where there are more animals first." It was the beginning of a logical if not gruesome assessment from the man who'd spent years protecting Dr. Kincaid. "They'll go first to where they've always gone—near the Village of Rabbits and the Village of Sheep. They've grown used to finding lots of bones near the cliffs there. My guess is they'll follow their noses to those places first and only stumble into the grove by accident sometime after that."

"That's good, I suppose." The faces of Briney and Maude in the Village of Rabbits came to Edgar's mind, and he felt terrible for being relieved that their village would likely be attacked before his own. "I mean, at least it will be good for the grove. They'll have a little more time."

"Did you tell them what I told you to say?" Dr. Kincaid asked Edgar.

"I told them to make as many spears as they could and to build fortresses from stones if they could find them," said Edgar. "And I told them not to use wood, because the Cleaners would eat right through it, and that stone was the only thing that would hold them back."

"And?" said Vincent, eyebrows raised as if testing the boy.

"And I told them not to try to hide up in the trees, because the Cleaners would knock the trees down. I also told them they could eat the Cleaners, if only they could kill them with the spears in the right way, and that the Cleaners were good to eat even though they were terrible to look at."

"Very good!" cried Vincent. "You've done well. All we can do now is hope they heed our warning and prepare themselves. One dead Cleaner can feed a lot of people, and if they can protect themselves and fight well, who knows what might happen?"

Edgar felt a growing sense of dread as Vincent tried to hide the truth. He knew that the Cleaners were huge, vicious creatures. Could the people of the village really survive if a thousand angry Cleaners found the grove?

Dr. Kincaid could see the boy wanted to stay, to fight and protect the people of the place where he'd spent most of his life. "Your path leads out of the grove, Edgar," Dr. Kincaid reminded him. "To the House of Power."

Maybe the House of Power really did hold the key to saving

Tabletop, and this gave Edgar hope. But he felt another pull to the House of Power: Isabel and Samuel. Edgar had a strong feeling that this was where both of them had gone. Friends can feel such things in times of peril, as if a long, thin string holds them carefully together, tugging at one another through the open space of a dangerous world.

The three of them were about to leave when Edgar turned back and pulled a clump of green figs from one of the trees. The figs weren't ripe yet and they were still attached to the vine. Edgar had a chunk of the slimy Cleaner remaining in his other hand, which he'd been saving for this moment. He put the Cleaner into a small sack made of sheepskin which he'd taken from the village, then pushed the gathering of figs down into the squishy meat of the Cleaner in the sack.

"We'd better be getting on," called Vincent. "It's a world of chaos we live in now, and we need to travel as far as we can under cover of night."

Sealing off the bag with a string, Edgar placed it in his pocket, and the three travelers went out into the open toward the Highlands.

CHAPTER 4

UNSEEN LADDERS

Lord Phineus had recently emerged from a treacherous journey into a world beneath the House of Power that had not ended well. He had screamed twice for Sir Emerik and was growing impatient. Gazing out into the night he could not see that the Highlands had begun sliding down *inside* of Atherton, that his once lofty home was now the lowest place of all. Already the Highlands were three feet lower than they had been when he ventured into Mead's Hollow. There were precious few who knew this secret, and Lord Phineus was not among them.

When Sir Emerik arrived outside the door to the main chamber he wasn't exactly sure what to expect. Lord Phineus offered no greeting. Instead, he began speaking as if Sir Emerik had been there all along.

"The problem is, you can't see where we're supposed to go," said Lord Phineus. "Only I know where it is. No one else."

Lord Phineus was covered in a cold sweat, his eyes swollen and rimmed in red. The frenetic and edgy way in which he spoke made Sir Emerik wonder if he was in the presence of a lunatic.

"Lord, what's happened to you? Are you all right?"

In truth, Sir Emerik had not the least concern over the well-being of his master. In fact, if Lord Phineus were to take ill, it would be all the easier to do away with him. But why had the man's demeanor changed so drastically in only a few short hours? Lord Phineus had always been so calm, logical, and calculating; now he was rambling, pacing, and speaking near nonsense.

"Did you hear what I said?" asked Lord Phineus. "No one else knows!"

"I'm sorry. I don't understand what you mean," said Sir Emerik. He was aware, suddenly, of all the candles in the room and how the light from them cast shadows on the walls showered with cascading ivy. It made the room feel alive with evil. Sir Emerik's eye twitched at the sight of so much fire so near.

"What's that absurd thing you're doing there?" said Lord Phineus. "That terrible twitch. Stop it at once."

Sir Emerik breathed deeply and stared at the floor. The twitching stopped, and when he looked up again Lord Phineus was bent over, scratching vigorously at his leg. "Something wrong, my lord?"

Lord Phineus's eyes were inflamed with blood. He wasn't feeling at all well. "The Crat," he mumbled. "I should have killed them a long time ago."

This made no sense to Sir Emerik, but he was more and more pleased to see that the man before him was not in his right mind. It might be easier than he'd thought to take control.

"There is yet another problem that must be overcome," said Lord Phineus. His mind seemed to be righting itself, if only a little, as he stood up and leaned heavily against the wall. "We'll need water to survive."

"But we have all the water we need!" Sir Emerik was almost too animated in his response. He had understood this to be a problem already solved.

"I've told you before of the secret place where the water finds its beginning," said Lord Phineus. Sir Emerik had to work very hard not to show his anticipation. Lord Phineus should have known deceit when it was before him, but it seemed that he did not. "The time has come for you to know of this place."

Sir Emerik couldn't stop a small rise at one corner of his mouth at the notion. Having power over the water had long been the one missing piece in his plans.

"Are there guards who can maintain order in the absence of us both? This will take some time."

Sir Emerik tried to contain his glee. "There are, lord. There's Tyler, a protégé of mine, a very good man at the gate. And there's Horace—you remember Horace, don't you?"

Sir Emerik was testing Lord Phineus to see just how mad he had become. Horace had been chief guard here for a long time, but he had been banned from the House of Power, like so many others, after the Highlands came even with Tabletop. He and the others had families who would gobble up resources and split their allegiance to Lord Phineus.

"What kind of absurd question is that?" said Lord Phineus. He was scratching his leg again and gazing knowingly at Sir Emerik. "You think I'm losing my mind."

Sir Emerik hesitated. In the split second of silence Lord Phineus removed a long blade from his boot, shot across the room with alarming speed, and pinned Sir Emerik against the door. The sharp edge of the weapon lay horizontal against Sir Emerik's chin.

"I know your intentions. You should not imagine them fulfilled."

The blade was pushed harder against Sir Emerik's chin and it broke skin. Sir Emerik whimpered as if he were a small, scared boy of six or seven. It had never crossed his mind that Lord Phineus might know of his deception.

"There are many lines and ladders in my mind," said Lord Phineus. "Yellow lines and ladders that are mine alone. They are hopelessly out of your reach."

Though his master was beginning to sound unstable again, Sir Emerik was strangely mesmerized by the voice as he felt blood dripping down his chin. It occurred to him that the world's radical change was a prophetic sign that it was time for him to seize power, and as long as he had water and no Cleaners could get into the House of Power, his world would be better than it ever had been before.

Lord Phineus stepped back, releasing Sir Emerik. He casually put the blade back in his boot and scratched his leg once more, as if the encounter had never occurred.

"You will come with me," Lord Phineus said at length. "And do as I say." Sir Emerik nodded in agreement as he held back the blood dripping from his chin.

Lord Phineus took hold of the statue that stood in the main chamber. Mead's Head. He turned the stone head right, left, and right again. Hearing the familiar click on the floor behind him, he turned and faced Sir Emerik with a grave and weary look on his face.

"I've lost control of the water," said Lord Phineus. "And you must help me get it back."

While Lord Phineus and Sir Emerik disappeared into Mead's Hollow in the dead of night there were two others who discovered that the Highlands were descending into the center of Atherton. Until then, only Samuel and Isabel had known for sure. But that was about to change.

"What do you smell?" asked Horace.

"I'm not sure what I smell," answered his companion, whose name was Gill. "Something . . . *different.*"

Gill was a wiry man, quick and stealthy on his feet. He had the unusual habit of sniffing the air around him in order to

MEAD'S HEAD

HOLD FIRMLY
THEN TWIST !!!

1.

2.

3.

43780?

33128?

REMEMBER
LISTEN FOR THE
"CLICK"!

MEAD

STAIRS TO
HOLLOW

IT IS
HERE

gain any insight he could, especially at night. His larger than average nose raised into the air as his long neck bobbed rhythmically from side to side. Gill had the look of an animal that had smelled something unexpected but could not see it. If he had ever experienced it for himself, he would have said the air smelled like a dirt road after a hard rain. But there had been no rain on Atherton—not ever—and he tried his best to place the smell somewhere simpler in his mind.

"Something is wet," he whispered into the night.

Horace moved forward cautiously with Gill close behind, and with each step the smell grew heavier around them. When they came to the very place where the Highlands had once risen into the sky, Gill knelt down and felt the moist new edge of Tabletop. He held the gritty mud on his fingers to his nose.

For a moment he thought they'd stumbled into a place where the two lands hadn't met flat against each other, but his mind was quickly changed. The Highlands had moved down inside of Atherton about the length of a man's arm, and putting his fingers at the seam on the bottom, Horace felt it ever so slowly grinding. He gazed to his left—across the deep grey of night—and could see a dark line of land running long and crooked.

Horace stood, feeling his lungs swell with the knowledge of a changing world.

"I must go to the House of Power and reason with them," he said. "We can't stay in the Highlands any longer. This place must be forsaken."

It was a rather gloomy way of putting things, and Gill shuddered as he stood.

"But what about those creatures—the Cleaners? This could be a good development. It could separate us from them."

Horace was unmoved. Staying within the sinking Highlands seemed to him the worse of two approaching evils. What would become of a people trapped in a sinking world with cliffs rising all around? There was something altogether wrong about the idea of being trapped, of descending into inescapable darkness. And there was something else, something deeper in his awakening soul. He felt a bottomless guilt at the very thought of leaving those in Tabletop alone to battle a coming enemy they could never defeat alone. The Highlands had to be left behind, because if they weren't, then Tabletop and everyone in it would be destroyed. All of Atherton would fail.

"If we are to learn anything from the past," he said, turning toward Gill with the best argument he could craft in short order, "we should know better than to think the Highlands will stop. Soon it may be too late to get the horses and the families out, and then what? Everyone will be trapped in a growing darkness, and who's to say the Cleaners couldn't find a way in? We have to escape this place before our chance has passed."

CHAPTER 5
A HOUSE DIVIDED

"You there!"

The sound of the voice startled Samuel and Isabel. The man who'd shouted the words was outside the wall, where the two could not see.

"I know that voice," whispered Samuel. "That's Horace!"

Isabel put her finger to her lips and pulled a hard, dry fig from her pocket, expecting something terrible to happen at any moment and getting ready to fight. The two stayed very still and listened to the voices in the dark.

"Get back!" screamed the guard stationed in the tower atop the gate. He was holding a sizable rock over his head. Samuel could see him looking down at Horace, a man who had, until only recently, been the main guard in the House of Power.

"Put the rock down, Joseph." Horace spoke with great authority. "It's me."

The man with the rock let his arm hang loose. He was a young man, only twenty-five, and he had no family to speak of.

"Horace? That you, Horace?"

Isabel leaned her head out of the ivy and glanced over the stone rail where she saw another guard running through the courtyard with a torch.

"Things are getting awfully busy around here," she said. "Maybe this is our best chance to find the source of water. That is, if you truly know where it is."

This came as something of a surprise to Samuel. *Can she really think I've lied to her?* She appeared to be losing confidence in him.

"Let's listen for another minute," said Samuel. "Then we'll go."

The situation at the wall grew more complicated as Samuel and Isabel looked on.

"It's Horace!" shouted Joseph from the tower.

"Get rid of him!" said the other who had run up with the torch. He was a little older than Joseph but not nearly as seasoned a guard as Horace. His name was Tyler.

Joseph turned back to Horace. "You know I can't let you in," he said. "Lord Phineus won't allow it."

"I need to speak with him," said Horace. His voice was stern and even. He knew the man above him well enough to know that he'd very much like to open the gate but that it might cost him his life if he did.

“I’m sorry, Horace, but he can’t be disturbed. It’s the middle of the night. Maybe if you come back tomorrow.”

Horace was a man in possession of a thunderously loud voice, deep and powerful and made for distance. He liked to use it to its full effect.

“You will open this gate and take me to Lord Phineus!”

Joseph was torn between the escalating demands of the men on either side of the wall. “Wait a moment. Both of you calm down,” he said softly, as if his quietness might bring things under control. But Horace only yelled louder, until finally Tyler could take no more and climbed up next to Joseph.

“Are you sure we shouldn’t be going?” asked Isabel. “I can’t imagine a better diversion.”

“Just another moment,” said Samuel. “I’ve a feeling this is important.”

“Horace, you must leave this place at once!” said Tyler when he’d arrived at the top.

“I have something to say, and I will be heard!”

Soon everyone who remained in the House of Power was awake and wondering what was going on outside. Even Samuel’s mother had come running from her room at the sound of Horace’s voice. She and a group of others stood by the giant gates and clamored for information.

“That’s my mother!” said Samuel, seeing her within the crowd below. Isabel had the feeling that Samuel might suddenly try to run or call to her without thinking about the consequences.

“You know she’s alive and well,” said Isabel, responding

with quiet force. "Trying to talk to her won't help us find the water. It will only get us caught. Better to wait."

Samuel was confused. This was a lot more adventure than he'd bargained for.

"Everyone please just *calm down!*" Joseph had abandoned his soft voice from the tower and resorted to hollering. Just when Horace was drawing in a giant breath in order to roar even louder than before, Joseph finally put an end to all the shouting. "Lord Phineus isn't here," he announced.

Tyler slapped Joseph's shoulder and glared at him as if he'd said something he really shouldn't have, but Joseph kept on. "We don't know where he is. And Sir Emerik is gone as well. We can't find either one of them."

Samuel now realized their best chance to enter the main chamber really had come. Still, he couldn't bring himself to leave his mother before knowing she was all right.

"Where do you suppose they've gone?" asked Horace, beginning to take command of the situation in the absence of power within the walls. "Could it be that they've left you and have plans of their own?"

"They're here somewhere," said Tyler, but he was lying.

"Are you sure of that?" asked Joseph. "You told me only an hour ago that they wouldn't return until morning."

Everyone heard—all the people who had gathered on the other side of the wall, and Horace, too—and control swiftly shifted entirely in Horace's favor.

"Open the door," said Horace. "I have something to show you."

"We're not opening this door!" shouted Tyler. "Come back in the morning and we'll discuss it. Until then, you can scream all you want. This door stays shut!"

"What do you want to show us?" asked Joseph, who was a more curious sort than Tyler.

"Come down here and I'll show you."

"Back away from the door," Joseph ordered. When he appeared to be pleased with Horace's location he climbed down the narrow stone steps.

"This is a terrible idea," Tyler said to no one in particular.

Joseph and another young guard from the House of Power removed the vast wooden beam that lay across the swinging wooden doors. Everyone backed away as one of the two heavy doors was pulled open just far enough for Joseph to slip out. At that moment Adele bolted from the crowd and into the opening, sliding outside as she shrieked at Horace, "Where's my boy? Where's Samuel?"

Horace had found her boy once before and she hoped he would know of his whereabouts again.

Samuel very nearly opened his mouth and yelled out, "I'm here, I'm here!" But Isabel immediately gave him a very stern look, telling him she might punch him if he made so much as a peep. And so he said nothing as he craned his neck to listen more carefully.

"Take this horse. I brought it for you," said Horace to Joseph. "Ride it to the edge—where the edge used to be—and you will see. I'll be here when you return, and then we'll have something to talk about."

Isabel heard the sound of hooves as Joseph galloped for the border of the Highlands. And then she heard Horace's voice again, louder than it needed to be, as if he knew that Samuel was hiding nearby and needed to hear him.

"You and your son will cross paths again," he said. "Though I believe you must leave the Highlands if you are to find him. We must *all* leave the Highlands."

"But she's the cook!" cried Tyler from his perch on the wall, his voice cracking. *I've already lost a guard,* he thought heavily. *Now Sir Emerik is going to kill me for letting the cook escape.*

Samuel had seen his mother escape the House of Power, and she was with someone he trusted. Now he held on tight to the words Horace had said. *You will cross paths again.* He turned to Isabel with a new resolve in his voice that surprised her.

"Follow me," he said as he began moving cautiously toward the main chamber. "It's time we made our way to the source of water."

CHAPTER 6

INTO THE HOLLOW

As Samuel and Isabel approached the stairs leading up to the main chamber they could see that the way was lit, though unguarded. Everyone had gone to the wall. Samuel's mother was safely away, and only the challenge of finding the source of water remained before him.

"This is our best chance," he said. They started off, fast but silent, and soon the two were up the deserted stairs, down the hallway, and in front of the door to the main chamber.

Samuel tried the handle and found the door locked as he'd expected. Lord Phineus had been mistaken to assume Samuel wasn't a clever boy, however, for Samuel had a secret known only to him, a secret left by his father, Sir William.

"This way," said Samuel, waving Isabel toward a second set

of stairs. At the bottom was a torch burning softly, and Samuel took it from its hold and carried it up the steps. They turned left at the top, and Samuel stood before the door to Lord Phineus's private room. To the right of the door sat a square box made of wood with a leafy green plant inside.

"We need to move that," said Samuel.

"How do you know?" asked Isabel.

"My father told me." He glanced at Isabel and saw that she was surprised. "He used to show me all sorts of secrets about this place before . . ."

There was a long pause in which the two looked awkwardly at each other.

"Before what?" asked Isabel.

Samuel stepped away from the wooden box he'd been trying to move. "A year ago he fell from the Highlands, back when there was a Highlands to fall from."

"I'm sorry," said Isabel.

Samuel shrugged and took hold of the box once more. It was full of dirt and very heavy, so Isabel came alongside and helped.

"Whose door is this?" asked Isabel, glancing up as they scooted the heavy box across the floor. She didn't like the dark look of it. The door appeared to be made of black wood, and there was a long crack down the middle that looked like a vein with blood running through it, as if the door were alive in the dancing flames of night.

"It's Lord Phineus's private room," said Samuel, trying to

move the box with one hand while he held the torch. He was not making much progress.

"I don't want to go in there," said Isabel, backing away. Samuel stopped trying to move the wooden box and looked at Isabel. It was unusual to see her lose her confidence.

"We're not going inside. There are things hidden here, things we need."

"Who hid them?"

There wasn't time to explain everything about his father—about how he had stood against Lord Phineus and paid a terrible price—so he offered only a little of his father's legend.

"My father hid these things when he became suspicious of the others," said Samuel. "He didn't trust Lord Phineus or Sir Emerik. He woke me late one night and showed them to me, in case anything ever happened to him, in case Lord Phineus tried to hurt me or my mother."

Isabel moved back toward Samuel.

"Why would he hide something there?" she said. "It's right in front of his door."

"My father was fond of hiding things right beneath people's noses. He thought it was the last place Lord Phineus would look. I hope he was right."

Isabel moved Samuel out of the way with one arm, then took the edge of the wooden box in her hands and slid it to the other side of the door.

"Hold this," said Samuel, giving Isabel the torch and kneeling down. The wall was made of stone blocks of two sizes. The larger stones were about the size of the box Isabel had just moved, but interspersed between those were smaller ones, the size of Samuel's hand. He took hold of one of the smaller stones and tried to jiggle it free.

"I'm sure this is the one," said Samuel. "It has to be."

Isabel knelt down next to Samuel, holding the flame closer. The stone Samuel was gripping didn't look like it was at all loose.

"Are you sure about this?" asked Isabel. "I mean, did you actually see your father put something here, or did he just tell you it was here?"

"I saw it," answered Samuel. "It was dark when he showed it to me, but I'm sure this is the one."

"Stand back," said Isabel. Samuel looked up, confused and irritated. Isabel thrust the torch back into his hand and walked quickly, almost to the end, where a window looked over the House of Power. When she turned back, Isabel had her sling in hand, already loaded with a black fig.

"Move to the side, and hold that torch near the mark," said Isabel. She began swinging the sling over her head, the circle it made in the air barely fitting into the width of the hall. It made a wonderful sound, a whirling echo that grew faster and faster down the deep length of the passage.

"You can't throw one of those in here," said Samuel, alarm rising in his voice. He was about to insist that she put the weapon away when he heard a *snap!* and then a crash as the black fig hit the stone wall. It ricocheted off the floor, up to the ceiling, and back through the hall toward Isabel. She ducked and the fig zipped past her head, then flew out the window.

"That made a lot of noise," said Samuel. "Someone might have heard."

Isabel peeked her dark brow around the corner of the window and saw the various lights aflame in the courtyard. It didn't seem to her that anyone had noticed the sound, although people were moving away from the wall now, returning to where they'd come from.

"Better make it fast," said Isabel. "See if it worked." She had the feeling that someone might have been stationed near the main chamber, someone who would probably return any moment.

Samuel knelt down with the torch and examined the small square stone. The black fig had hit it dead center and left behind a spiderweb crack.

"You're a really good shot with that thing," said Samuel as Isabel came up beside him. "I hope you never have a reason to use it on me."

Isabel smiled vaguely. She liked being praised for her strength, especially by older boys who thought that girls were weak.

Soon the shards of the broken stone were removed, and they found three items hidden inside a hollow. Samuel quickly put all of them in his pocket, and then they both struggled to get the wooden box back in place. The two moved cautiously down the stairs, hugging the wall as they went.

No one had arrived yet at the door to the main chamber. Samuel took out of his pocket the first of the four things his father had hidden for him. It was a key made for unlocking the door to the main chamber. It worked beautifully, and when the two were safely inside Samuel breathed a sigh of relief.

"No one comes in here uninvited," he said. "We're alone now, only we need to put this torch back where we got it. Someone will see it's missing."

The two searched the chamber and quickly found a second, unlit torch against one of the ivy-covered walls. Samuel touched the end and found it was moist with fuel. After lighting it, he sent Isabel quietly to return the one they'd been using.

While she was out of the room, Samuel wondered if he should tell Isabel everything his father had told him. He looked at the objects in his hand. One was another key, oddly shaped; another was a weapon, sharp but small; and the last was a folded piece of paper. He slipped all three items back in his pocket.

When Isabel returned she shut the door but neglected to lock it, rushing back to Samuel's side.

"We're okay," she said. "No one saw me." She turned her attention to the statue before them. It was the head of a man, made of a white sort of stone, sitting on a pedestal. Isabel thought the man had big ears.

"What's that say?" she asked. Isabel couldn't read the name etched into the white stone.

"Mead," said Samuel.

"Who's Mead?"

Isabel hadn't heard a name like that before and it made her nervous.

"I don't know," said Samuel. "But I think we're about to find out."

He took hold of the head as his father had shown him when the two had secretly come to the main chamber in the deep quiet of a past night. He was reminded of how his father had stood next to him, guiding smaller hands. A hot feeling welled up in his throat. Memory had a special way of hurting sometimes.

"Do you need some help?" asked Isabel.

"No!" he shouted, surprising himself and Isabel. "My father showed me how. I can do it."

"No one's going to come in here, like you said," offered Isabel. "Whatever it is you're doing can take as long as you need."

Something clicked on the floor behind the two, and Isabel swiveled around. "What was that?"

Samuel stepped in front of her and pointed to the floor amid the twisting ivy. "It will take both of us to remove the cover, but it's unlocked."

"What's unlocked?" asked Isabel. Dread was rising in her voice as she stood next to Samuel, staring down at the tangled web of ivy that parted over a space not much wider than her head. Samuel knelt down, pushing the creeping ivy aside, and revealed the door leading to Mead's Hollow.

"The source of water is somewhere behind this opening," said Samuel. "My father told me how to find it." Samuel pulled the slip of folded paper from his pocket. "He wrote it down for me, so I could find my way."

There was a sound coming from outside the door, as if someone wearing heavy boots were approaching. Samuel shot a glance past Isabel's head.

"You locked the door, right?" He didn't think anyone would try to enter, but with Lord Phineus and Sir Emerik away, maybe someone would be so bold as to try. Isabel shook her head no.

The two went directly to work lifting the stone slab, frantic but careful to stay as silent as they could. Isabel was sure she did not want to make the journey to the source of water, but it was a place to hide, at least for a moment.

The sound of boots on stone stopped outside the door to the main chamber, then seemed to move from side to side, as if the person outside were unsure about trying to enter. A soft knock came on the door.

"Lord Phineus? Are you in there?"

It was Tyler, who was actually hoping not to find anyone. He thought he'd heard a strange scraping sound coming from behind the door, but he couldn't be sure. He hadn't slept in a long time. Maybe his mind was playing tricks on him.

Samuel and Isabel had already started down the steps leading into Mead's Hollow when Tyler put his hand on the latch to the door. Samuel crouched on the fourth step with the torch in one hand, while Isabel sat above him on the second step.

"Close it!" he whispered harshly.

Isabel slid it across the floor until it clicked into place. But the clicking sound sent panic rising within her and she tried to push up, regretting the decision she'd made. Suddenly, she didn't care if she was caught; she only wanted to make sure she could get out. Isabel pressed all of her weight against the stone above her, but it would not budge.

"Please, Isabel," whispered Samuel. "Be quiet. There are things down here you don't want to wake up."

Isabel turned to Samuel, the whites of her eyes wide and shining in the flame. She had been scared before, but never like this.

Tyler was surprised to find the door to the main chamber unlocked. He was also apprehensive about going inside and called out instead. "Is that you, Sir Emerik?"

No sound came from inside, and Tyler slowly peered around the corner of the door into the room, holding a flame into the air before him. There was no one, only the dark empty space of the main chamber and the window behind it. He ran his hand over his forehead and felt a cold sweat. Through the window he heard a commotion at the wall. Joseph had returned, and with him news of whatever Horace had wanted him to see.

Tyler closed the door and ran for the stairs, hoping the night would somehow come under his control as he made for the wall below.

CHAPTER 7

DAWN BREAKS ON A CHANGED WORLD

By the time Tyler raced down the stairs and through the courtyard, everyone had returned to the wall where the giant doors stood secure to hear what Horace had to say. Tyler could already hear his unbearable, booming voice. For a man like Tyler, left in command of a great many things and losing control of them all, it was a maddening sound.

"Don't anyone touch that door!" he howled on his approach. He went immediately up the narrow steps to the top of the wall and looked outside. Joseph had indeed returned.

"Open the doors!" cried Horace into his cupped hands with a bellow that felt like it would blow Tyler's hair back or knock him clean off the wall.

"Shut up, Horace! I can't take any more!" Tyler declared. He had been holding a rock in his hands, squeezing it as his nerves frayed, and without thinking he threw the stone hard and fast. Tyler was not a terribly good shot, and the stone, which was about the size of his fist, went right past Horace and hit the horse instead. The horse bucked into the air, then jerked the rope out of Joseph's hand and bolted into the darkness.

Horace watched the horse run away, then turned back to Tyler. "You must come out of the House of Power!"

Joseph put a hand on Horace's shoulder, asking him to please stop for a moment. He understood what Horace was doing, but he was just about as tired of hearing Horace yell as Tyler was.

"Horace is right, Tyler," Joseph said to the man standing above him, speaking in an even tone. "We have to leave this place, and quickly."

Tyler was resolved to keep his post—to make Sir Emerik proud of him and hold the House of Power from its enemies—but if others wanted to leave, he knew he couldn't make them stay. He didn't have the sort of authority that would force them to obey out of fear or respect. Who could have guessed things would have unraveled as they had in the middle of the night, and so quickly?

The group that had remained in the House of Power since the Highlands had fallen into Tabletop was comprised almost entirely of young men without families, along with a handful of women without husbands or children. Two of these men removed the beam that secured the doors, swinging them open. Everyone but Tyler streamed out and stood before Joseph and Horace in a circle three deep.

It was there that they were told the Highlands were sinking into Atherton.

Horace laid out the plans of where they were going and why, along with his conviction that the Highlands might very well be inescapable by morning. He was emphatic in his argument that the people in Tabletop could be trusted, and he explained how Lord Phineus had tried but failed to poison everyone in the three villages beneath the waterfalls.

Some in the group were not entirely convinced they should leave the safety of the fortress or that they could ally with the people of Tabletop. Among them were some of the guards—their lungs still tight from coughing—who had been hit with black figs and orange dust in the recent confrontation with the villagers. But their fears were overshadowed by the thought of being trapped in a sinking prison of walls and darkness. The very idea of it was haunting.

"We must take as much food and water as we can carry from inside," said Horace.

"What if we run out of water? What then?" asked one of the guards.

"We no doubt choose between the lesser of two evils," said Horace. "Stay here and sink into oblivion, or leave and risk a shortage of water."

And then Horace said something no one had expected.

"A falling Highlands may mean rising water. It's possible we could build a new basket system that can be lowered into the abyss to attain water. Better to be dipping into a giant well than be stuck at the bottom of one."

Few had thought of this possible eventuality. The idea of a dark, watery grave was universally terrifying.

"What of the horses?" asked the man who'd been watching over them. Many of the horses were kept in a stable outside the House of Power, but there were ten or more inside, held at the inner stable on the other side of the courtyard.

"If you want them to live, you'll need to get them out," said Horace.

But the time for getting horses or anything else out of the House of Power had passed, for as the group turned back to retrieve horses and supplies, they saw the doors slamming shut. There was a mad dash toward the closed doors as Tyler lifted one end of the timber and dropped it into place. Then he darted to the other end of the timber, hefting it into the air with all his might as the crowd outside barreled forward and crashed into the doors. One of the doors began to swing open, but Tyler pushed hard against the beam of wood and wedged it tightly, locking himself inside.

He could hear the sound of angry voices outside, but it was muffled from where he stood, and this gave him a small measure of satisfaction. He backed away from the doors, so very hungry and tired, and walked unsteadily into the courtyard until he could hear the voices no more.

And so it was that while Sir Emerik, Lord Phineus, Samuel, and Isabel descended into Mead's Hollow, a fourth village sprang up on Atherton. On the far side of the Highlands, as far away from the other villages of Tabletop as could be managed, there came into existence the Village of Horses. The village was comprised of all the people from the Highlands along with the horses that could be found outside of the House of Power. When the last of the horses leaped for the edge, the Highlands were a full five feet below Tabletop.

An hour later dawn was about to break on Atherton. Everyone in the Village of Horses stood at the edge looking down at their old home, filled with dread as they considered the day that lay before them. The Highlands were almost twenty feet beneath them now, and they could actually see them moving down ever so slowly, a gurgling, grinding noise coming from under their feet.

There was something at once beautiful and terrible about seeing their home collapse. It was a lonely place to look at in the coming light of morning, deep shadows casting over a once superior realm. And yet the House of Power had never before been seen from above, and it was a magnificent thing to behold with its gleaming white stone walls and green gardens, its rising turrets and winding staircases. From above it had the appearance of a magical, stately place being overcome by an evil darkness.

"What will become of us?" asked Gill of no one in particular.

"That all depends on the choices we make," said Horace, who stood nearby. "It's a brand-new day, a chance to set things right."

Gill scanned the line of trees that surrounded the Highlands. They had once stood high and mighty around him—forty feet or more—but soon he would be staring down at their tops. He turned to say something to Horace and saw that he had moved off and was staring toward the far edge of Atherton with a troubled look on his face.

Horace's closest allies, Gill among them, approached him as a group. "What is it?" asked Gill, gazing as Horace did toward the edge of the world. "What do you see?"

Horace knew what might be coming. They had talked at length in the night of what was to happen next, of how the people would need to be told of the coming danger, and of what each of Horace's men must do. He turned to his men and spoke with fear in his voice, echoing the words he'd heard Maude say in the Village of Rabbits.

"We must all unite against the one foe. It's our only chance."

The Cleaners.

"Get some horses ready," said Horace. "It's time."

When morning came to Atherton it felt as if a new world was being lit for the first time. All the changes that had come before seemed to rush into the one charged moment of dawn. From every vantage point, the same message was clear and sharp as a knife.

Atherton was not the place it had once been.

Briney and Maude, the keepers of the inn, stood motionless

and silent in the Village of Rabbits, staring at the line of trees where cliffs had once risen into the sky. The Highlands lay dark and wide against the rising sun, and it felt like much of what had made this secret place so powerful had fallen away along with its descent. "I miss the cliffs," said Briney, putting an arm around his wife. "It was a place to put my back against where no one could sneak up behind me."

This feeling was shared by many. Three lands previously separated by tall cliffs were now together as one. It was unsettling for people like Briney and Maude who'd lived in the safety of the middle, in the peaceful round world of groves and pastures that had been Tabletop. Danger seemed to close in from all sides as it never had before, because the world of Atherton was flat.

Or was it?

"Those trees don't seem as tall as they did last night, before dark," said Maude, narrowing her eyes toward the Highlands and trying to remember. "I'm sure of it. Those trees are shorter."

Briney looked at his wife and moved his hand to the small of her back.

"How long has it been since you slept?" he asked.

"I'm not seeing things, Briney!" The strain of all of the upheaval was apparent in Maude's trembling voice. Briney had always been the more sensitive of the two, and he didn't like what he was hearing. He was sure she was exhausted, that her eyes were playing tricks on her. Maybe it would calm her down if he looked to the Highlands again and pretended to believe her, so he gazed hard in the direction of the trees, which stood clustered all along the edge of his sight.

There was a strange sound coming from a long way off, right along the line where the cliffs used to be. Briney and Maude both looked toward a small group of men on horses, the pounding of hooves growing nearer.

"That will be Horace," said Maude. She could see it was him by the shining bald head atop the lead horse. "I wonder why he didn't come across the middle of the Highlands, as he did before."

This was Maude's way of telling Briney she had been right. The Highlands had indeed begun to slide down inside of Atherton — why else would Horace take the long way around?

Maude turned in the direction of the Flatlands, her mind suddenly caught by another idea.

"I hope he has some good news," she said. "I'm not certain everyone in the Highlands is ready to put the fighting behind us."

Briney tried to remember how far away the edge of Tabletop leading down to the Flatlands had once been. He replayed in his mind the images of the creatures Maude had described in the night.

"The Cleaners are coming, aren't they?" he said.

There was a long pause in which the two found each other's hands and held tight.

"They're coming," answered Maude.

Somewhere off in the distance, in the craggy rocks of the Flatlands, a Cleaner caught the scent of horses on the air. It was a new smell for the creature, one it liked. Darkness was on the decline in Atherton and the time for eating had arrived. The beast clicked its sharp, crooked teeth together, calling its horde near, and a pack of evil monsters began moving toward the Village of Horses.

CHAPTER 8
THE FALLING ROPE

"It must be thirty feet to the bottom, and it's still moving," said Dr. Kincaid. He had arrived at the edge of the Highlands with Vincent and Edgar. The three companions were astonished to see how far the Highlands had already crashed inside Atherton.

"This is taking place faster than I'd expected," added Dr. Kincaid.

"You *knew* this was going to happen?" asked Edgar. He stared first at Dr. Kincaid and then at Vincent. He could see by the looks on their faces that they'd known all along.

"Why didn't you tell me?" said Edgar.

"It would have only confused and frightened you more," said Dr. Kincaid. "I'm trying to tell you things as you need to know them, no sooner. And besides, I'm finding Atherton not always as I expect. Some of my information is turning out to be . . . unreliable." He stepped closer to the edge of the cliff. "I imagined we'd walk right in without any problem, but it appears the Highlands are descending quite a bit faster than I'd calculated."

"It will make everything more difficult," added Vincent.

Edgar looked over the edge into the Highlands and felt a sudden exhilaration, forgetting for a moment the chaos of the changing world around him.

"I can climb over this ledge. I can get down there."

Vincent scanned the line of trees on the other side and wondered who might be waiting within them. Then his eyes settled on the boy. "The longer we wait, the more distance there is to climb down." Vincent looked at Dr. Kincaid, who was mumbling to himself, and then back at Edgar with an expression that asked, *Even if we could do it ourselves, how are we going to get Dr. Kincaid down there? He's too old.*

Edgar crouched down and scanned along the floor of the Highlands. "There!" he said, pointing. He had spied one of the giant baskets that used to hang down from the Highlands. The contraption was created for Highlanders to receive food from those in Tabletop, who alone harvested figs and supplied rabbit and lamb meat for the privileged living above them. It was strange to see the basket lying there on its side, discarded and useless, when it had once acted as the only lifeline between the two realms.

Edgar didn't wait for Vincent or Dr. Kincaid to answer. He wanted to make quick work of the thirty feet, grab the rope attached to the basket, and bring it back. Without further thought he threw his legs over the edge and started sliding down until Vincent caught hold of Edgar's good arm. He gazed long and hard into Edgar's eyes.

"Are you sure you can do this?" he asked. "It's a long fall to the bottom if you miss a step." Edgar looked down and saw that there were plenty of places to put his feet and hands. He nodded.

"And are you sure this is a risk worth taking?" asked Vincent, looking now at Dr. Kincaid. "Our way is more treacherous than you anticipated."

Dr. Kincaid bent down on one knee, ignoring Vincent and placing all of his attention on the boy hanging precariously from the ledge. "Do you think the Cleaners can be overcome?"

Edgar thought about the question. The Cleaners were giant, ferocious creatures designed to find and kill anything in their paths. They had always been trapped in the Flatlands, but the Flatlands had risen and a thousand Cleaners had been unleashed on the world of Atherton.

"No," admitted Edgar. "Even with every person on Atherton in the fight, I don't think we can survive against the Cleaners."

"You're wrong," said Dr. Kincaid, touching Edgar on the shoulders. "They *can* be overcome. The answer lies in the House of Power." He glanced over the edge. "Only you can take us past an obstacle of this kind."

Edgar's eyes sparkled beneath raised brows, and a wide smile revealed a gleaming row of teeth. He was about to climb, something he thought he'd never do again, and Dr. Kincaid needed him to do it. Without Edgar, their journey was over. It was he alone who could save the grove, the other villages, *everything.*

Edgar drew in a deep breath and Vincent let him go. The moment Edgar had all his limbs on the wall he felt fully alive. There was a comfort in climbing that he couldn't explain, as if he were doing the one thing he was put on Atherton to do.

And yet, there was also a new sensation against his hands and feet that worried him. This wall was not like the others he had climbed. All of the other walls had been dry, but this one was damp and slippery, with bits of mud and mossy green patches between the rocks. The way down to the Highlands felt, and even smelled, soggy. It made Edgar think he could lick the stones before his face to quench his growing thirst.

"This won't be a problem at all," said Edgar, trying to encourage himself as well as his companions. He could already see the route he would take and that it would not be difficult for him to make it to the bottom as long as he didn't slip on the moist surface.

As he went, it crossed his mind to take a longer way so that he could keep climbing for the sheer joy of it, but the wall began to shake in his hands and the slippery hold of one hand almost came loose. If the wall leading down to the Highlands were to continue shaking or become more violent, he could imagine his hand with the missing pinky letting go. That would be the start of problems he wasn't sure he could handle.

Edgar focused more precisely on the task at hand, feeling the Highlands slowly grinding beneath him as they sank farther. He found to his surprise that he was taking not the fastest but the safest route he could find, and yet it was a daunting challenge. Still twenty feet from the bottom, both feet slipped free and he dangled from only his hands. He struggled against the slippery mud to hold his grip and managed to regain control, but his heart raced at the thought of such an unexpected, close call.

There were no more problems the rest of the way down as Edgar adjusted to the new feel of the rock face. Once he was standing at the bottom, he sighed with an uncharacteristic relief, gazing up at his two companions.

"This place will need to be renamed," yelled Dr. Kincaid from above. "It's feeling rather odd to keep calling it the Highlands, don't you think?" He was trying to keep the mood light, easing his own worry that the boy wouldn't make it back with the rope.

The tree trunks and mechanisms that had once held the ropes and lowered the baskets had been torn apart by the falling world, and the end of the rope lay frayed and loose on the ground. Much of the rope had been wound onto an enormous wooden core and ripped free, but Edgar thought there was enough rope attached to the basket to reach the top. He took the frayed end and tied it in a knot around his waist, then tried his best to untangle the mess at his feet.

When he was satisfied there was enough to make the climb all the way to the top, he began working his way up the wall of stone. He was a startlingly fast study, and this time he seemed to better understand how to overcome the slick surface.

As Edgar rose higher, the rope caught in the pile and he had to turn and hold on with one hand, yanking the rope back and forth until it was untangled. Soon he was a few feet from the top and the rope began to tighten around his middle. Looking down, he saw that he'd reached the end of the rope. The other end was tied firmly to the large, heavy basket on the ground below.

He was so close to his goal, and yet the wall kept moving down. It occurred to Edgar that if the Highlands were to really start falling, crashing into the center of Atherton with some speed, he would be pulled off the wall by the rope, the basket acting like an anchor yanking him into the open air.

"Can you untie the rope from around your waist?" asked Vincent. He was just out of Edgar's reach, lying on his stomach with one arm hanging over the edge.

Edgar held on with his injured hand, feeling the sting of rock against the scabbed bump where his pinky was missing. With his other hand he frantically began untying the two knots he'd put there. The wall was moving down inch by inch, slowly but steadily, and every moment counted.

Just as he was getting the first knot undone the Highlands lurched violently and the rope tightened, very nearly pulling Edgar free from the cliff. After the cliff dropped the length of Edgar's forearm in the space of a split second, the tremor halted as quickly as it had begun. Both Dr. Kincaid and Vincent were on their bellies, frantically calling and reaching out to the boy beneath them.

Edgar was such a calm climber that it seemed more like he was moving in water than air. He had shifted two steps down and was already through the second knot. He held the rope at his side, glad to be free of it.

"On the count of three," said Edgar. He held the frayed end of the rope beneath his knees and counted, heaving it up over his head. Vincent caught the flying rope without trouble, but he hadn't thought of how to secure it. His eyes darted around in search of some way to hold the few feet of rope he had to work with.

"Use these," cried Edgar. From his pocket he pulled out two sharp wooden stakes. He had found them on the ground below, where they had once been part of the pulley mechanism. As he tossed them up they flew over Vincent's head and Dr. Kincaid retrieved them.

"Such a resourceful boy, don't you think?" asked Dr. Kincaid.

"You'll find the wall is a little wet," said Edgar. "It might be slicker than you expect."

This seemed not to interest Dr. Kincaid and Vincent as the two men found a rock big enough to pound the stakes through the rope and into the ground. They did it quickly, but even as they did, they could see that it wouldn't hold for very long. The Highlands were slowly descending, and the rope was tightening from the weight of the basket.

"Go!" cried Vincent, nearly pushing Dr. Kincaid from the ledge. The old man took the rope, clearly worried that it would not hold his weight, and he threw his legs over the ledge. Soon he was shimmying down the side of the wall, the rope growing tight and stretching in his hands. When he was far enough along to make room, Vincent started down. He didn't realize he'd be falling on top of Dr. Kincaid if the rope snapped free.

Edgar had stayed on the wall, working his way down next to Dr. Kincaid, helping him to choose places to put his feet. The two of them were about ten feet from the bottom when the rope began to make a tearing sound from above.

"Hurry!" yelled Vincent. "It's going to snap any second now!"

Edgar looked down. The basket that had been lying on its side was now upright and weighing heavily on the rope. Dr. Kincaid looked at Edgar in a panic. The rope was about to snap in two.

"Let go of the rope and hold on right here," said Edgar, his voice calm but filled with authority. Dr. Kincaid followed Edgar's lead.

"Now here," said Edgar, guiding the old man free of the rope and out from under Vincent. They were only five feet from the bottom, but a fall that far for a man of Dr. Kincaid's age could easily be a bone-breaking event. Vincent was closer to ten feet above the ground, and when the rope snapped in two he fell down the rocky face of the cliff. Dr. Kincaid was just barely out of the way, and he watched the descent of his protector as he flew past, arms and legs flailing, as if in slow motion.

Vincent landed in the basket with a crash. The rope followed, coiling inside on top of the fallen man as the basket leaned to one side and toppled over. When Vincent did not emerge right away Edgar feared he'd been injured. Vincent was by far the strongest among the three, and there wasn't much hope of an old man and a young boy traversing the threatening world of the Highlands without Vincent's help.

Edgar looked back at Dr. Kincaid and saw that the old man's grip was beginning to falter.

"How far to the bottom?" asked Dr. Kincaid.

"Only a few more feet," said Edgar. Dr. Kincaid looked down and saw just how close he was to the bottom, a little embarrassed to have been so afraid. He was able to navigate the remaining small distance without any help from Edgar.

The two went directly to the basket and peered inside. Vincent wasn't moving.

"Why's he not moving?" said Edgar.

"I don't know," said Dr. Kincaid, concern rising in his voice. "Maybe he stabbed himself with one of his own spears."

There was movement from under the rope as Vincent came to. He moaned as he lifted his head, and when his face came into view, blood was pouring out of his nose like water.

"What happened?" he said, smearing the blood around his face, not realizing what a mess he was making.

"He's broken his nose," said Dr. Kincaid. When Vincent heard this, he felt the bulging arch of his nose and winced in pain. He rolled out of the basket and onto his feet, then threw his head back and held his nose shut.

"Thith ith going to thwell up really big," said Vincent.

Edgar felt himself wanting to laugh unexpectedly. Even though it wasn't really funny, he experienced a rush of giddy relief after their harrowing descent to the Highlands.

"It already has," said Dr. Kincaid. "Nothing else feels broken?"

Vincent glanced at Dr. Kincaid and saw that he was unharmed and looking surprisingly well. The old man was always looking surprisingly well. Vincent took his fingers from his nose before answering.

"I'm fine. This will stop bleeding soon enough."

There was a sigh of relief among the three of them, but it lasted only a few seconds. From deep below the Highlands there came a bottomless, gurgling hum that didn't stop for several minutes. The walls lurched out of the ground, slimy with mud. The soggy smell swelled strong and sharp in Edgar's nose, and he couldn't say if it was the smell of Atherton being born or withering away.

Very quickly they went from being thirty feet below Tabletop to a hundred feet, and Edgar wondered how in the world he would ever get his two companions back out again.

The three moved through the trees wordlessly and with great care, expecting to be overtaken or trapped by an enemy at any moment. When they reached the other side of the line of trees and gazed out over the beauty of the Highlands, it was Vincent who spoke first.

"There's no one here," he said. "They've all gone into the House of Power."

"Even the horses are gone," said Edgar. He was looking off

toward the stable, the place where he'd first seen the giant four-legged animals he thought might try to eat him. It was silent there, too. He couldn't imagine the horses crowded into the courtyard of the House of Power, trampling the flowers and making a terrible mess.

"I don't think we're going to find anyone here," said Dr. Kincaid, stepping out from the shelter of the trees and into the open field that lay before them. "This place has been deserted."

Samuel and Isabel were on a remarkably different path from Edgar as he moved beyond the trees and into the realm of the House of Power. Samuel was trying his best to lead the way through the gloomy world of Mead's Hollow in search of the source of water. His father had told him where he must go and had instructed him on the many dangers to be avoided, but it was slow going in the underbelly of Atherton. They moved with a stone wall at their backs, feeling their thirst growing, following a path that would soon bring them face-to-face with Lord Phineus.

CHAPTER 9

AN UNNATURAL QUIET

The people who lived in the Village of Rabbits were farmers who raised rabbits all day long. There was hardly a fighter among them — save Maude — and it had been quite a stretch to get them to stand firm against the recent attack from the Highlands. The fight had given them some courage and vigor, but it had also showed them the bleakness of war. People had died, and the violence had left them wishing they'd never have to defend themselves again.

They had spent a long night doing as Dr. Kincaid and Vincent had instructed, but the effort seemed futile to almost everyone in the village. They had taken what wood they could salvage from the broken-down houses to make what might be called spears by someone with an active imagination. Most felt that if there really were giant creatures on the way to the village by the hundreds, makeshift shelters and pointy sticks would not protect them.

When morning came upon them there were three hundred people milling around outside the inn, all of them waiting for word of hope from inside.

But there happened to be on that morning one who didn't stand waiting to hear how the leaders inside the inn would decide her fate. She was a child of seven, and she loved her rabbits more than anything in the world. She especially fond of one particular rabbit, Henrietta, that was about to have babies.

The children were being watched carefully with so much danger afoot, but this particular girl had a way of slipping away unnoticed. She drifted away from the large group, kicking a pebble and pretending to play by herself. There came a moment when no one was watching closely, and she slid behind a house that was leaning unsteadily to one side. She skirted along the row of houses, noticing as she went that almost all of them were falling apart or already in a pile on the ground. The crashing world of Atherton had done its best to level the Village of Rabbits, and it had come very close to doing a perfect job of it.

As she approached the last house on the end of a row her heart leaped. This was her house, and it was still standing. There was a long narrow room that was open on one end and attached to the house, with maybe twenty rabbits in hutches along the walls. It was shaded from the sun toward the back where the rabbits were, just the way Henrietta liked it.

"Henrietta?" the girl sang softly. Just then she heard a strange sound, like two bones clanging together very quickly from somewhere in the dark corner of the skinny room. She stepped forward carefully, peering through shafts of light that were creeping into the dusty air of the space. The sound came again, and this time the girl screamed like she'd never screamed before. Something had latched onto Henrietta, holding the rabbit between its crooked teeth.

The girl fled back to the inn for help. Whatever it was didn't follow her. Instead, it slunk back into the dark corner and devoured the beloved pet.

A group from the village soon arrived with sharp sticks and rocks. They pried the flimsy walls down and opened the room to the light of day, and there in the corner, clicking its bloody teeth, was the thing they'd been told about. It was a Cleaner.

The moment the walls were down it began racing in search of a new dark spot to hide in. The Cleaner cowered in the middle of a circle of men as they threw rocks at it. Soon the Cleaner was beaten enough that the men could approach it and poke it with the sharp sticks they carried. And then, without further violence, the Cleaner was dead.

There came a howl of excitement from the crowd. This was the monster that would come in great numbers to tear apart the rabbits and the children?

"I think we could handle a hundred of those," cried one man.

"A thousand!" yelled another. There was genuine happiness in the group, except for the girl, who had lost her Henrietta and could not be consoled.

Then through the hollering crowd strode Briney, Maude, and Horace with a few of his men. The crowd parted like water as the group who'd been conferring inside the inn came to the middle of the circle and stood before the fallen creature.

"Killed it, did you?" said Maude. She was not in a favorable mood.

"We did!" came the cry of several men, holding their sharp sticks over their heads like great conquerors.

"It would have been more useful if you'd let it live. We could have studied its movements."

This took a little wind out of the group. A quiet passed over them.

"You know what this is, don't you?" asked Maude. She had seen a Cleaner from a distance and been told much more about them by Vincent. The night before, he had visited her while Edgar was in the grove.

"Why, it's a Cleaner, like you said," answered one of the villagers.

"It's a *baby* Cleaner," said Maude. She walked a few paces and stood over the fallen creature. "This thing must have wandered off from its den in the middle of the night, following the smell of rabbits." Maude looked hard at the circle of people around her. "Imagine something bigger, with teeth as large as those sticks in your hands, and you're getting closer to the truth of what we face."

"How much bigger?" asked a woman holding the crying little girl who had loved Henrietta. The dead Cleaner was about four feet long and thick around the middle, and it had a disgustingly huge mouth full of jagged teeth.

Maude didn't hesitate. "Eight or ten feet long, probably four hundred pounds. And aggressive. You won't be throwing rocks at a pack of full-grown ones when they show up here. You'll be running for your life."

The short-lived glee was now completely gone from the group. Maude wondered if she'd told them too much. There could be a real risk of hysteria if she wasn't careful.

"You need to form groups and go through all the houses. Make sure there are no more juvenile Cleaners hiding in the village. And someone should check with the scouts to see if they've heard or seen anything approaching."

They had been smart enough to set up a line of villagers around the village and toward the Flatlands, a line that this one delinquent Cleaner had managed to avoid in the night. Big Cleaners were not quiet on their approach as a group, or so Vincent had told her, and hopefully the scouts' forewarning would allow them a small amount of time to prepare.

"Give us just a little longer and we'll have our plans set," finished Maude. She turned to Horace and Briney and the group started back for the inn. She stopped short and called back to them.

"I'm told you can eat them," she said, "but I'm not going to be the first."

The villagers all looked back at the ghastly thing that lay dead on the ground, its slimy green insides oozing out into the dirt, and nobody dared even think of eating any part of it.

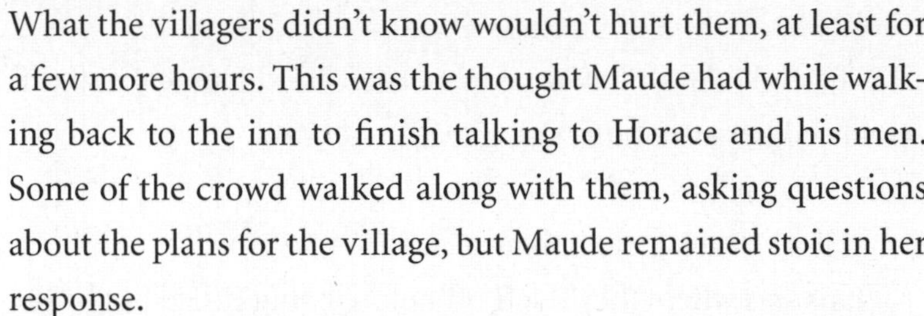

What the villagers didn't know wouldn't hurt them, at least for a few more hours. This was the thought Maude had while walking back to the inn to finish talking to Horace and his men. Some of the crowd walked along with them, asking questions about the plans for the village, but Maude remained stoic in her response.

"We need more time," she had kept telling them. She had wasted no time speaking her mind to Horace and his men the moment they were back inside the inn and the door was closed behind them.

"They have no chance," Maude had said. "No hope whatsoever."

"We don't know that," Briney had replied, coming to the defense of the villagers, as usual.

"They can't build a shelter of stone that doesn't fall over," she began. She was building up a head of steam and her voice rose as she continued. "Did you see those weapons? I told them to make spears and they walk around with sticks in their hands. And even if they could make real spears, they don't have the courage or the training to use them. This village couldn't fight off ten Cleaners, so what's going to happen when a hundred of them show up? They could be here in an hour or a day, but I know they're coming. Either way, we don't have time to whip this village into fighting shape. It can't be done."

Briney sat down. Then his chest began to sink inward, and soon he was staring at the floor. She was right. The village and everything in it would be destroyed. Maude put her hand on Briney's shoulder, and her emotions threatened to get away from her.

"The Highlands have been deserted," said Horace, and this refocused her attention on the matter at hand.

"*Everyone* has fled?" she asked.

"All who haven't lost their minds."

This was where they'd left off before being called out by the villagers. Now that they were back, Maude wanted more answers to questions she'd been thinking about.

"Where have all the people and those big animals, the horses, gone to?" asked Maude. She stumbled on the word "horses," still getting used to the very idea of these foreign creatures.

One of Horace's men who'd been silent until then now spoke up. He was black-bearded and wide across the face and shoulders, and his bright eyes cut through the darkened room.

"We took them out of the Highlands on the other side," he said. "As far away from here as we could get them. The people of the Highlands fear you, as they feared Lord Phineus, and fear is fertile ground for fighting."

Horace broke in. "Once there were three villages on Tabletop, and now there are four—at least for a short time. The people of the Highlands are far away, but we need to find a way to bring them to us. We'll need the horses."

"Who leads this group if not Lord Phineus?" asked Maude.

The man with the black beard looked at Horace. "He leads us."

It was mildly comforting amid all the bad news to know that Maude had befriended the leader of a people she feared. She paused a moment, gathering her thoughts, and then she asked Horace what he thought they should do.

The plans he had were not what she'd expected, but there was something in them that rang true. It was a real solution that just might work. It had the advantage of at least getting them more time.

"The only problem is that I'm not sure those in the grove or the Village of Sheep will go along with a plan like that," said Maude. "Someone will need to go ask them."

CHAPTER 10
FLYING ROCKS

Edgar glanced over his shoulder, and he saw that he and his companions were utterly trapped in the Highlands. For some reason he thought of the old wooden cup he'd always carried to Mr. Ratikan's house when it was time to get his water ration. He felt small, as if he were looking up from the bottom of the wooden cup, unable to escape.

"How are we going to get out of here?" asked Edgar. It struck Edgar as odd that they hadn't been more focused on this very obvious and disastrous problem looming close in their future. They would need to get out at some point, and Edgar was the only one of them who could climb.

"We'll figure that out when the time comes," said Vincent firmly, as if it were a question he was unwilling to address even if he knew its answer.

The giant wooden doors to the House of Power sat closed in front of them, and there was not a sound from inside the courtyard. The only noise came from around them, an echoing murmur of rocks grating against rocks as the Highlands continued their slow descent.

How far could it fall? thought Edgar. He made quick work of the wall, climbing up to the top and turning back. Vincent carried with him a length of the rope that had snapped loose at the cliffs, and he flung the end up to Edgar. Soon the rope was secure, and Vincent was inside the fortress with Edgar. The two removed the beam over the wooden gate and opened it.

"Let's be slow in our exploration," said Vincent, motioning Dr. Kincaid to pass through the doors and into the courtyard. "There might be someone inside with a weapon, waiting for just such a moment as this."

Already the courtyard was beginning to show signs of neglect. The brightly colored flowers seemed particularly delicate. The petals were brown and flaking at the edges and the long stems drooped toward the ground. The hedge was parched and leaves hung limp from small trees planted between the stone walkways. And there was a fountain to one side that was empty. There was a sadness about it, as if it had lost its reason for being. It was the deadest-looking thing in the courtyard.

The House of Power was showing the symptoms of death more sharply than other places in Atherton, as though the truth of its great beauty were being brought to bear: It was a fragile beauty, held together by great effort. The Highlands lacked the rugged sense of having been useful. It was a place with a colorful candy coating, hiding very little underneath.

"This place had a shabby kind of splendor, even at its best," said Edgar, pride welling up inside him. "The grove is still beautiful, even without any water." He touched the bag that held the three young figs and felt them squishing around inside, and he felt a little closer to home.

"Where has all the water gone?" asked Vincent. He looked at Dr. Kincaid with some alarm, and it seemed to Edgar that Vincent had expected the fountain to be bubbling with life. "I assumed that Lord Phineus was holding all of the water in the House of Power for himself and his loyal followers."

"I was thinking the same thing," said Dr. Kincaid. "I hope there are no more surprises awaiting us today."

Vincent was already moving slowly ahead. "Do you know the way?" he asked. "I can't be sure."

"I know the way," said Dr. Kincaid. "Follow the center path. It will snake back and forth through the ivy-covered terrace and end where the stair begins. We must go up the stairs in the middle."

Edgar was startled that Dr. Kincaid would be so familiar with the House of Power. Hadn't he been trapped in the Flatlands with Vincent since Atherton's beginnings?

"There doesn't seem to be anyone here," said Vincent. "Maybe the lack of water has turned out to be a good thing for us after all. There was nothing to keep them here, and it has made our approach all the easier."

Vincent continued winding his way through the courtyard

with Dr. Kincaid and Edgar following close behind. With not a soul about the place, he became increasingly relaxed. At one point he stopped and looked back at his companions.

"How does my nose look?" he joked. It was absolutely dreadful and made Vincent seem like an entirely different person. His nose appeared to be even wider than it was long, which was saying a lot because Vincent had a very long nose.

"You look fine," said Dr. Kincaid. "Can we please get on with it?"

Dr. Kincaid had seemed more nervous and quiet than Vincent along the way. Edgar wished he knew where they were going and why, but throughout their journey the older man had steadfastly refused to supply any useful information, so Edgar had given up asking. Wherever their ultimate destination was, the idea of getting there had turned Dr. Kincaid a little cold, and the old man wasn't quite the fatherly figure he'd seemed to be when they'd first met.

At last they came up along a high white wall alive with climbing ivy, the green vines snaking brightly against the white stone. Vincent reached out and touched the wall, and when he did, a rock the size of Edgar's head crashed down from above. It struck Vincent on the top of his shoulder and he howled in pain.

"Get away from there!"

Looking up, the three companions saw a man's head sticking out. It was Tyler, and he was about to hurl another rock from above.

Vincent pushed Dr. Kincaid toward a nearby wall with

open archway doors in it. Another rock crashed on the stone floor of the courtyard as Vincent and Edgar followed quickly behind Dr. Kincaid.

They were in Samuel's deserted room. Everything was still there, including most of the books.

"Don't you come out of there unless you want another on your head!" Tyler was not in his right mind. Alone and scared in the House of Power, he'd hoarded some food and water, hoping to survive the changing world and see what fortune it would bring.

"How bad?" asked Dr. Kincaid, looking at Vincent's shoulder.

"It's not broken, just badly bruised. I'll be all right."

"So you can still protect us?" asked Dr. Kincaid.

Vincent tried to move his arm back and forth and winced in pain. "I just need a minute," he said.

Edgar fished around inside the pocket on the front of his shirt and pulled out his sling and a black fig. "I can protect us."

Dr. Kincaid beamed at the boy, then turned his eyes on Vincent. "You stay here. The boy and I can handle one rock-throwing maniac."

Vincent protested, but he knew Edgar's skill with a sling, and soon Dr. Kincaid was running out into the courtyard waving his arms and dodging flying rocks. Tyler appeared to have quite a collection of smaller stones and he knew how to use them. Dr. Kincaid was hit once square in the back and was just barely able to dodge a near direct hit to the head.

"Ha-ha-ha-ha!" howled Tyler from above. But he hadn't

seen Edgar sneaking out into the open to hide behind a row of hedge. Tyler could hear the sound of the sling swishing over Edgar's head and the *snap!* of the black fig as it came flying toward him, but it all happened so fast. The fig smacked him flat on the forehead and he fell out of Edgar's sight. There was a dead silence in the courtyard.

"I got him," said Edgar, looking into the room where Dr. Kincaid had taken shelter again with Vincent. "You can come out now."

Dr. Kincaid and Vincent emerged from Samuel's room, glancing up warily at the possibility of a heavy falling object. Then Vincent, with a burst of renewed vigor, charged up a flight of white stairs off to his right in search of the culprit.

When they arrived they saw that Tyler was not dead, but also not moving. Behind him sat a pile of rocks, a box filled with stale bread, and a rather large wooden bucket half filled with water.

"Edgar, you first, and quickly!" said Dr. Kincaid.

Edgar approached the water and cupped his hands inside, quickly gulping down as much as he could hold. He took a loaf of the stale bread, a kind of food he'd tried only once before, and he tore a large bite off with his teeth, chewing vigorously.

They ate and drank hastily, leaving most of the food behind. All three of them wondered who the person was and why he had stayed. He had the look of a man without a family, and they felt sorry for him.

"We'll leave him be," said Dr. Kincaid, "with water and some of the bread. He's going to need it. Now, follow me." There was a new resolve in his voice and a feeling in the air of having arrived at the very place where the answers they sought could be found. The three of them departed with a growing sense that this man was the only enemy they would find in the deserted House of Power.

Down the stairs they went, to the very end of the courtyard and into a rotunda with three sets of stairs. Dr. Kincaid hesitated only a moment—glancing in every direction—and then started up the middle set of stairs, two steps to a stride. At the top he continued on until he arrived at the door to the main chamber.

Dr. Kincaid looked back at Edgar and Vincent. All the color had gone out of his face.

"It begins," he said, and he put his hand against the door, pushing it open.

CHAPTER 11

A PLAN SET IN MOTION

Maude had never been on a horse before and it was a harrowing experience. She was riding with Horace, her arms wrapped around his waist as they raced across the barren landscape. There was no saddle, only a rope between the horse and the man, and the animal was difficult to control, even for a skilled rider like Horace. The speed at which they traveled was alarming, and Maude was convinced a fall like that would kill her. As this thought grew in her mind she tightened her grip around Horace's middle until he could barely breathe.

"We're almost there," he said, trying to comfort her. "You're a natural rider. Soon you'll be doing this without me."

"You can keep your horse," said Maude. "I'm perfectly content to raise rabbits."

Maude felt Horace's body shaking with laughter.

"You won't think it's so funny when I fall to my death and pull you right off with me," she said. This made him laugh even more, and she took one hand from around his waist and slapped him in the back of the head. Horace thought this was the funniest thing yet, and he nearly laughed himself right off the horse.

He pulled up short of the Village of Sheep and let the animal walk as they drew near. "I think we've run her hard enough," said Horace. "Best we give her a rest."

The two had already ridden to the village at the grove and talked through their plans, but their job was only half done. Already midmorning had arrived and with it the growing threat of Cleaners finding them. Now there was only Wallace, the leader in the Village of Sheep, to convince.

"He's the wisest among us," said Maude. Horace knew she was speaking of Wallace without her having to say his name. "If he's unconvinced, our plan will fail."

"I believe you're right."

The two dismounted the horse and began walking. Soon they spotted a group of four people approaching from the village, but Wallace was not among them.

"It's me, Maude, from the Village of Rabbits!" hollered Maude. The four took this as a good sign and advanced more quickly. They'd seen horses the day before when they'd fought back those in the Highlands, and the sight of the big animal made them nervous.

"Where's Wallace?" asked Maude as the two parties neared each other. "We need to talk with him right now."

The four from the village hadn't had the occasion to witness Maude's direct approach to things, and it took them somewhat by surprise. "What's he doing here?" said one of them, looking at Horace, then at the horse.

"We don't have time for this," said Maude, her voice rising just enough to let them know she meant business. "Take us to Wallace or we'll sic the horse on you."

Horace rolled his eyes and tried to explain the animal was harmless, but this got him nowhere.

"You're not bringing that thing into the village. What if it tries to eat the sheep?"

Horace smiled and explained that horses don't eat other animals, but the men were unmoved.

"You'll have to leave it here."

"If I do that it will run away," said Horace.

The four men conferred briefly and the unluckiest among them was chosen to hold the horse while the rest went to find Wallace.

"This is ridiculous," said Horace, observing the terror of the poor man who'd been chosen. Horace handed over the rope and told the man to stay clear of the back legs.

"She'll just stand there as long as you don't make any sudden movements," said Horace.

The group moved off while the man holding the rope stood perfectly still, glancing sideways at the glossy shine on the horse's neck. The animal turned and sniffed the man's face, blowing his hair back through thick nostrils, and the man nearly jumped out of his pants.

"Don't feel too bad," said Maude as they departed. "At least you don't have to ride it." She was walking unnaturally bow-legged, feeling the tightness in her legs.

The Village of Sheep was beginning to look dry, less green, and a little worse for the wear. Soon the group found Wallace, who was standing among his sheep in one of the few remaining patches of green grass. He seemed genuinely happy to see them, though Maude and Horace were both alarmed by how little he and the rest had prepared.

"Wallace, what have you been doing all night?" said Maude. "This place doesn't exactly look fortified for an encounter with Cleaners."

"I've been waiting for you," he said.

"That's not much of a plan," said Horace. "I expected more from a man of your intellect."

Wallace scratched the red hair on his head, smiling.

"You're a man of action, and I was sure you would come with plans of your own," he said. "One good plan is better than two competing ones. It saves an awful lot of time, and time has recently become more valuable."

Horace was visibly pleased. If Wallace had forgone making plans and fortifying his village, it meant that the man trusted Horace to lead and that he was not attached to the idea of staying. These were significant steps in the right direction as far as he was concerned.

"Can I speak openly?" said Horace, gazing off at the three men who'd accompanied him and Maude. Others from the village were creeping quietly closer to hear what was going on.

“Come with me,” said Wallace, and he led Horace and Maude away to a rise out in the grass, where the three sat down together.

“Fresh air makes me think better, what about you?” asked Wallace, gulping a deep breath of air and releasing it with a great sigh.

Horace was a gifted communicator, and so it was that he was able to use few words to describe the escape from the Highlands, the formation of a new village, and the encounter with a young Cleaner in the Village of Rabbits. When he came to the plan, Maude broke in.

“We can’t know everything,” she said, concern in her voice. “There are some things we have to guess.”

Wallace gazed at the woman before him and understood her motive.

“You wonder whether I’ve guessed the same as you,” he said, an unnerving sort of coolness in his voice. “We shall see.”

Horace had the distinct feeling that Wallace had indeed made a plan after all, only he hadn’t chosen to share it. Somehow Horace felt the two men had thought of very nearly the same thing.

“The Cleaners,” started Horace, “are our biggest threat now. It is as Maude said—we must all unite against the one enemy—if there is any chance of surviving in these hazardous new surroundings. In another time or place we might have fought for what remains or kept our distance from one another, but this threat comes to kill each and every one of us.”

Maude was still the only one among the three who had

actually seen a Cleaner, but she was incredibly persuasive when she knew she must be. "They will devour everything in their path," she said. There was finality in her voice.

"But there are three things that work to our advantage," continued Horace. "The first is that they appear to be dormant or at the very least quite a bit less dangerous at night. We must use this information wisely." Horace said this with a nod toward Wallace. "The Cleaners crave meat and bones. They are carnivores. Maude has even seen them go after the weakest among them, so they make no distinction between what kinds of meat interest them. *All* meat interests them."

This highly gruesome idea hung in the air on the pale green hill for a few seconds before Horace completed his thought. "They will follow the scent of food."

Wallace only nodded as if Horace had spoken a rather obvious truth.

"People don't smell as strong as animals do," said Horace. "And there's no way to quickly get rid of a smell that's been festering for a very long time. I surmise that the Cleaners will go first to the Village of Rabbits and the Village of Sheep, because these places have the scent of food they will like. They might catch the scent of the horses and come by that way as well, but the really pungent odor of food is in the two villages, and it cannot be erased overnight."

Horace was coming straight to the point now, and kept right on going.

"The grove will be the least interesting to the Cleaners. We may see a small number of them there, but the really big groups will go there last, after . . ." He realized he was touching on a difficult subject.

"After they consume everything in my village," said Wallace, "and hers." He nodded at Maude.

"Unfortunately, I believe that's correct. And I don't think there's anything that can be done about it."

"I completely agree," said Wallace. "Go on."

"If we all converge on the grove but leave most of the animals behind, there is a chance of gaining an upper hand. The Village of Rabbits has already begun to empty out. Everyone is on the move to the grove. Even Gill, one of my men, is moving the Highlanders as we speak."

"You must keep the horses, all of them," said Wallace, breaking in uncharacteristically. "They will be needed."

"We are of the same mind," said Horace. "For now, they are all on the way to the grove, where I hope they'll be happy to eat the figs off the trees and gain some strength."

"Continue," said Wallace.

"I think we can hold the grove," said Horace. It was his most bold statement yet, one he wasn't entirely sure of. "The trees will be of some help, and the greater number of us to fight with the aid of horses. I believe it's our best chance."

Wallace sat motionless, looking out over the green grass that was starting to turn brown in patches.

"So it is to be an exodus," said Wallace. There was a calm force in his voice. "And then a stand to the last."

Horace nodded slowly, not sure if he'd convinced the shepherd to leave his flock.

"Your plan gets us all through today and into the first night in a changed world," said Wallace. "Who knows what another morning will bring that will force us to change course?"

Wallace had hit on precisely the thing Horace had been stewing about all morning. Atherton was changing rapidly and unpredictably. It was a variable that had to be accounted for.

"You said there were three advantages we held over the Cleaners. What is the third?"

And then Horace told of what he thought this third advantage was, and in the telling he could see that Wallace thought the same thing.

"It's time I said goodbye to a good many of my sheep," he said, a weary pitch to his voice creeping in. "We must be on our way."

Cleaners were on the move, a wild fury boiling between them as they climbed over one another to get in front of the pack. The slippery suction cups on their long underbellies were scouring the dust as they went, searching for the trailing scent of food. They made a terrible slurping sound that blended with their clattering legs and snapping jaws. A deadly smell hung in the air.

The Cleaners lunged at one another, biting with their sharp teeth. They were almost three hundred in number, heading directly for the Village of Rabbits, and they had never been in such a rage. It was a slow journey, because one of the beasts would lash out at another and a war would break out between them until one was felled, and the Cleaners that were near heaped into a pile over the victim and devoured it. The race for fresh food sizzled in their tiny brains like acid, driving the Cleaners into an unprecedented frenzy.

They smelled food, lots of it. It was food they would have.

PART TWO

MULCIBER

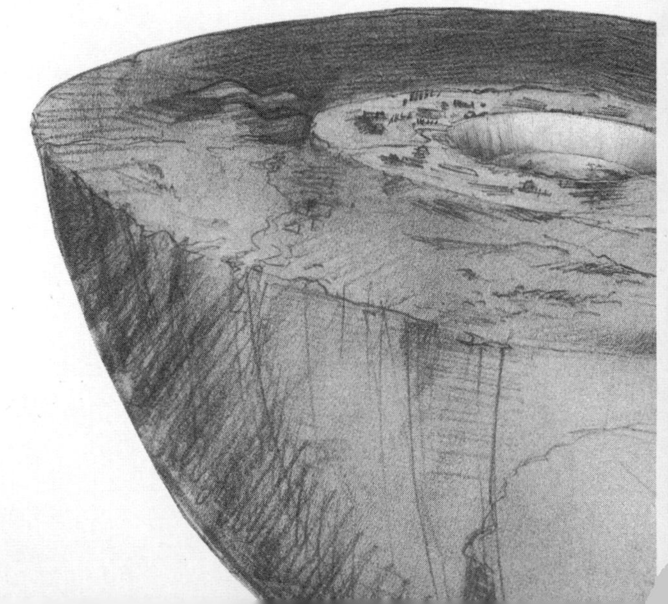

Do I contradict myself?
Very well then I contradict myself,
(I am large, I contain multitudes.)

WALT WHITMAN'S *SONG OF MYSELF*
AS QUOTED BY
DR. MAXIMUS HARDING

CHAPTER 12
TWO PARTIES UNITE

Dr. Kincaid went directly to Mead's Head when they entered the main chamber in the House of Power and ran his hand along the chiseled hair of the statue.

"Just as I left it," he said with some satisfaction. He glanced at Edgar, who was looking back and forth between the bust and Dr. Kincaid.

"Is that *you?*" Edgar asked.

"It most certainly is," said Dr. Kincaid. The old scientist was in a high state of anticipation. "And it appears to be unharmed, which means it might still work as it once did."

"But how . . ." What Edgar was seeing threw his mind into a state of confusion. How could a statue of Dr. Kincaid's head have been in Lord Phineus's chamber all this time, while Dr. Kincaid was in the Flatlands?

Before Edgar had a chance to voice his puzzlement, the floor beneath the group of three began to quake, slow at first but growing more violent. The three stumbled across the room to steady themselves by grabbing vines on the ivy-covered wall.

As the quake grew in intensity, Edgar glanced out the window of the main chamber. The Highlands were crashing fiercely, faster than he had ever seen or imagined any part of Atherton falling. It felt like a near freefall, and as they descended, shadow fell on the Highlands. Edgar could not understand the sound it made. If ever he had heard a massive wave breaking against a shore, he would have said it sounded like that, only the wave would have been filled with boulders the size of houses, exploding all around him.

The Highlands came to a brutal stop, which threw the three companions onto the floor of the main chamber in a heap. Edgar banged his head against Lord Phineus's table on the way down and it nearly knocked him unconscious. The sound of liquid and stone lingered, slowly dying in the air, and Edgar felt as if the brains in his head were sloshing back and forth.

Vincent was the first to rise and look out the arched opening, but soon all three were standing there. Dr. Kincaid put his arm around Edgar.

"Are you all right?" he asked, examining the round bump forming on the boy's forehead. It was bruised, but there had been no blood.

Edgar nodded, but looking out the window made him think differently. They were so deep inside Atherton now, deeper than he could have imagined was possible. Light poured in weakly from above, but frightening shadows now filled the once majestic Highlands.

Edgar looked directly at Dr. Kincaid, rubbing the bump on his head. "I'm not sure I can climb out of here," he said. He could see that the walls in the distance were wet and slippery, and rock fragments were crumbling off and falling into the Highlands as he spoke. "This might be beyond what I can do."

Dr. Kincaid knelt down before Edgar and put one hand on each shoulder, examining Edgar's head. In his mind he pronounced the boy fit for travel.

"One disaster at a time," he said, and then he was quickly up on his feet and moving toward Mead's Head. He turned it back and forth, unlocking the secret passage in the floor, and then he turned to Vincent.

"Have you got what we need?"

"I do indeed," said Vincent. He had been carrying a pack and two spears all along, but now he dropped the spears as if he planned to leave them behind. From the bag he removed a selection of weapons Edgar had never seen. One was a whip, long and leathery, which Vincent coiled in a circle and held in one hand.

"He's quite talented with that," said Dr. Kincaid. "Sort of like you with the sling and the black figs."

Edgar was so confused that he simply watched as Vincent held his bag in the same hand as the whip and put his other hand inside. When his hand emerged it clutched a magnificent knife the likes of which Edgar had never seen or imagined. The blade was a foot long, made of something that reflected the weak light in the room.

"What are you going to do with that?" said Edgar. "You can't get close enough to a Cleaner to use it."

Vincent didn't answer but instead looked at Dr. Kincaid. "I'm ready," he said. "Open it up."

"Open *what* up?" said Edgar. There was a deep ache in his forehead and it was making him irritable. He was growing tired of being kept in the dark.

Dr. Kincaid stepped over the ivy-covered floor near the wall and removed the cover to Mead's Hollow.

"We'll need light," he said.

Vincent handed the knife to Dr. Kincaid and went into the outer hall without hesitation as Edgar approached the hole in the floor. He saw the words chiseled into the stairs leading down but could not read them.

"It's called Mead's Hollow," said Dr. Kincaid. Vincent returned with a torch from outside and held it down into the dark passage. "It's here, beneath the House of Power, that we shall find Dr. Maximus Harding."

Edgar was thunderstruck. "What's he doing down there?"

Vincent uncoiled the whip in his hand, playing it back and forth on the stairs like a snake.

"That's exactly what I've been wondering," said Dr. Kincaid.

From the moment the door to Mead's Hollow had been closed Isabel was unable to shake the feeling that she would never get back out again. It created a knot in her throat that would not leave, a knot that was telling her to cry and curl up into a ball in the dark where no one could find her. But Isabel forced the knot deeper down her throat, willing herself to go on.

She and Samuel had been in Mead's Hollow for hours. At first there had been a steep switchback path surrounded by walls on every side. Down, down, down they'd gone, past the bottom of the House of Power and into Atherton itself. In the silence of her own thoughts Isabel wondered just how deep the Highlands had fallen into the middle of Atherton.

There came a moment when the air turned cold and the space changed in tone. Without warning, their way went from confined to abysmally wide open. There was but one wall to lean their bodies against, and as Samuel held the flame out and away from it, the darkness seemed to go on forever. Isabel had the feeling that if she walked out into the open space it would swallow her up. And what was worse, there was an almost unbearable sensation that the whole world of Atherton was crashing in around her. She clung to Samuel, desperate to find a way out of Mead's Hollow.

"How much farther?" she asked, her voice drifting softly in the wide open space.

"We've got to be getting close," answered Samuel. "I can't imagine it being much farther."

The two had followed the instructions that had been given

to Samuel by his father a long time ago, and Isabel was beginning to think Samuel had read them wrong.

"Are you absolutely sure we're going the right way?" she asked. There was a part of her that had no idea why she was trying to find the source of water to begin with. It was a journey begun with a purpose, but the purpose was starting to feel a little beside the point. Even if they could find it and make the water flow once again, the Highlands were sinking, so what good would it do? And how would they ever get out?

Samuel didn't answer Isabel. She'd already asked him the same question three times. The truth was, he wasn't at all sure. He only knew what his father had written down on the note, most of which he didn't think he should share with Isabel:

— Find the blue line and follow it. Never waver from the blue line.
— If you see the Crat, click your teeth fast and loud; it will keep them away for a while. This is a secret known to me alone.
— Do not allow yourself to be bitten by the Crat. A scratch can be overcome, but a bite cannot.
— If the Crat attack, you must not try to run. Put your back against the wall and fight them.

"What about the yellow line?" asked Isabel, startling Samuel from his thoughts. He held the flame out from the wall of moist stone they walked beside. There, on the floor of rocks they walked along, was a line of yellow running off into the darkness where they could not see. The air felt vast and open in that direction, as if it might go on for miles.

"My father said to never leave the blue line," said Samuel. "Wherever the yellow one leads, I don't think we want to follow it."

He brought the flame back in front of him and saw that it was waning. The sticky fuel supply, a substance like a glob of black mud at the tip of the torch, was growing smaller and wouldn't last forever. Soon it would be out, and then what would they do?

"I think we should go back," said Isabel. She eyed the blue line on the wall, which snaked like a thin ribbon of translucent blue rock cutting through the wall at eye level. It would lead them out of this place.

"We have to be close now," said Samuel. "My father said it would take a few hours, so it has to be . . ."

The sound of the Crat crept up on them like a shadow and Samuel was cut short. *Eeeeeeeeek! Eeeeeeeeek!* There were three or four of them, and they were near. The Crat made a shrieking sound, though not very loud, like a tiny person with a head the size of an eyeball screaming. It was, strangely, a sound of bitter sadness, as if whatever were making the noise wanted not to kill them but to rub up against their legs and be picked up.

Isabel and Samuel began slamming their teeth together in the air, opening their mouths as wide as they could, and the Crat seemed to stop. Samuel held the torch out, putting his back up against the wall, and peered into Mead's Hollow. He saw something move, darting across his line of sight and then back into the dark where it was lost. Whatever it was had a very long, hairless tail and black eyes that shone in the firelight.

Isabel was surer than ever that they should turn back. It would take hours to follow the blue line out of Mead's Hollow, but at least they knew the way. She dreamed of going back to her parents, to the grove, to her life the way it had been before Atherton started crashing in on itself. But she also knew that none of these things were possible. Even if she could get out of Mead's Hollow, she was still trapped in the Highlands, and even if she could find a way out of the Highlands, there was still no water in the grove.

"Why are we doing this, Samuel?" she asked. "Do we really think we can find the source of water? And what if we do? What difference will it make?"

Samuel didn't listen. There was something else occupying his every thought.

"Look there," he said, pointing into the darkness. There was a dot of light, flickering but steady. It was not moving. "What do you think that is?" asked Samuel.

"Maybe it's the source of water. There might be a door by that light."

Samuel held out the torch and looked at the ground before his feet. There was another yellow line leading out into the dark. In fact, there were many yellow lines, all leading away from the safety of the wall at their backs.

"We can't go out there," said Samuel. "It's not what my

father said." He glanced at the wall again, saw the blue line leading on, and touched it.

"But it's a *light,* Samuel. Something's over there."

The two argued in whispers, but it was a quarrel they didn't need to have, for the light began to move toward them. Soon it was noticeably closer.

"Someone's down here," said Samuel. His voice was electric with fear.

Isabel was naturally prone to acting on instinct in the face of oncoming danger, and she took out her sling. Her hands shook so violently that she had some trouble getting the black fig properly loaded.

"It can only be two people," said Samuel. He was afraid to even say their names, but he whispered them anyway. "Sir Emerik and Lord Phineus."

The sound of the Crat started filling the air, as if a great many of them were surrounding the approaching light. The flame began to twirl around in a circle, and Samuel could only imagine that whoever was out there was trying to keep the Crat from biting them. They could hear the sound of the flame swishing through the open space.

"Hello, Samuel." The cold voice of Lord Phineus came from a few feet away.

Suddenly, the torch was ripped from Samuel's hand and a blade poked playfully at his chest. Isabel screamed. She had not screamed in a very long time, and all the terror she'd felt came out at once as she beheld the twisted face of Lord Phineus in the dancing flames. The scream echoed into the vast and powerful space.

"Nobody can hear you," said Lord Phineus. "At least no one who can do you any good."

Lord Phineus looked positively insane, the black point of the widow's peak on his forehead dripping with sweat over his pale face. His eyes were swollen and glistening.

"What are you doing down here?" he asked. There was a strange sort of glee in his voice.

The sound of the Crat grew nearer, and Samuel could hear Sir Emerik in a rage trying to drive them away.

"Back! Back, I tell you!" *Eeeeeeeek! Eeeeeeeek! Eeeeeeeek!*

It was horrible to listen as Sir Emerik approached, but Lord Phineus seemed unaware of the chaos around him.

"I asked you a question," he said, pushing the tip of the dagger harder against Samuel's chest. "What are you doing down here?"

Eeeeeeeek! Eeeeeeeek! Eeeeeeeek!

The Crat were nearly on top of them, and Isabel began banging her teeth together so violently it startled even Lord Phineus. He began to laugh like a madman, which gave the whole of Mead's Hollow a feeling of mayhem. It was a symphony of maddening noise in a place not accustomed to such a racket.

As if to answer in reply, Atherton itself began to quake and shudder. It would not be outdone by mere mortals. Very soon the deafening sound of rushing water and crashing boulders filled the air, and the floor felt as if it were being pulled out from underneath them in fits and starts.

Meanwhile, Sir Emerik crawled clumsily toward the group, one hand swinging the flame all around him. But the Crat had gone away, and as Atherton settled into a dull, echoing roar, he looked up and saw Samuel.

"You!" screamed Sir Emerik. "It's only *you?*"

Sir Emerik looked at Lord Phineus, who had stopped laughing and was leaning heavily against the wall.

"You sent me out there so we could catch two foolish *children?*"

Allowing himself to be unguarded with no wall at his back turned out to be a bad decision for Sir Emerik. At that moment a Crat came from behind and leaped onto his back, clamping its teeth into him. He squirmed and shouted, waving the flame in every direction until the Crat was struck with the torch and released him.

"I'll only ask you once more," Lord Phineus said to Samuel, unmoved by his companion's plight. "Why have you come here?"

Samuel felt momentarily as helpless as he had when Lord Phineus taunted him in the House of Power. "We're looking for the source of water," he confessed, shaking.

Everything had gone quiet. The Crat were gone and Atherton was at rest. Lord Phineus knelt down and put his face a few inches from Samuel's. White fluid dripped from Lord Phineus's nose, the end of a trail that started in the corners of his eyes.

"Then you will be pleased," said Lord Phineus. His eyes glared heavily at the boy. "The blue line stops here, Samuel. You've found what you came for."

Lord Phineus hauled Samuel along the wall a few more feet and yelled behind him to Sir Emerik.

"Seize her!"

Sir Emerik took hold of Isabel and led her forward. He did not look well. What hair he had was matted grotesquely against his face. His eyes were bulging—not as much as Lord Phineus's were, but bulging nonetheless. And the terrible twitch remained, jolting in the firelight.

The men dragged Samuel and Isabel along until they arrived in front of a door. The door was of average size top to bottom and side to side, but it had a feeling of thickness that could not be measured. There was a latch of a kind Samuel had never seen. Putting down his torch, Lord Phineus took hold of it.

"You came looking for the source of water," said Lord Phineus. "You shall find something altogether different."

He jerked the heavy door open forcefully. When the door was open far enough Samuel was thrust inside and Isabel thrown in behind him. Lord Phineus followed, for he had reason to want to see the boy's reaction to what would be found inside. But this was a disastrous mistake. The moment he entered, Sir Emerik slammed shut the door and locked the three inside.

Every part of Sir Emerik shook with excitement. He had finally rid himself of Lord Phineus.

“No one remains! I am lord now, Lord Emerik, Lord of the Highlands!”

But the truth was Sir Emerik had been bitten by the Crat, and his weak mind was already awash in madness. He heard a familiar, quiet sound coming from the distance in Mead’s Hollow.

Eeeeeeeek! Eeeeeeeek! Eeeeeeeek!

Sir Emerik touched the wall at his side and began running.

CHAPTER 13
THE SECRET AT THE SOURCE

Sir Emerik ran until his breath was gone, and still he heard the sound of the Crat behind him. They were on him, and this time they would not relent. Ten, maybe more, huddled in close. They had been denied a victim among many opportunities for too long, and Sir Emerik felt a deep concern that this time the creatures would not relent.

This was the first time Sir Emerik could really see the Crat. They were not as small as he'd supposed. The Crat were a full three feet long—five if you counted the hairless tail twitching behind—and powerfully built. They were black, which made them hard to see, but now it seemed that they *wanted* him to see them.

If Sir Emerik had ever seen a large house cat or a common

city rat, he would have said the creature before him looked like both at once. This would have been correct, because that's exactly what the Crat were—a hybrid species dreamed up by Dr. Maximus Harding and left to roam Mead's Hollow. He'd had great hopes for the Crat but found them wild and unpredictable. And yet, as with so many of his creations, he could not bring himself to destroy the Crat. He preferred to hide his flawed inventions, and Mead's Hollow had seemed as good a place as any.

Sir Emerik whipped the torch back and forth and managed to set one of the Crat on fire. He watched it roll and scream and smelled its burning hair. It reminded him of having his own hair burned off by Edgar, and for a moment he was distracted, letting down his guard.

It was then he felt the pain. Looking down, he saw the Crat at his boot. Its long, sharp teeth had pierced the leather, and jaws that seemed capable of crushing gravel into dust were clamping down around his big toe. He kicked furiously and set the beast on fire with the torch, but it would not let go. It wasn't until Sir Emerik batted the creature repeatedly with the torch that it finally released him. He kicked the flaming animal out into the darkness and to his astonishment it ran off, rolling the fire off its back as it went, until he could see it no more.

"Get back! Leave me alone!" he shouted. Having witnessed the man set fire to not one but two of the Crat, the creatures seemed to rethink their idea of taking him down. They screamed horribly but moved off.

REMEMBER THE RULER OF PANDEMONIUM

BEWARE OF THE CRAT!!!

REJEWSKI — CRYPTOGRAPHER, 1932

MEADS HOLLOW

CRAT

REVIEW – ENIGMA MACHINES

COMBINE REIHENSCHIEBER WITH BAZERIES

Sir Emerik felt a searing pain inside his boot, as if all of the skin had been torn off his toe. It was a pain that matched very closely that of the wound on the shin of his opposite leg. He had been bitten twice now.

Sir Emerik heard the snapping sound of a whip from somewhere in Mead's Hollow. "Who could that be?" he muttered to himself. He looked toward the sound and saw light coming his way. "Maybe it's that Tyler come to find me. How long have I been down here?" Sir Emerik heard the whip cracking again. "Tyler!" he howled. "Tyler, I'm here, against the wall! Follow the blue line!"

Sir Emerik felt suddenly better, as if he might escape Mead's Hollow after all. He remembered that he was in charge, that he was Lord Emerik now and would rule, if only he could get out. And then it was as if these indulgent thoughts of power were almost too much for him to bear and his head were swelled to overflowing. His brain felt full of a liquid rumbling, like it was turning wet and about to run out of his nose. He was slowly losing his mind.

Eeeeeeeek! Eeeeeeeek! Snap! Snap! Snap!

The Crat and the whip traded turns echoing through Mead's Hollow while Sir Emerik stood with his back to the wall, waiting for Tyler to find him.

But of course it was not Tyler who came upon this broken man, but Edgar, Dr. Kincaid, and Vincent. Vincent cracked the whip several times for good measure, and what Crat remained scattered at this new threat.

"Who are you?" said Dr. Kincaid, gazing at Sir Emerik as if he didn't belong in Mead's Hollow. "Who let you in here?"

Sir Emerik did not answer. His eyes lay heavy on Edgar, and he was consumed with one thought—to take the torch in his hand and set Edgar on fire. How could this terrible boy have climbed down in the Flatlands and yet be standing before him? Sir Emerik's face contorted with rage, and he lunged toward Edgar.

Edgar was a very quick child, as we have come to know, and he dodged the oncoming flames without difficulty. Vincent snapped the whip toward Sir Emerik and caught him with a stabbing pain in the ear. Trying to set Edgar on fire qualified as a violent act, and Vincent acted in kind.

"Who are you?" Dr. Kincaid asked once more.

"It's Sir Emerik," said Edgar. "He serves Lord Phineus."

This seemed to baffle Dr. Kincaid even further. "But what's he doing down here? He shouldn't be here."

There was a little anger in his voice, as if he felt Mead's Hollow was a sacred place for only a few and that he alone could invite people into it. It struck him that Sir Emerik was not the kind of person he would invite.

"Children!" cried Sir Emerik, touching the new wound on his ear inflicted by the whip. "Children will be my undoing!"

He was raving, but something about what he'd said made Edgar jump. "What do you mean?"

"I mean Samuel and that girl, and now *you!* Why must you all torment me?"

This was a shocking piece of news for Edgar. Could Samuel and Isabel be trapped in Mead's Hollow?

"You mean there's *more?*" said Dr. Kincaid, bewildered by the idea of so many people wandering around in such a forbidden place.

Even as he was losing control of his own mind, Sir Emerik had the capacity to dream up evil schemes. He stared at the group before him and heard the distant scuffling of the Crat.

"I will tell you where to find the boy and the girl, but you will let me pass. I must get free of this place, and of him!" Sir Emerik pointed to Edgar is if he were a monster, and wished with everything in his black heart that the Crat would tear the boy apart.

"You've been bitten, haven't you?" said Dr. Kincaid. "You should know it won't end well. A few hours, a day at most, and you'll be finished."

"Shut up, old man!" cried Sir Emerik. "I've never felt better in my life. And you should be more polite when talking to the lord of all Atherton. There are many who fear me."

Dr. Kincaid didn't have the slightest idea what Sir Emerik was talking about.

"He's of no use to us," Vincent assessed. Dr. Kincaid nodded and stepped back, giving Vincent authority to do as he pleased.

"You must let me go first, then I'll yell back to you," said Sir Emerik, starting along the wall with the blue line. Vincent cracked the whip, then took Sir Emerik by his filthy robe and held him out toward the open of Mead's Hollow.

"Speak," said Vincent. "Or I'll throw you into the dark and you'll be dinner for the Crat. Tell us where the children are!"

Eeeeeeeeeek!

Sir Emerik heard the Crat coming nearer, and his blood went cold. He couldn't get the words out fast enough. "That way, you'll find a door. The door to the source of water. The four of them are locked inside."

"What do you mean, the *four* of them?" asked Dr. Kincaid.

"Just let me go! Please let me go!" Sir Emerik was crying out with such agony that Vincent simply couldn't take it any longer. He hauled Sir Emerik along the wall, toward a far-off exit, and thrust him to the ground.

"Do not try to follow us," he commanded. "You won't like it if I see you again."

There were two torches now, and Edgar threw one toward Sir Emerik. It sparked on the ground and was picked up, and then Sir Emerik was gone, racing for the door that led out of Mead's Hollow.

The group of three moved on, cracking the whip as they went and occasionally connecting with a Crat coming too close to Vincent's watchful eye. Soon they were at the door, a door Dr. Kincaid knew well.

"What did he mean by four?" said Dr. Kincaid. "I thought there were only two—Samuel and Isabel."

"I think I know who will be the third," said Edgar. "But I have no idea who might be the last."

It was true Samuel and Isabel were trapped in a room with Lord Phineus, but as it turned out, there was something very special hidden in that room besides water.

The room itself was not like anything Samuel or Isabel had seen before. There was light, even though the room was far underground beneath the Highlands and there were no torches. What they saw was a different kind of light, creeping out from somewhere beneath a series of nine perfectly circular pools of water in the room. The pools were scattered randomly across a large, open area that was black and cold. It was haunting to behold—an unnatural path of round, watery light on the floor—and it made Isabel shiver. She leaned out over the first pool and thought it looked bottomless.

"What's happened to this place?" asked Isabel. No one answered her.

There were chunks of wood and stone and frayed lengths of rope lying along the edge of the pools, as if once there had been some water-releasing system in place. Atherton's collapse had destroyed whatever it had been, and Isabel had a lingering sense that the water was trapped here, in the nine pools, never again to flow freely. The children's eyes moved curiously around the room, momentarily forgetting that they were not alone.

Lord Phineus was locked inside the vast room with them, and it had produced a chilling effect on the master of the fallen Highlands. He had moved off alone into a dark corner near one of the pools, intent on nursing his wounded mind. Lord Phineus knew there was someone else in the room, someone the children didn't know anything about, but Lord Phineus was not

prepared for the attack from behind, the ropes that tied his hands, the firm push to the ground.

"Who's there?" asked Samuel, gazing into the dark corner of the vast room of circular pools and paths.

"It's a trick," said Isabel. "Lord Phineus is fooling with us."

She was searching around for something she could use as a weapon and struck upon a long splinter of wood from one of the pulleys. Out of the darkness came the shadow of a man, tall and lanky.

"Get back, Lord Phineus! Get back, I tell you!" cried Isabel.

She very nearly began stabbing the stick toward the approaching figure when Samuel spoke.

"Wait," he said hesitantly, as if he might be seeing a ghost. "That's not Lord Phineus. It's someone else."

"Someone else indeed," came a familiar and friendly voice from the past. Into plain view strode Sir William, Samuel's long-lost father.

"Samuel!" he cried. There was a year's worth of emotion in his voice. "Samuel!" he cried again, running around the rims of the pools and watching his boy do the same until they met.

Sir William knelt down and Samuel rushed into his arms. The two embraced, and it looked to Isabel as if Sir William would never let his son out of his arms again.

CHAPTER 14
THE YELLOW LINE

There was an all-too-brief moment of happy catching up between the father and the son, in which Sir William was overjoyed to learn that Samuel's mother was alive. Sir William looked unexpectedly well, for he had been drinking all he wanted from the source of all water. And there had been plenty of food, delivered in reasonably large quantity by Lord Phineus himself. He would bring supplies and the two would make adjustments to the flow of water together, adjustments that required two men to achieve.

Lord Phineus brought their happy reunion to a stop by shouting from where he sat at the edge of the third pool. As Samuel turned toward the awful voice it appeared to him as if Lord Phineus had been tied up and was struggling to free himself. A great many beams, frayed ropes, and metal gears were piled up around him. His boots were in the water, and his robe dangled heavy and wet over the edge.

"Is he trapped?" asked Samuel, looking to his father for an explanation.

"Untie me, you fool!" screamed Lord Phineus, his black boots splashing water as if he were a three-year-old having a tantrum. "We can't stay in here!"

"He's not as strong as he once was," said Samuel's father. "It wasn't as hard to gain control over him as I thought it might be."

"Was he bitten by one of those creatures?"

Sir William nodded. "I believe he's going mad before our eyes."

"Release me!" cried Lord Phineus again. He seemed to lose some of his vigor and hung his head, his chest heaving in and out.

Isabel had been listening carefully to everything going on around her, but she had remained aloof, standing with her back against the door.

"Who is this pretty girl you've dragged down here with you?" asked Sir William. His voice was gentle as he reached out toward her. He could see that she was afraid of him.

"I'm Isabel, and he didn't drag me along." Isabel wanted not to trust this man before her, but with his kind blue eyes and shaggy beard he looked more like he belonged in the grove than in the halls of power in the Highlands. "I came looking for the source of water so I could release it again," she continued. "The grove is drying up."

She hadn't yet taken Sir William's hand when it was held

out to her, and seeing she was a spirited sort of girl, he pointed his hand instead at the first pool of water.

"It looks to me as if you could use some water yourself. You'll find none better."

Samuel went straight to the pool and began lapping up water into his mouth and came up with a huge *aaahhhhhhh!* But Isabel was afraid Sir William might push her in.

"Samuel said you disappeared over a year ago," she began. "That you'd fallen from the Highlands. He and his mother thought you were dead. They felt lost without you for so long. What have you been doing down here all this time?"

"That's a fair question," answered Sir William. He ran his fingers through a beard flecked with grey that made him look older than he was.

"I was brought here against my will." He looked at Lord Phineus, who had grown disturbingly quiet. "He made things very clear. Either I come here and turn the water off or on as he commanded, or Samuel and his mother would *accidentally* have a tragic fall over the edge of the Highlands."

Sir William looked at Samuel. "If I'd tried to escape, you and your mother would have been killed. I had no choice but to remain here and do his bidding."

Then Lord Phineus must have been as evil as she'd always imagined, Isabel thought. Satisfied with Sir William's explanation, she started toward the pool of glowing water to drink her fill. Sir William smiled and touched her on the arm. "Everything will be all right. I'll make sure nothing happens to either of you."

It was the first time since leaving home that Isabel felt a keen sense of being protected. She hadn't realized how much she'd missed the care of her parents, and it made her wonder what Edgar's life as an orphan had been like.

Soon the reunion turned to darker matters. They were trapped behind a locked door, Atherton was violently collapsing in on itself, and Cleaners were on the loose. But though the news was harrowing and hard to imagine for Sir William, he never stopped encouraging Samuel and Isabel, and they felt mysteriously safe in a world gone crazy.

At length Sir William glanced across the pools of water at Lord Phineus and found that he should have been paying more attention to his captive. Now that his eyes had adjusted to the meager light in the room, he could see that his captive had been quietly working on the ropes and was very nearly free of them.

"Stay here!"

Samuel and Isabel nodded their agreement and watched as Sir William rushed between the pools to Lord Phineus. As if suddenly a lunatic, Lord Phineus began shouting but not forming words, struggling to free himself from the ropes that ensnared him. In the tussle, Sir William slipped and crashed into the water of the third pool as Lord Phineus kicked frantically with his black boots. One of the boots caught Samuel's father across the face and he went under.

"No!" cried Samuel. He began running toward the scene with Isabel close behind. "Leave him alone!"

But Samuel needn't have worried. Sir William had kept in very good condition as the keeper of the water. Lord Phineus was no match in his altered state of mind, and when Sir William exploded out of the water the tide quickly turned in the fight. Sir William turned Lord Phineus over and slammed his face into the stone floor. He tied his hands to a beam once more and sat him up.

"Stay put. I won't be so friendly next time."

"Cut me loose!" cried Lord Phineus. "I must leave this place!"

In the midst of all the hysteria, something happened that even Sir William could not have imagined.

The heavy locked door leading into the room began to move.

Isabel was the first to notice the door opening, which also made her the first to see Edgar barge into the room. She was speechless for a long moment—everyone was—but finally, it was Isabel who said something.

"Can it really be you?"

"I could ask you the same question," said Edgar. This was how he'd always talked to her, and it didn't cross his mind to change his ways now. But for Isabel, this was one time she could not allow herself to pretend as if she didn't have feelings for the boy standing at the door. She ran to Edgar and embraced him. To Edgar's great surprise, he hugged her back.

"I believe I'll be all right now," she said, gathering herself as she stepped back and looked at Edgar. "We're going to get out of here."

Everyone went about the quick business of hearing how in the world they'd all arrived in the same place. "I told you he didn't fall!" said Edgar on hearing the news that Sir William was Samuel's father.

Dr. Kincaid and Vincent, shaking their heads in disbelief, had moved off toward Lord Phineus. They seemed to have a great deal of curiosity about him. The two of them were standing over Lord Phineus, trying to talk to him, but it seemed as if Lord Phineus would not listen. He was kicking at the water and yelling at them to leave him alone. Whatever Dr. Kincaid and Vincent were saying, it could not be heard by the others from across the long room.

As Edgar watched this puzzling scene he began to sense that something was moving. It was the water in the pools. The light was shimmering and shaking on the walls and the ceiling, and suddenly, Sir William was alarmed.

"Move toward the door!" he screamed. The smile had vanished from his face as Atherton came alive again. The water in the pools began to slosh back and forth lazily at first and then began bouncing unnaturally.

"The water's too high!" said Sir William, pushing the children back against the wall and staring into the pools.

"What do you mean?" Vincent shouted from across the room.

"The water was always somewhere far below, deep in the nine holes, but it's finally come to the very top. We're about to be flooded!"

Vincent gave his whip and the one lit torch they had among them to Dr. Kincaid, then he rapidly untied Lord Phineus and hauled him up on his feet. The captive struggled mightily at first, but Vincent knew well how to contain a man half his strength. He held his arms back in such a way that the slightest fight from Lord Phineus produced sharp pain from his knuckles to his shoulders.

When the nine pools began overflowing, the three men were nowhere near the door. In the blink of an eye the room became like a storm on an ocean, water flowing out of the glowing holes faster than anyone could have imagined possible.

"Take the children out!" cried Vincent. "Get them past the door, into Mead's Hollow!"

Sir William guided Samuel, Isabel, and Edgar toward the exit. They were propelled off their feet by the rush of water, and the three of them tumbled into Mead's Hollow where the storm had room to run shallow and wide.

They were soaking wet when Vincent came out into the dark with Lord Phineus. He had managed to keep the flame alive through the torrent of water by holding it high above his head. Throwing Lord Phineus against the wall, he gazed back at the door in search of his companion.

Atherton shook mercilessly, falling farther as waves of water reached as high as the middle of the doorway. Everyone had reached the other side of the door when they realized that Dr. Kincaid was not among them.

When Atherton began to settle into a low hum, the water flowed through the door more slowly, and finally, Dr. Kincaid came tumbling out into Mead's Hollow, coughing and wheezing. Sir William pulled Dr. Kincaid out of the line of rushing water and slapped him on the back hard and fast.

“Stop that!” cried Dr. Kincaid, spitting and belching up water. “I’m fine. I only need a moment to recover.”

There was a brief silence as everyone listened to the gurgling and grinding of Atherton coming to a halt.

“We almost lost you in there,” said Vincent, still holding Lord Phineus so that his face was against the wall. “You must be more careful.”

“Tell that to Atherton!” howled Dr. Kincaid. Seeing all eyes on him, he was a little bothered by the attention he’d drawn to himself. He rose to his feet.

“Turn him around. He must look at me!”

Lord Phineus did not comply easily. He did not want to look at Dr. Kincaid. When he finally did there was a moment of terror on his face, then recognition.

“Mead’s Head!” he cried out. “How can it be you have Mead’s Head?”

But Dr. Kincaid was in no mood to answer the questions of a lunatic. He looked Lord Phineus square in the eye and commanded him to move.

“To the yellow line!”

Edgar, along with everyone else, had no idea why Dr. Kincaid wanted to follow the yellow line or why he suddenly thought Lord Phineus would listen to him. So it came as a surprise when Lord Phineus seemed to noticeably deflate. He began mumbling about Mead’s Head, yellow lines, and ladders. And then, to everyone’s amazement, he obeyed the command.

“I’m going to need light,” he said. There was a terrible, quiet anger in his voice. “If you expect me to go out there.”

Vincent held the only light they had among them, but he didn't want to give the light to Lord Phineus, for fear that he would stick the torch directly into the water and snuff it out. The man was crazy. He probably wanted them all to die.

Vincent held the light over the watery ground. There was still an inch or more of water covering everything he could see, but the yellow line heading out into the wide open of Mead's Hollow could be clearly discerned. He handed the torch to Sir William and had him stand nearby.

Lord Phineus did not hesitate when he saw the line. He began staggering toward it, with Vincent holding him tightly from behind. Everyone fell into step behind them, until all the light from the room was gone and only the one torch remained.

CHAPTER 15

ONE VILLAGE REMAINS

The world outside was rapidly changing as Lord Phineus led a group of people through the underground realm of Mead's Hollow. It was midday, and the grove was bustling with activity. Everyone from the surrounding villages had come together amid the trees—three hundred from the Village of Sheep, about the same from the Village of Rabbits, and two hundred more from the Highlands. There were more than a thousand in total including those already living in the grove.

Everyone had either been given a task or guided into the safest places to hide. Some were working with the remaining animals, building pens and holding areas deep in the thickest part of the grove where their smell would hopefully remain contained. Many watched the perimeter of the grove, searching the landscape for anything that moved. Others were building things with parts of broken-down houses: makeshift shelters, spears or clubs, and ladders leading up into the largest trees.

One of the great advantages of coming to the grove was the trees that could be opened up and gutted. The orange insides mixed with a tiny bit of water was a quick and easy source of food, and it helped a great deal considering how little water and food they had been lucky enough to bring with them. They had been told not to kill and cook any of the animals. The smell would travel on the air even more than that of the live animals, and this would almost certainly attract Cleaners.

Gill, who almost always remained on a horse, traveled back and forth from the edge of the Highlands and around the grove. Throughout the morning Atherton shook violently, then settled, then shook again, and each time Gill returned to the edge of the Highlands to see how much farther it had fallen.

"How deep will it go?" he asked himself, gazing down into the shadowy land that had once been his home. He detected a scent with his long nose. There was something different in the air, very subtle but close. He made his way around the edge of the grove toward the Flatlands, feeling a little more nervous.

While everyone else was busy with the work of fortifying the grove, Maude, Horace, Wallace, and Isabel's father, Charles, sat together on the porch of Mr. Ratikan's house. It was the only part of the house that hadn't been torn to pieces by Atherton's violent changes. As they made plans, there had come an unexpected moment of silence in the group, and Charles sniffed the air.

"I can already smell the rabbits," he said. "They really do stink."

“That’s not rabbits—it’s the horses,” said Maude, feeling protective of the small and harmless animals she’d worked with for as long as she could remember.

“No, I believe it’s the sheep,” said Horace. “The sheep smell more than I’d expected.”

Wallace was the first to smile, but then the others followed, recognizing that their petty argument was beside the point. “We couldn’t leave them all behind,” he said. “There have to be some for a fresh start, when we find our way out.”

“We’ll need to tell the others soon,” said Horace. He was thinking of the many families in the grove, including his own son and wife whom he’d hardly seen since the trouble began. “We can’t stay here forever.”

Charles was the most concerned about their plans. His only child, Isabel, was missing, and he wanted to give her every chance of being found.

“We don’t need to leave for a while yet,” said Charles. “We could last a few days, maybe longer.”

Maude had never had children and could only wonder what it would feel like if one of her own were missing in a land teaming with Cleaners. And yet she could not help telling the truth as she saw it, her lack of tactfulness on full display.

“We risk losing everyone if we stay on too long,” she said. “Isabel could be anywhere.”

This did not comfort Charles. He knew it was true, knew that she might already be dead, and he felt helpless. He glared at Maude, but she would not look at him.

“Gill’s the best tracker among us, and he’s searching for

Isabel," said Horace. "If she's out there, that nose of his will find her."

"What if she's in one of the other villages?" pleaded Charles.

"She's not," said Maude. "We moved everyone out. She's just not there, Charles."

Charles paused a moment, not sure how to proceed. "Do you think"—he stood and rubbed his hands nervously on his legs—"do you think she could be down *there?*"

No one answered, but there had long since been a feeling among the group that Isabel was very likely trapped in the Highlands and that she would never escape.

"Is there any way to get down inside?" he asked, his mind turning to desperate measures.

"The only way I know of would be Edgar," answered Maude. "He could do it, but he's missing just like Isabel. People in the grove say they saw him last night, but now he's gone again. Nobody knows where he went."

Charles stepped off the porch and began walking into the grove.

"Charles, we need you here—we have to . . ." Maude started, but Wallace stopped her.

"Let him go," he said. There was an awkward silence and then Maude was distracted by something. She sniffed, staring off into the trees.

"What's that smell?" she asked.

Horace caught the same scent as Maude, the same troubling smell that Gill had barely been able to discern from outside the grove. Horace stood up, scratching his bald head.

"Someone is cooking meat," said Maude. She'd cooked a thousand rabbits in her days and nights at the inn, and she knew the smell of meat on a fire.

Without waiting for a response, Maude bolted through the trees, darting this way and that for fifty yards or more until she came to the foot of a second-year tree where a woman and two children sat together. Horace came up behind Maude and the two stood there, nearly speechless.

"The children were hungry," said the woman at the fire. She held in her hand a stick, at the end of which was a whole rabbit, sizzling over the flames. "They haven't eaten anything but a wad of orange dough in two days."

"You stupid woman!" yelled Maude, appalled at the selfishness of this defiant act. "You've put us all in danger!"

"Maude," said Horace, his voice quiet and calm. "Let this woman feed her children. They deserve a moment's peace."

Maude was about to protest, but her eyes fell on the children and her voice caught in her throat. There were so few children on Atherton — not even a hundred — but how scared they must be! There was a girl and a boy, both very young. They were dirty and thin. And they were terrified.

"I'm sorry," said Maude. She began to tear up — but only a very little — then she turned and walked away.

"Put the fire out the moment you finish," said Horace. The woman nodded, smiling at her children, and Horace followed Maude through the trees.

Most of the Cleaners on Atherton were already busy at their gruesome work in the Village of Rabbits or the Village of Sheep, chasing what they could catch and tearing apart with their monstrous teeth everything in their path as they scrambled over and under one another in search of food. These Cleaners were very focused on the task before them, and they would not be easily distracted.

But they were not the only Cleaners on Atherton. There were a few that always rose later than the rest, that often had their food brought to them, and these were the oldest and largest of them all.

The smell of cooking rabbit drifted ever so silently over the trees and out of the grove, toward the Flatlands. And there the smell caught in the wet nose of a very large Cleaner that was chewing on a dry and dusty bone. This was an angry Cleaner, for it had grown accustomed to having food brought to it by the weaker among them, and in the feeding frenzy it had been forgotten.

The Cleaner reared its head and half of its body a full six feet in the air, pulling a row of suction cups off the ground and pulsing them sickeningly in the air. When it dropped back down its full twelve feet of length made the sound of breaking bones as it lurched forward on its mission. Seven more frightfully large Cleaners formed a line behind the first, and the group began charging for the smell of cooked meat in the grove.

CHAPTER 16
MULCIBER

"What's that you're doing?" asked Vincent. Sir William was chomping his teeth together loudly. Samuel and Isabel had joined in as Lord Phineus led the way deeper into the unknown realm of Mead's Hollow.

"It keeps the Crat away," said Samuel.

"He's right," said Sir William, beaming at his boy. "It's a little trick I discovered by accident down here on one of my early journeys to change the flow of water. Lord Phineus and I were surrounded by a pack of the Crat and I was beating them away with a club. For some reason I started snapping my teeth at them. I guess it was involuntary—a sort of fear gripped me and made me act like a cornered animal. But the interesting thing was, the moment I made that sound, they ran away."

Vincent glanced back at Dr. Kincaid and could tell the two were thinking the same thing.

"It must be an innate fear of Cleaners," said Dr. Kincaid. "The Crat didn't last long in the Flatlands."

"Tell me about the Cleaners," said Sir William. He had heard only bits and pieces of the news of these coming monsters and he was curious about them. He began clapping his teeth together again as Vincent provided a brief explanation of what a Cleaner was, what it ate, and how it behaved.

"And there are about a thousand of them upstairs," Edgar added. "On their way to destroy the grove and the other villages."

"That's terrible!" said Sir William, between clapping teeth. "Can they be stopped?"

Dr. Kincaid glanced back at Sir William. It was cold underground in Mead's Hollow, and Dr. Kincaid was shivering, his clothes heavy with wetness. "There's only one person who can answer that question."

"Who?" asked Sir William, but he got no reply. Vincent had seen something and was directing everyone's attention to it.

"There it is!" he said. At the same time Lord Phineus wavered off the yellow line, away from where Vincent pointed.

"Where do you think you're going?" asked Vincent, tightening his grip on Lord Phineus.

"You can't make me open that thing," he said. A new darkness had entered his voice. The force of his personality had returned, as if it had only been sleeping and gaining strength. "Return me to the House of Power," he demanded.

Vincent kicked the legs out from under Lord Phineus and put a knee in his back, holding him against the wet stone surface of the floor. "I'm afraid you're going to have to do as you're told." He lifted Lord Phineus by the back of his robe and dragged him forward, kicking and screaming, until the yellow line ended about ten feet farther into the darkness.

What everyone saw on the ground at the end of their path was a large, solid yellow circle the width of a man's outstretched arms that contained eight dials with letters on them. The dials were glowing as if there were a light somewhere beneath them, shining up into Mead's Hollow. Edgar went directly to the circle and felt all around it, touching the dials and finding that they snapped from letter to letter. Though they were made of a clear substance, he could only see half of each one, because the other half was hidden beneath the ground. As he clicked one of the dials, new letters appeared and others disappeared beneath the yellow circle.

"What is this thing?" asked Edgar, looking directly at Dr. Kincaid.

Dr. Kincaid didn't answer at first. He watched as Isabel and Samuel crouched around the circle and spun the dials back and forth.

"I'm too old to climb out of the Highlands, Edgar," said Dr. Kincaid. "I think it may be too big a task even for you." He smiled at the children, and his teeth chattered slightly from the dampness. "So we must find another way back to the Flatlands."

"Wait," said Samuel. "Is this a door? A way out?"

"Indeed it is," answered Dr. Kincaid. There was a gleam in his eye. "Move away from it now."

Edgar, Isabel, and Samuel stood together and loomed over the yellow circle as Dr. Kincaid moved in front of Lord Phineus. Vincent held him firm in his grasp.

"You must open that door," said Dr. Kincaid. "You must open it right now."

The lord would not look him in the eye.

"Pandemonium," mumbled Lord Phineus. Then he flew into a rage and Vincent could barely contain him. "*Pandemonium,* I say! That's what you aim to bring to my kingdom! You will not have it! It's mine and mine alone!"

"You know how to open that door," said Dr. Kincaid, his patience stretched. "The password is eight letters and you know them!"

Lord Phineus laughed. Only he knew how to open the yellow door, no one else.

"I know that word," said Samuel. "I know where it comes from."

Dr. Kincaid looked up. "What word?"

"'Pandemonium,'" he said. "I know that word."

Lord Phineus stopped laughing and looked at the boy. There was a crack in his confidence.

"You are a very stupid boy," said Lord Phineus, trying to rattle Samuel with the cruelty of his voice as he had done so many times before. Vincent still held Lord Phineus by the arms and he wrenched them back.

"How do you know that word?" asked Edgar. "Did someone say it to you?"

Samuel answered without hesitation. "No. I read it."

"Read it where?" Edgar prodded.

Samuel thought about all the books he'd enjoyed during his life of ease as a child of the Highlands. There had been so many. But that word. "Pandemonium." Where had he read that word?

And then, like a sharp bolt of lightning, a vision of the book came to him.

"It wasn't a normal book. It was more like a verse. I remember that it was very hard to follow and I didn't finish it. It's called *Paradise . . . Paradise something,*" said Samuel. "It's big — a whole book — but it's only one poem."

"Of course!" Sir William chimed in. "I've read it as well. *Paradise Lost.*"

"Yes! That's it!" cried Samuel.

"Shut up!" demanded Lord Phineus. "Not another word!"

Sir William and Samuel knelt at the yellow door and touched the dials.

"'Pandemonium,'" said Sir William. He looked at his boy. "That was a dark and terrible place in the poem, the most terrible place of all."

"And the ruler of that place, do you remember his name?" asked Samuel.

Sir William thought back, tried to remember, but could not.

"I remember it," said Samuel. "I do, I remember it!"

"Don't you speak that word!" screamed Lord Phineus.

"The ruler of Pandemonium is called Mulciber," said Samuel. "That's eight letters, and there are eight dials."

"Don't open that door!" growled Lord Phineus. He watched as Dr. Kincaid turned the dials.

Dr. Kincaid spelled the word in his head—m-u-l-c-i-b-e-r—the ruler of Pandemonium, and he turned the dials to match the word. He came to the last letter, paused with a glance at Lord Phineus, and turned the final dial to spell the name Mulciber. Steam poured from the edges of the circular door as it began to rise ever so slightly. Sir William clutched the edge of it and began to lift it open.

"Don't!" cried Lord Phineus. "You can't have him back!"

"What's he talking about?" asked Isabel. She had been silently observing, trying to catch a clue here or there to the mystery that was unfolding around her. Lord Phineus turned and lunged at her like a wild animal, trying without success to break free of Vincent's iron grip.

When Sir William had opened the mysterious entryway there was light in Mead's Hollow as there hadn't been before. A pale orange glow emerged from the circle in the ground. It might have been beautiful for a moment, except for the sudden sound of the Crat that exploded all around them. They had been near—nearer than they realized—and the light sent them into a frenzy. *Eeeeeeek! Eeeeeeeek! Eeeeeeek!* Everyone, even Lord Phineus, began crunching the air, trying to scare the Crat away.

"Everyone down the ladder!" cried Dr. Kincaid. "Now!"

He pushed Isabel, Edgar, and Samuel toward the light in the

floor and there they saw a yellow ladder leading down. It hung in the air, ending well above the bottom, almost as if it were floating.

"Give me my whip!" shouted Vincent. Sir William took hold of Lord Phineus and Dr. Kincaid tossed the whip to Vincent. He cracked the whip over and over again toward the swarming Crat as the three children hurried down the ladder. They were followed closely by Dr. Kincaid, but the old man stopped with only his head poking out into Mead's Hollow and he spoke to Lord Phineus.

"You must come with us," he said. "It's the only path left to you."

Lord Phineus looked up, his eyes swollen and rimmed in red. Sir William pushed him toward the circle of light.

"You should not have opened that door," warned Lord Phineus. "I tell you, you can't have him. You won't find him! I won't allow it."

"Get down here this instant!" screamed Dr. Kincaid. He moved down the ladder without another word. Sir William nudged Lord Phineus to the very edge of the opening.

Eeeeeek! Eeeeeek! The Crat were circling very close, and Vincent was having trouble snapping them all away with his whip. Sir William saw one dart into the light and come for his legs. He kicked with all his might and sent the creature flying into Mead's Hollow. He'd had enough.

Sir William had been shoving Lord Phineus toward the opening until finally the captive tumbled in, grabbing the ladder to steady himself. Sir William descended after him, forcing him farther down with the heel of his boot, until the two of them were through and only Vincent remained in Mead's Hollow.

As Vincent made his way toward the opening, Atherton began to shake, moving like a rolling earthquake. The motion knocked Vincent right off his feet. The Crat were bowled over as well, disoriented and unable to attack. One of the Crat tumbled into the hole, landing on its feet next to Lord Phineus. It bit once and Lord Phineus shrieked, kicking the awful creature against one of the walls. The lone Crat darted into a corner, looking for a dark place to hide.

Vincent crawled toward the hole, rolling off course as he went, until finally he reached the yellow ladder. When he was almost all the way inside, he looked back. He could not see the water but he could hear it coming. He took the door by a handle on the inside and he flung it down over his head, shutting himself and the others away.

As Vincent neared the bottom, he saw that the lone Crat was huddled in the corner of a long corridor. Vincent uncurled his whip and snapped at the Crat until it lay lifeless.

"How lovely," said Lord Phineus, a viscous sarcasm in his voice, "that you're always here to protect us."

Vincent had a very real desire to turn his whip on Lord Phineus.

"That way," said Dr. Kincaid, seizing control of the situation. He pointed down a corridor that looked to Edgar as if it sloped downward. The entire floor along the way was illuminated from the bottom with soft orange light. It was a stone floor, but it held wide, clear sections of what appeared to be a murky sort of glass.

"There's no place for him to hide," said Dr. Kincaid, staring at Lord Phineus. "Let him lead the way, and keep a close eye on him."

Vincent snapped his whip, startling Lord Phineus into motion, and the group began to move forward, toward where the light fell away.

Edgar fell into step beside Dr. Kincaid and the two walked in silence for a minute or two. When Edgar spoke, he chose his words carefully.

"How did Lord Phineus know how to open the door?" asked Edgar, a new thought rising in his mind. "Did he lock Dr. Harding down here?"

Dr. Kincaid smiled and pulled on his big earlobe, looking down at the boy.

"I believe he did just that," said Dr. Kincaid.

"Mulciber, is it?" whispered Sir Emerik. He had long since abandoned his torch and traveled in utter darkness and quiet through Mead's Hollow. He had stayed close to the others all along, but he'd hung back when they reached the round yellow door—far enough away to avoid the circle of Crat, but near enough to hear the word. "Mulciber!"

The water had come like a flood, but Mead's Hollow was vast and empty and it would take a great deal of water to fill it.

Sir Emerik stood in an inch of liquid that sloshed at his boots, listening for the sound of the Crat.

"I shall wait a moment, until they've moved away from the door."

There was only one thing that remained in Sir Emerik's mind. One task he must complete before dying, for he knew he was terribly ill, that the Crat had poisoned him beyond repair. He would die, but not before taking his revenge on the one who'd ruined him. Sir Emerik ground his teeth together and reached down into the water, spinning the dials to spell the word that would let him in. He felt the door move on the last letter, wrenching it up with all his strength.

I must kill that wretched boy, Edgar.

CHAPTER

17

DR. HARDING'S LABORATORY

The group of three children, three adults, and one raving madman walked the orange corridor for a few minutes and found that it was quickly descending deeper into the ground. Chunks of stone had fallen from the ceiling and the walls, and they had to maneuver around them.

"Where are we, Dr. Kincaid?" asked Edgar. He had maintained his position next to the old man, hoping to gather some clues to their whereabouts. Samuel and Isabel were near, listening carefully as the two spoke.

After a few steps more in silence Dr. Kincaid offered a little something. "*Inside* Atherton."

Edgar pondered the idea of the two words. *Inside Atherton.* It was a very big idea that he didn't know how to begin exploring.

Dr. Kincaid went on. "You remember all our conversations about Dr. Harding and the Dark Planet?"

"Tell me again, won't you?" said Edgar. He wanted Samuel, Isabel, and Sir William to overhear so they would understand as he did that Atherton was not what it seemed.

Dr. Kincaid glanced back at the others watching him. They needed to know—not everything, but *something*—and now was the perfect time to tell them.

"The Dark Planet was dying," said Dr. Kincaid as they descended the long corridor. "But there was a young man, Dr. Harding—*very* smart—who found a way to make a new world. While the Dark Planet grew darker, the place Dr. Harding made grew larger. It was filled with clean air and water and all sorts of magnificent inventions."

He had almost gotten lost in his thoughts for a moment, but now he stopped and stared at Edgar, Isabel, and Samuel. "Dr. Harding created Atherton. He brought you all here and made you forget your terrible past. And then, for reasons I don't understand, he mysteriously disappeared."

Samuel, Isabel, and Sir William didn't know what to say. They'd thought it was possible from the bits and pieces they'd gotten from Edgar. But the plain truth of it was like being hit over the head with a heavy object. Atherton was made by a man, Dr. Harding, and the man had vanished. And what was more, Atherton was not their true home, the Dark Planet was.

Dr. Kincaid felt he had said enough. He left the group and moved quickly up the corridor to where Vincent kept a watchful eye on their prisoner.

"Lord Phineus," said Dr. Kincaid. Lord Phineus had been hobbling along mindlessly and hadn't looked back as they walked the corridor. But when he stopped and peered back into Dr. Kincaid's eyes, the light in the room seemed to turn him into a monster. His mind was flooded with the sickness of the Crat, sweat beading down his pallid face and dripping from his chin.

"We come to the very place where you locked him away, do we not?" questioned Dr. Kincaid. "It is here we shall find the good Dr. Harding."

Lord Phineus was unmoved. "I'm not taking you in there," he said coldly.

Dr. Kincaid nodded at Vincent and he uncoiled the whip.

"You treat me like an animal!" screamed Lord Phineus. "I won't have it!"

He lunged for Dr. Kincaid, but Vincent cracked the whip and Lord Phineus jumped back.

"Take him," said Vincent, looking to Sir William.

"Wait a moment." It was Dr. Kincaid. He moved closer to Lord Phineus, almost close enough to touch him. "Your time has come to an end," he said. "There is no escaping me."

A change came over Lord Phineus, as if he was only just realizing that something drastic had occurred. Without the aid of anyone pushing or pulling him along, he advanced three or four more steps. The orange corridor made a sharp turn to the right and Lord Phineus disappeared around the corner.

Everyone followed warily behind him. There was another corner, and another, each one turning back against itself until

Edgar came around a last one. He entered a vast room that took his breath away.

The room was shaped like a giant rectangle, and throughout it were columns, each extending ten feet wide, filled with books, thousands upon thousands of books. The light on the floor had grown more yellow, almost white, glowing from behind cloudy, thick glass. But in this room, the floor was covered in numbers—five-digit numbers, scrawled wildly all over the immense floor before Edgar. Light from below shone straight through the numbers in the floor and their shadows struck the ceiling. The ceiling was lower here, only a foot or two over Dr. Kincaid's head, and it was white like the stone used to make Mead's Head. Edgar gazed above him at the countless rows of five numbers, eerie in their crudeness and random shape and size, that filled every part of the ceiling.

"What is this place?" said Sir William. "It looks like the home of a lunatic."

"How right you are," said Dr. Kincaid. "As Edgar could tell you, all of these numbers unlock something different in Dr. Harding's brain. Each one hides an invention, a process. These numbers are the keys that unlock the mysteries of Atherton, but only one person can use them."

Along the walls of the room there were stone tables and instruments Edgar could not understand. Lord Phineus stood facing away from them, gazing at something on one of the tables. Sir William and Vincent were directly behind Lord Phineus, watching for any sudden movements.

"Where's Dr. Harding?" said Edgar. Samuel and Isabel were

standing nearby, listening for an answer. The three of them thought maybe Dr. Harding was hidden behind one of the columns, or perhaps he was dead, left alone for too long in this madhouse of a laboratory. They were very curious to observe him.

Dr. Kincaid looked at all three of the children, smiled awkwardly, and then pointed toward Lord Phineus. "He is there, of course."

"Where? I don't see him," said Isabel. But Edgar had already put two and two together. He looked at Lord Phineus who was tinkering with something at the table.

"Lord Phineus and Dr. Harding are one and the same," said Edgar. "How can that be?"

Dr. Kincaid nearly laughed. "Could it be any other way?"

CHAPTER 18 UNLOCKING DR. HARDING'S BRAIN

"You can't have him back," said Lord Phineus, his voice creeping into the room with a familiar, maddening tone. "His mind is gone. It belongs to me now."

Dr. Kincaid dropped to one knee and spoke to Isabel, Samuel, and Edgar as if they were younger than they really were.

"I must talk to him alone," he said to them. "You may look around and touch the books, but don't play with the things on the stone tables, and don't wander off too far."

Samuel went immediately to the columns of books, while Isabel and Edgar walked past the first of many tables to gaze at the tools and strange objects. They were lost in a world of someone else's making. There were containers of dirt and rocks and seeds. There were models of Atherton at various stages carved from wood and clay and drawings on countless pieces of paper.

Many of the drawings and models were of things that looked frightening: weird plants and trees, winged creatures, Cleaners. Soon Isabel and Edgar drifted apart, each compelled to look in different directions of the vast laboratory.

Dr. Kincaid advanced across the room and stood with Vincent and Sir William. "Leave me with him," he said. "There are things he and I need to discuss."

Sir William began to protest, but Vincent knew better. He guided Samuel's father several steps away, far enough to give the two men of science some space, but near enough that they could pounce on Lord Phineus if necessary.

Dr. Kincaid had no fear of Lord Phineus and came very near to him. But Lord Phineus lurched back against the stone table as if he were trying to keep away from someone who could hurt him.

"Something has happened to the man who built this place," said Dr. Kincaid. "Something that made him lock the yellow door so that he could not be found."

"Stop talking to me," said Lord Phineus. He clapped his hands over his ears. "You can't have him back! Don't you see? There are things he can't know, things that will drive him mad!"

"What would make him lock the door?" repeated Dr. Kincaid, pulling as he often did on his drooping ear. "He burned all the journals and with them all the numbers. But he could not burn the numbers in this room, could he?"

Lord Phineus had been averting his eyes from the host of shadowy numbers that hovered like dark clouds above him.

And yet he had not been able to avoid them. There were too many. The numbers, Mead's Head come to life in the form of Dr. Kincaid, the bite from the Crat—all these things were starting to break Lord Phineus wide open, revealing another man.

"Why don't you look at the ceiling, Dr. Harding?"

"Stop talking to me!" said Lord Phineus. "Atherton is mine and mine alone. You can't have it back!"

"Oh, but I can, and I will," vowed Dr. Kincaid. And then he began reading the numbers on the ceiling out loud, first in a whisper and then a dull voice, and finally, he was yelling the numbers with all his might.

"54329. 21395. 44350. 88604! 56123! 43986!"

"Dr. Kincaid, that's enough!" cried Vincent, afraid of pushing too hard and destroying Dr. Harding, along with everything else on Atherton. "He's not unbreakable. He's still a man."

Lord Phineus had sagged closer and closer to the floor as each number cut deeper through the black fog surrounding his mind. The fog had cleared little by little at the sound of every number, revealing trap door after trap door opening into knowledge he'd hidden away.

But Vincent was right, Dr. Kincaid had to stop, for some of those doors held dense pockets of information that even a brilliant mind could barely contain. Dr. Harding's reentry into the world was happening much too fast, and it threatened to kill the already weakened man who lay slumped on the floor in front of Dr. Kincaid.

Vincent lifted Lord Phineus's head, holding him steady. He appeared to be unconscious and he was pale as a ghost. "You've gone too far," said Vincent, looking at Dr. Kincaid. "He's no good to us if we drive him insane."

But Dr. Kincaid was unmoved. He reached his hand back and slapped Lord Phineus hard on the face, then held him by the chin and said his true name with untold authority.

"You are Dr. Maximus Harding, and you will come out!"

Lord Phineus opened his bloodshot eyes and stared at the man before him. He coughed and touched his face where he'd been hit. And then he spoke.

"What have you done, Dr. Kincaid?"

"I've woken you up," said Dr. Kincaid with a smile. "It's so very good to see you."

Dr. Harding shook his head and rubbed his eyes as though he'd been sleeping for a year, then he rose to his feet with great effort. Everything about him was changed. He was still sick — so very, very sick—but he was no longer Lord Phineus. His expression had always been cruel even in his kindest moments, but the cruelty had vanished, replaced by solemn regret, something that didn't belong on the face of Lord Phineus.

"Why, Maximus? Why did you do this?" asked Dr. Kincaid.

"Because of you," said Dr. Harding. He leaned heavily against the stone table at his back. "And the boy."

Dr. Kincaid suddenly wished he could be alone with Dr. Harding. He didn't want Vincent or anyone else to hear about this most delicate part of their complicated history.

Dr. Harding seemed to be getting a little of his strength

back. He rubbed the sweat out of his eyes and his expression grew stern. "After everything I did for you," he said. "For *them!*"

Them, Dr. Kincaid knew, were the rulers of the Dark Planet who had demanded so much. It was true. Dr. Harding had been terribly used, especially near the end.

"I didn't intend for things to develop as they did," admitted Dr. Kincaid.

"You were supposed to protect me," said Dr. Harding, the words coming out like those of a young boy who'd been betrayed. He scratched fiercely at his leg, and when his hand came back out from beneath his robe, it was covered in blood.

Dr. Kincaid felt ashamed. The boy genius he had found so long ago was terribly injured in every way a man could be. Mind, body, and spirit were broken, and it was Dr. Kincaid's fault.

"I didn't know they would use you that way," said Dr. Kincaid. "I told them not to push you so hard, to let you rest. But they wouldn't listen. I told them even a brilliant mind can be broken if it's not cared for. *Especially* a brilliant mind."

"Why did you do it?" asked Dr. Harding. He was back at the topic of the boy, Dr. Kincaid could tell, and he tried to veer him off the subject.

"What's going to happen to Atherton?"

"Where is the boy?" demanded Dr. Harding. He was unmoved in his resolve to discuss the matter.

"How do we overcome the Cleaners?" shouted Dr. Kincaid. "You must tell me, or everyone will perish!"

There was a drawn-out silence. Dr. Harding leaned against

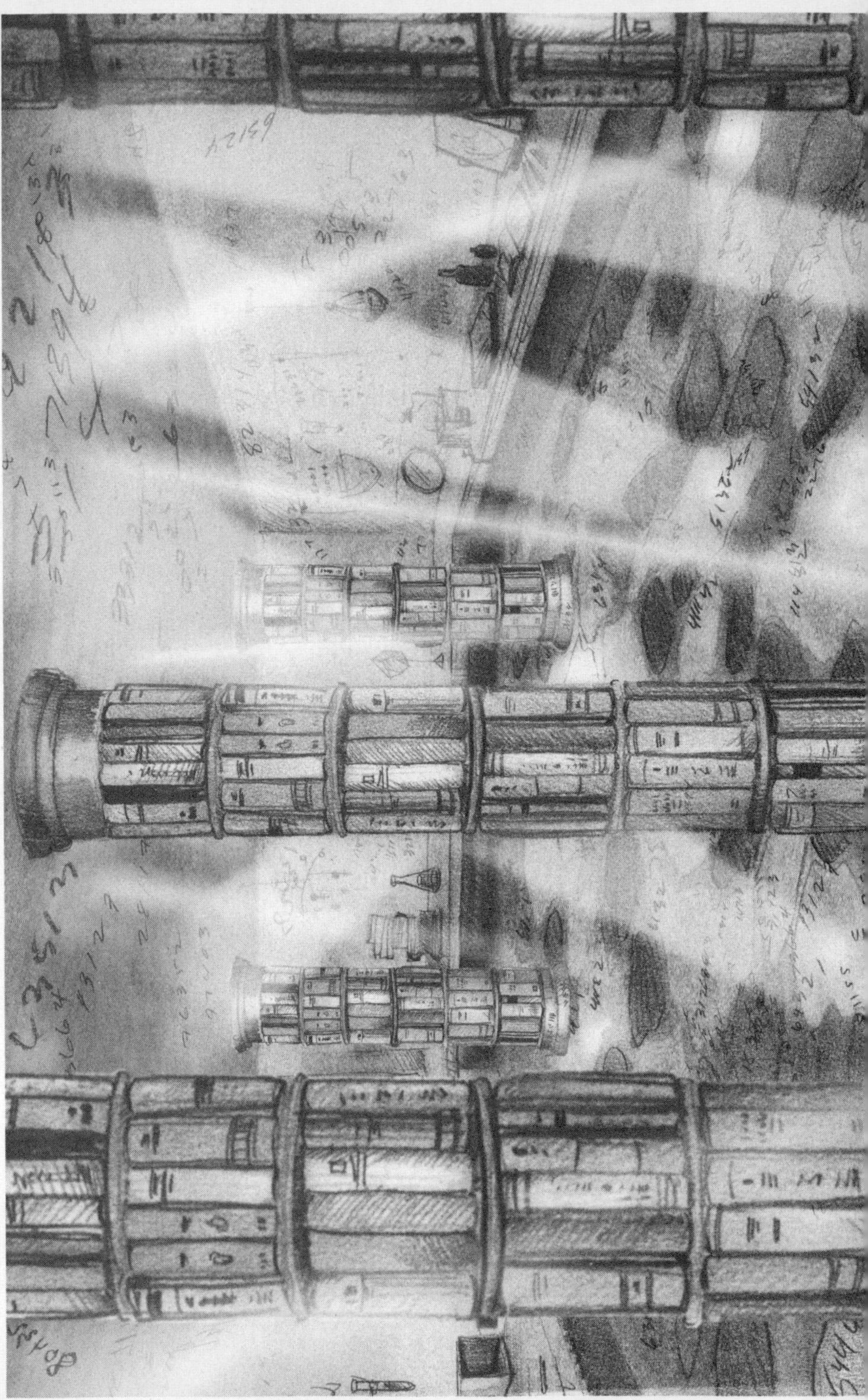

the stone table for support. He was growing weaker, though his mind was refreshed. He looked at the ceiling, rolling equations over in his mind and thinking of all that he had created. He was a gentle man, nothing like Lord Phineus, and he loved the feeling of his mind filling with knowledge.

"The Crat have bitten me, haven't they?" asked Dr. Harding, coming to a number that opened his mind and showed him how he had created the Crat. Dr. Kincaid nodded silently, wishing it were not true.

"Well, then," continued Dr. Harding. A quiet understanding had overtaken him. "It's only a matter of time. You know that."

Suddenly, there came the sound of shouting from Samuel and Isabel, who were running through the laboratory, darting back and forth between columns. The big room was full of echoes and it wasn't until the two were very near that they could be understood.

"He's been taken!" cried Isabel. She was in a high state of panic. "Edgar's been taken!"

"What do you mean, taken?" said Vincent. It seemed impossible. He hadn't watched carefully because the yellow door was shut tight and locked. No one else could come in, or so he'd thought.

"Taken!" repeated Isabel. "I tried to stop him, but he was too big."

"Stop who? What do you mean, Isabel?"

"We shouldn't have left him alone, but Samuel wanted to

show me the books." Isabel couldn't bring herself to say what had happened. The mere thought of it frightened her beyond reason.

"Sir Emerik!" cried Samuel. "He came down and took Edgar."

"Where have they gone?" asked Dr. Kincaid, certain of the answer.

"Back into Mead's Hollow," said Isabel. Her voice was shaky and quiet. "We followed to the ladder, but Sir Emerik told us he would hurt Edgar if we tried to stop him or cried out for you."

"I should have killed that man when I had the chance," said Vincent, feeling as if he'd failed in his duty. "I'll kill him this time." He was already starting for the orange corridor when the determined voice of Dr. Harding stopped him.

"No, you won't."

Dr. Harding was standing up straight again. He seemed to have gathered a new strength at the sound of Edgar's name as he shared a bit of surprising information with everyone in the room.

"Mead's Hollow will soon fill with water. After that, there's no way out of the Highlands."

"You might be surprised," said Vincent, thinking of Edgar's unmatched climbing skills.

Dr. Harding stared at Dr. Kincaid, who had once been like a father to him. He'd brought the full measure of Dr. Harding's brilliance into use to save the Dark Planet. But ultimately Dr. Harding had failed everyone. He hadn't left his life behind and become Lord Phineus because of the crushing weight of so much knowledge or the relentless pressure from those who needed him to succeed. These things played a role in his evolving insanity, but there was something else, something taken from him, that had finally broken him.

"I'm only going to live a few more hours," said Dr. Harding. "I want to see my boy on Atherton."

"He doesn't belong to you!" cried Dr. Kincaid. "He's not yours to save!"

"And neither does he belong to you," said Dr. Harding. His voice was calm but direct.

Vincent moved between the two men, sensing a showdown about to erupt, and he spoke the truth of the matter.

"Edgar doesn't belong to either one of you. He belongs to Atherton."

Samuel and Isabel looked on, confused and frightened by everything they were hearing.

"As far as I'm concerned he belongs to the grove, and someone needs to get him back." It was Isabel, and she was angry. "If one of you doesn't go, I will. I won't let Sir Emerik take him. I won't!"

Isabel's words echoed around the stone pillars and the room fell silent.

"Nine three four five two," said Dr. Harding. "That one tells me a lot. It tells me how to escape the Cleaners."

He pointed to a far corner of the room where the numbers could hardly be seen.

"Eight seven four nine one," he said. "That one opens a very big door to a vast room in my mind. In there I see what I devised, how I built Atherton to move, why it moves, and when it will stop."

"Stop talking about useless numbers!" cried Isabel. She couldn't believe what she was hearing and wished they would simply leave in search of Edgar, but Dr. Kincaid was unmoved.

"Tell me these things," said Dr. Kincaid, utterly focused on Dr. Harding. "I must know them!"

"I will tell you if you release me to get the boy," said Dr. Harding. "But you must send me alone. You must all move on, away from here, before it's too late."

Dr. Kincaid felt like a man crushed under the full weight of all the misery in Atherton.

"I don't trust him one bit," said Isabel. "I can't tell if he's Lord Phineus or Dr. Harding. And what if he is Dr. Harding? What difference does *that* make? He could still hurt Edgar if we let him go."

Samuel agreed. All of his life he'd known the man before him as the cruel Lord Phineus. No matter what anyone said, he was having a hard time believing he could be anyone else.

"We'll go instead," said Samuel, looking up at his father. It was a courageous notion, but one Sir William had no interest in pursuing.

"That's a valiant idea," said Sir William, "but I'm responsible for you and Isabel, and I can't think of a more dangerous place than Mead's Hollow. I can't take you back in there and I won't leave you behind. I'm afraid we can't be the ones to help your friend."

“Fine!” shouted Isabel. She couldn’t stand that Edgar was getting farther away while they stood arguing. “I’ll go alone, without any of you!”

Out of habit she pulled a black fig out of her pocket and set it in her sling. Her hands were shaking, though she couldn’t have said if it was anger or fear that caused it.

Dr. Harding knelt before her. “Isabel.” He had a powerful but gracious voice up close, and it seemed as if he knew her better than she’d expected. “Whoever goes out there won’t be coming back,” he went on. “But I made Atherton, and I know how to save him.”

There was something about his voice and the way he looked at her that made her tremble. She was at once awestruck and comforted by the close presence of Dr. Harding. *Could it really be true? Could this man have made Atherton?* She was determined not to believe it but found it impossible not to.

“It’s my final wish,” said Dr. Harding. “Please, just let me go and find Edgar.”

Isabel nodded, convinced that if Edgar was to be saved there was only one person who could save him.

“Bring him back,” she said. “Bring him back and I promise to take care of Atherton for you.”

Dr. Harding smiled for the first time, and he nodded at Isabel as he stood.

Dr. Kincaid tugged on his ear, surprised at the momentary despair he was feeling, and then he, too, nodded his approval.

“I’m sorry, Dr. Harding—I truly am. I thought you could

save the world." He laughed at the thought of it, seeing at once his own folly. "But it turns out no one man can do that. Atherton is irreparably turned to wreckage, like the mind of the man who made it. Even you can't fix it."

"Now, now, Doctor," said Dr. Harding. "Don't be too sure. It may not be as broken as you suppose."

And then Dr. Maximus Harding told everyone quickly and with purpose what was going to happen to Atherton and how the Cleaners might be overcome. They all sat spellbound in disbelief at the boldness of Dr. Harding's intellect. And when he was through, they truly believed there was yet a chance.

"I'm not going to live very much longer," he finally said. "You must let me be on my way."

They took him up the narrow corridor, and they told him how Edgar could climb if only he could get out of Mead's Hollow.

"He's an amazing boy," said Dr. Kincaid as Dr. Harding made his way up the ladder. "I believe you can save him."

Dr. Harding seemed to mentally check the time as he felt Atherton lightly shaking from where he stood at the top of the ladder. He dialed in the letters—m-u-l-c-i-b-e-r—and the round door opened with a wet, hissing sound. Water poured in around the edges like a little river and Dr. Harding cupped one hand, drinking his fill.

"When you feel Atherton move once more—I mean *really* move—you must be away from here. The next thing that happens will be more violent than all that has come before."

Dr. Harding hobbled up and out of the opening, glancing

back only once, and was gone with the slamming of the door. It wasn't until then that Dr. Kincaid really broke down and cried. Vincent came alongside his old friend and put an arm around him.

"We'll never see the likes of him again," said Dr. Kincaid, for he knew Dr. Harding would be dead before night fell on Atherton.

CHAPTER 19

A CLEANER IN THE GROVE

Gill had never raced a horse so fast in all his life. He had already passed into the trees, and it was hazardous going between the branches. He was hollering as he went for anyone who might be in the way, zigzagging down row after row of second-year trees until he reached the clearing where Mr. Ratikan's house had once stood.

"HORACE!" he yelled. He wasn't one for yelling very often, and it came out papery and weak even at his best effort. But Horace was sitting before a table with Maude and Wallace and knew Gill was coming before hearing the call. It was hard to miss the pounding of horse's hooves through a grove of trees.

"I'm here, Gill," said Horace. He and Wallace stood up and walked off the porch with Maude right behind. "What's the matter?"

Gill pulled on the rope around the horse's neck and came to a stop in the clearing. The animal was soaked with sweat and breathing heavily, its broad tongue searching the air for something wet.

"Cleaners," said Gill as he dismounted and stood in front of them. "Cleaners are coming, *big* ones."

"How many?" asked Wallace.

"And *how* big?" asked Maude.

"It looked like eight or nine, but I couldn't be sure." He looked at Maude. "You said they were six or seven feet long, but these looked larger than that."

"How much larger?" asked Horace, concern rising in his voice.

"I don't know. *Bigger.* Maybe ten feet, but I didn't get that close." Gill sniffed the air and caught a scent that shouldn't have been there. "Who's cooking rabbit?" he said. "That's a bad idea."

Nobody answered him.

"How long before they reach the grove?" asked Wallace.

Gill tried his best to guess, because he really couldn't be sure. Cleaners moved faster than a man but quite a bit slower than a horse at full gallop.

"I'd guess half an hour, maybe a little less."

Horace was quick to action in a military sort of way. He sent Maude and Wallace to different parts of the grove to maintain order. They would carefully hide the mothers and children up high in the biggest of the third-year trees, for though these were not especially good places to hide, they were the best places available to them. They would set up groups of men around the trees in ever-widening circles, and if there were women among them who wanted to fight, they would let them fight. Better to protect the children in the face of a coming fury that could bring an end to everything.

And finally, Wallace and Maude were to make absolutely sure that Horace's wife and young boy were safe. Horace simply could not go to them now, not as the commander at so perilous a time.

"Wallace," said Horace as his friend was about to depart deeper into the grove. "Your peaceful ways are needed now more than ever. The people will need to feel comforted."

Wallace stepped closer and touched Horace on the shoulder. "I'm glad a person like me can be of some use at a time of war. It can feel as if there's no place for me, but you help me find my way. I can ask no more of someone I would follow."

He said these things to bring encouragement to a man thrust into leadership at a hazardous time.

"If you can make them feel as I do when you speak to me, you'll have done well," said Horace.

After Maude and Wallace parted, Horace turned to Gill. He waited until they were completely alone before speaking.

"Bring the fighting men to me, all who remain from the Highlands and the few we picked from the rest," said Horace. He was suddenly a commander speaking to a soldier, full of authority. "All of the horses, the longest spears, those who have mastered the sling and the black fig—get them all here this instant."

Gill mounted his horse and started off, but Horace stopped him before he was free of the clearing.

"Wait!" he said. "Bring as many live rabbits as can be carried."

"Whatever for, sir?"

Horace waved him off and turned back to the porch of Mr. Ratikan's broken-down house, mumbling to himself. Ten minutes passed and he began to feel uneasy, wondering if Gill had been right about the timing of the coming Cleaners. He heard the sound of many hooves in the grove, coming at a charge, and was stern-faced and solid as a rock when the group of men on horses burst into the clearing.

The horses looked tired just from the short gallop through the trees, and Horace knew that they needed water he could not provide. This would be one of maybe two good fights he could get out of them. After that, he wasn't sure how he could even keep them alive.

Gill dismounted and pulled along with him two horses, his own and one he'd brought for Horace. They all waited, looking at Horace in the quiet peace of the clearing, as their leader listened to the sounds of the grove. At length, he spoke.

"It would be best if our enemy were turned back," he began. "If they make it into the trees, it will be harder to contain them, and there is a chance they could get as far as the outer circle that guards the children. If even one Cleaner were to make it that far, it might get past other circles and find its way to a tree that holds a child." He paused before stating the obvious. "That would be unacceptable."

Everyone nodded their agreement, gazing back into the grove and thinking about the difficulty of containing a large, wild animal within the trees. But there was one from the grove who did not agree.

"What you say is true, to a point," said the man. "But don't forget we'll have to be out in the open with them if we leave the grove. There is safety in these trees you shouldn't overlook."

Horace nodded. He had thought of this, thought of the risk and the possible reward of fighting from within the grove. In the end, he had abandoned the idea.

"We can't risk having them loose through the trees. There are endless entry points, and they all lead eventually to those we must protect. We have to try, at all cost, to keep them from the grove."

The man, though not entirely convinced, signaled his approval.

"Who among you have mastered the sling?" asked Horace.

Six hands went up quickly and decisively, another four rose halfheartedly and stopped at half-mast. Horace called the six forward, then turned to Gill.

"Where are the rabbits?"

"Here, sir!" cried a man from the back. He and two other men dismounted their horses and came forward with squirming sacks of rabbits.

"How many in each bag?" asked Horace.

"About fifteen, sir."

"Back on your horses and keep the rabbits with you."

Then Horace proceeded to lay out his plan in the two or three minutes he was willing to risk before leaving for the very edge of the grove. After that they set off, most of them unsure of what they were about to encounter.

"I'm not sure this is going to work," said one of the men with a sling.

Horace had heard this several times already, and he would have none of it. "You will make it work."

Together they were ten men alone in the open of Tabletop — the three men who carried the sacks of rabbits with the six men who had claimed to have mastered the use of a sling, along with Horace, who was the only one on a horse. Fifty yards behind the ten men were forty men on horses, standing at the ready, spears in hand. The edge of the grove sat another fifty yards beyond that. And then there was what lay in front of Horace and his nine men. The Cleaners had come into view.

They were close enough that Horace could hear the snapping of their jaws and the clanging of bony legs. And he saw on their approach that they were massive in size. He could tell by their movement that they saw him and his men not as an enemy but as a source of food, for they showed no sign of slowing to regard the situation before them. They charged on as a herd of wild animals that had spotted easy prey and wanted only to be the first to sink their teeth into it.

"Do it now," said Horace. "Before they get much closer."

There were two men with slings for each man with a sack of rabbits, the teams set apart by ten feet between them. Rabbits were quickly taken from the sacks and placed awkwardly into the slings in such a way that their bellies fit inside and their legs dangled loosely over the edges. The moment the rabbits were in place they were swung in a circle overhead, spinning faster and faster, and then they were released with a *snap! snap! snap!*

Three rabbits flew wildly through the air, legs searching for something to hold onto, until they bounced and rolled on the ground in the distance. Two of the three hobbled up, limping but alive, and began moving about. The third lay motionless.

"Again!" cried Horace, "but with a little less force this time."

He wanted the rabbits as a diversion, not a meal, and they needed to be kept alive and darting in every direction if his plan was to work.

Three more rabbits were loaded and flung out into the open, and the result was the same: three more rabbits that were injured or killed in the effort. The Cleaners were gaining speed, a plume of dust building behind them, and Horace saw that another method would be needed.

"Give me the sacks!" he yelled, "and get back to your horses!"

The men hesitated only briefly, then handed the heavy sacks to Horace before dashing off in the direction of the grove. Horace could barely hold the sacks in one arm as he kicked his horse and sprang into action. The sacks dangled precariously at his side, threatening to catch in the horse's legs as he drove headlong toward the pack of oncoming Cleaners.

When he was but twenty yards off he pulled up short, stunned by the absolute fury of the creatures coming toward him. He turned the bags over one at a time and let loose the fifty or more rabbits that remained. The moment they were out of the bags they spread out chaotically over the open expanse of the Flatlands.

Horace raced for the grove, looking over his shoulder as the Cleaners came upon the sea of dancing food. The creatures reared up and began trying in vain to capture the rabbits in their smashing teeth. Cleaners were fast, but rabbits were faster, and while a few were soon devoured, many more darted between and jumped over the Cleaners, sending the mad beasts into a furious rage of spinning and slashing.

"Now!" cried Horace. He reared his horse back toward the Cleaners as Gill came alongside him and handed him a long, sharp spear. All the other horsemen came up in three lines behind them as he had instructed, and Horace's army made for the mayhem in the Flatlands. The Cleaners were so busy slashing and biting at the rabbits and at each other they scarcely saw the attack coming before the horses were right in their midst.

The battle did not go well for either party. Nearly all of the Cleaners felt the sting of a spear, but only two of the eight were killed immediately with a spear to the mouth. Five of the remaining six were injured but not killed, and the last, the biggest among them, was not harmed at all.

As the rabbits became a secondary concern and moved out of harm's way, the men on horses and the stunned Cleaners went into a prolonged battle of cutting teeth and lunging spears. Gill was jabbing at a Cleaner before him when from behind an even larger Cleaner reared up into the air and opened its hideous mouth. It stood upright at shoulder level to Gill, dripping slime from its suction cups, and it lunged toward his back.

But Horace had seen what was happening and came galloping at a full head, and as the beast came forward, it met a spear down the throat and through the brain, tumbling down off the back of Gill's horse.

The battle raged on in the open before the grove, but the largest of the Cleaners was also the smartest, and without anyone's noticing, it moved off with surprising swiftness, away from the violence. It moved with purpose, toward the shelter of the trees where it could hide.

Finally, at great expense to man and horse, the remaining giant Cleaners were either killed or turned back. Four of the eight were dead or dying on the bloodied ground and three had been forced back with near mortal wounds. They hobbled off, barely alive, and the men who remained dismounted, trying to save those who had fallen.

"Back on your horses!" cried Horace. Of the fifty who had begun the fight, only twenty remained, and many of the horses had been felled or were running wild in the open with the rabbits.

"But we can't leave them!" said one of the men. "Some are still alive!"

Horace turned to Gill, who had remained on his horse.

"There were eight. I counted them!" said Horace. "Only

four lay dead and three have crawled away, but there were eight. I'm sure of it."

Everyone turned at once and looked toward the line of trees. Nothing was there, nothing moved.

In the end Horace left two men with the fallen army to do what they could. He took the rest on horses and sped back toward the trees.

A Cleaner—the largest among them at twelve feet—had escaped into the grove unnoticed.

CHAPTER 20

A MOTHERLESS WORLD

Edgar's wrist was almost as sore as the place where his pinky was missing by the time Sir Emerik had dragged him all the way back to the opening of the main chamber in the House of Power. He had been biting the air with his teeth for the better part of two hours and his jaws were tight and sore. He felt as if he'd been chewing on a tough chunk of mutton served to the food line at Mr. Ratikan's porch, one that simply would not go down his throat no matter how hard he tried.

They'd had no light at all for a while, but Sir Emerik seemed to have gotten his bearings about the place and he strode fast and with purpose until the dim light of the source of all water could be seen. They'd gone right to it, touched the wall with the blue line, and followed it all the way out of Mead's Hollow. Edgar could tell when they'd arrived inside the House of Power because it was very steep there, rounding back and forth, until they arrived finally at the main chamber.

Sir Emerik threw Edgar onto the floor in front of him and climbed out of Mead's Hollow. He was breathing hard, covered in grime and sweat, licking his lips in search of water.

"Never again!" he said. "I will *never* go down there again!"

He stepped away from the opening and searched the room for water. He seemed unaware or uninterested in the amount of light that crept into the room. Finding a flint on the table and a torch with a heavy stone bucket of fuel, Sir Emerik soon had light to aid him in his search. He found a similar stone container of water beneath the table, half filled, and he gulped and coughed. It struck Edgar as odd that both containers, the one for the fuel and the one for the water, were made of thick stone with heavy wooden lids that fit tightly. It was as if someone had known Atherton would quake uncontrollably and regular buckets would tip over and spill.

Night had yet to come to Atherton, though it was nearing as Edgar leaned out the window and saw the tube of dim light pouring in from far above. The Highlands were dreadfully far belowground, hidden almost entirely in a heavy blanket of shadow. It was a desolate place, and as he looked intently along the black walls that surrounded him, he was unsure if he could climb out if given the chance.

"Anyone out there?" cried Edgar.

Sir Emerik advanced to the window and pushed the boy aside. From below there came a voice filled with surprise.

"Sir Emerik? Is that you? I'm coming, sir!"

It was the one person who had stayed behind, and he was running through the courtyard in search of the voice. He advanced up the stairs and was soon knocking on the door to the main chamber.

"It is you!" cried Tyler when Sir Emerik opened the door. There was a big lump on his forehead, and Edgar was reminded of how he'd hit the poor man with a black fig.

Despite his hasty arrival, Tyler seemed unwilling to enter the room. "You don't look so good, Sir Emerik," he said with some unease. Sir Emerik didn't smell right, he thought. Was the man in front of him rotting away?

Emerik strode directly to Tyler, his eye twitching ever so slightly, and bellowed into the man's face, "Call me *lord,* you fool!"

Tyler stood shaking in the doorway. It had not been a good day, and the raving lunatic who stood before him was only making things worse.

"Yes," said Tyler, bowing, "*Lord* Emerik."

Sir Emerik proceeded to slam the door in Tyler's face. Then he yelled with a force that could be heard all the way into the hall outside the room. "Bring me something to eat!"

Sir Emerik strode to the wall and took the torch he'd lit. "Oh, how I've waited for this moment." The twitch returned to his eye as he waved the flame happily out in front of him. "You remember how you tied me up and burned my hair off? You remember that, don't you, Edgar?"

Edgar was breathing hard, backed up against the window. It

was too far to jump, and he didn't think he could slither out and climb down, though the thought crossed his mind as he glanced behind him through the opening.

"Get away from the window," said Sir Emerik. He moved as fast as the Crat and poked the flame into Edgar's face until the boy was against the thick ivy on the wall. "Now," said Sir Emerik, glee building in his voice. "Now let's burn *your* hair off and see how you like it!"

Sir Emerik lunged for the boy playfully, laughing and coughing up watery blood from some broken place inside, thinking only of how grand it was going to be to torture Edgar and then kill him with his bare hands.

Edgar was nothing if not quick like a rabbit, and he dodged the oncoming flame as it was thrust toward him. Sir Emerik cackled as he prodded with the torch, hitting the drying ivy on the walls and setting off little fires around Edgar's head. Edgar lunged for the torch and nearly knocked it free from Sir Emerik's hand. He followed with a punch to Sir Emerik's stomach, and the self-proclaimed ruler of the Highlands doubled over for an instant as Edgar stepped back toward the wall.

Sir Emerik screamed, his eyes bulging wildly. He lunged forward hard and fast, almost falling headlong as Edgar darted quickly to one side. Edgar watched in stunned silence as Sir Emerik slid down the wall and crumpled into a heap on the floor, the butt of a knife sticking out of his back.

Behind him stood Dr. Harding.

"Why did you do that?" asked Edgar, as incredulous as he

was surprised to see the man's sudden arrival. His voice was shaking and unsteady. Edgar wasn't sure if he was looking at a friend or a foe, and if the knife might be aimed at him next.

"Because I'm not who you think I am," said Dr. Harding. He slowly sat down on the floor of the main chamber and it looked to Edgar as if he were an irreparably damaged man.

Edgar was quick to action, taking the butt of the knife in his hand and pulling it free from Sir Emerik's back. He held it close to Dr. Harding's face. Was this Lord Phineus, or maybe a mad scientist who only wanted to harm him? If he could escape the room he could make it to the wall. And if he could make it to the wall, there was a chance he could get out.

"You don't want to use that," said Dr. Harding. "Let's just sit and talk a moment. I only want to help you."

This could not be Lord Phineus. There was compassion in the voice of the man slumped on the ground in front of Edgar, something not possible for Lord Phineus. Edgar placed the knife out of Dr. Harding's reach, then found the torch and came near the ailing man on the floor.

"Let me get you something to drink," said Edgar. He was reminded that Tyler might return soon with food, but he pushed the thought aside as he went to the bucket and brought back a cup of cold water. Dr. Harding gulped heartily, coughing as Sir Emerik had, and it seemed to revitalize him.

He smiled at Edgar.

"Do you know who I am?" asked Dr. Harding. He squinted at the boy in a kindly way, not sure of what Edgar knew.

"You're Dr. Harding," said Edgar. "You made this place."

"I made more than that."

"What do you mean?"

Dr. Harding scratched at his leg and wiped his hand on his sleeve. There was a dreary pause before he spoke.

"I mean I made *you,* Edgar."

Edgar was at once confused and excited by the idea. "You mean you're my *father?* How can that be?"

A moment of regret rose in Dr. Harding's eyes.

"He took you from me. I was doing all right until then, keeping my mind on the work, not reading things I shouldn't read or adding more numbers, more rooms."

"You're scaring me," said Edgar.

"Dr. Kincaid took you from me. That's what drove me to burn the journals, to burn all the numbers and the rooms in my mind. I was filled with anger for what he'd done—what they all did. They used me! And they took the one thing I cared about. They took *you.*"

"Are you really my father?" asked Edgar. Something about the way Dr. Harding spoke made him uneasy. He didn't *feel* like Dr. Harding's son, and this bothered him a great deal.

"That depends on what you mean by father," said Dr. Harding, looking down at the floor and scratching again at his leg.

"Are you my father or not? It's a simple question."

Dr. Harding gazed at the boy before him, full of emotion and longing. He wanted only to hold him and talk with him as he thought fathers and sons should do.

"I made you, Edgar, like I made Atherton."

Edgar thought about this idea and didn't like it one bit. "How did you make me?"

Dr. Harding turned away, unable to look Edgar in the eye. "Well, to be fair, Dr. Kincaid helped," said Dr. Harding. "He's a smart man. I told him I wanted a companion—a son, not a wife—and he agreed to help me. But then things began to unravel here, on Atherton. There was so much pressure to get it right, so much work to be done. He said I was neglecting you and that you might get hurt. Dr. Kincaid thought it was best to take you away, to hide you from me. He was wrong."

Edgar suddenly had a hopeful thought, one that he imagined might make him feel better. "If you made me, then who is my mother?"

If there was a question Dr. Harding had hoped to never hear, it had just been asked. Every boy wants a mother, especially one who has been living like an orphan most of his life.

"You have no mother," Dr. Harding said. "I *make* things, remember? I suppose that's my curse."

Edgar couldn't believe what he was hearing. *I'm* made—*like a house or a wooden bowl.* Had he been made with strange tools and gadgets such as the ones he'd seen in the laboratory beneath the House of Power? It was a terrible thing to realize. *Is this why I feel so lonely, why I feel happiest alone, climbing high on the cliffs of Atherton?* At that moment it felt to Edgar as if all of Atherton was motherless. No wonder it was so broken, a motherless world driven by a man of science. How could it have been any other way?

Edgar wanted something, *anything* he could hold on to that would make him feel like a normal boy.

"Have I ever been to the Dark Planet? Did I live there once?" He had been so sure when he'd dangled his feet over the edge of Atherton and looked down at the world beneath him that it had once been his home. He'd wanted to go there.

"You were the firstborn of Atherton," Dr. Harding almost sang the words as he recalled the idea of Edgar coming to life in the laboratory beneath Mead's Hollow. "There's no darkness in you, no mark of the Dark Planet, and that makes you very special. I made Atherton for *you,* Edgar, before you were created and then after. Atherton was always for you. And so you and Atherton are mysteriously linked. I'm not entirely sure the two of you can survive without each other."

Edgar was too confused and tired to say anything in response.

"We have a little time," continued Dr. Harding, trying to make amends. "The next really big change won't start until after light tomorrow. You could get some rest." Edgar listened as Dr. Harding's voice became mystical, as if he'd passed into a room in his mind that he'd waited a very long time to open, and peeking inside had found the dawn of time hiding there. "The first day of creation has passed. The Highlands are safe until the second day comes."

There was a quiet knock at the door, and Dr. Harding lunged across the floor for the knife.

"It's food," said Edgar, touching Dr. Harding gently on the arm. "You don't need to worry."

Edgar went to the door and opened it, took the stale loaves of bread that were offered, and asked Tyler to come back in the morning. At first Tyler was unsure, but then he saw Lord Phineus on the floor glaring at him and he nodded, running off down the stairs.

The two sat together against the ivy-covered wall, the boy and his maker, and they ate dinner. Dr. Harding told Edgar about himself and his life, the things he could remember. It was hard to keep his broken mind focused and at intervals he trailed off into things Edgar didn't understand, but it was very much like the kind of conversation a boy and a father ought to have: a little laughing, some whispering of secret things, a hug. To sit with Dr. Harding in the quiet of the House of Power and not to feel afraid or alone, if only for a moment, was a great relief to Edgar.

"I understand you can climb out of here," Dr. Harding remarked at one point when Edgar leaned over into Dr. Harding's arms, so very tired. "That will be easier when there's some light and after you've had some sleep."

It was then that Dr. Harding told Edgar about how Atherton would continue to change and how to defeat the Cleaners, but the boy was quickly drifting off, and the words were heard as a dream that may or may not be remembered come morning.

Dr. Harding stayed awake long after Edgar was sound asleep, watching the boy and smiling at the wonder of what he'd made.

CHAPTER 21
THE CAVERN

It was Vincent who was clearly in charge from the very moment Dr. Harding closed the yellow door and locked everyone below Mead's Hollow.

"We have to go quickly," he began. "If what Dr. Harding said was true, there's not much time for us to take what we can and be gone."

Dr. Kincaid nodded, though he was still in something of a daze. Dr. Harding was gone, never to return, and he couldn't be sure if anything the man had said was true. Dr. Harding had gone mad not once but twice, first after losing Edgar and becoming Lord Phineus, and then after being bitten by the Crat. Dr. Kincaid felt a terrible sorrow at the loss of such a great mind. Lost in these thoughts, he began to walk down the orange corridor in silence and Isabel fell in step beside him.

"Will he find Edgar?" she asked.

Dr. Kincaid didn't know very much about children, but he was aware that sometimes they looked to adults for a glimmer of hope that would sustain them.

"Dr. Harding is the smartest man alive," said Dr. Kincaid. "Rest assured, Sir Emerik hasn't a chance."

"If only he can get out of Mead's Hollow, he'll be able to climb to the top. He could tell my parents that I'm all right."

She was worried for Edgar, but in the past few hours she'd become even more concerned about her own family. She wanted desperately for them to know she was okay, and that got her thinking about whether she actually *was* okay.

"Dr. Kincaid," she said as they rounded the corner into the laboratory, "how are we going to get out of here?"

He glanced at her and patted her gently on the back.

"Wait and see," he said, with the maddening air of secrecy she had come to expect.

When she entered the laboratory, Vincent was busy gathering things into a bag with straps that enabled him to carry it on his back. Pointing to a pile of such bags, he ordered everyone to pick one up and follow him. The bags were open at the top, but there were strings to tie them shut, and each person took one, following in a line behind Vincent. Most of what he placed in the bags were things Isabel and Samuel didn't recognize, and they were left to imagine that he wanted to preserve relics from the laboratory that might be useful later: tools, drawings, artifacts, models.

He came to the end of the table farthest from the entry and there he opened a wooden panel. Inside was a row of spears of a kind no one had seen before. The ends were capped with a hard, clear substance, and removing one with a *pop,* Vincent revealed a sharp, metal tip that ran six or seven inches down in a jagged line.

"Take the cover off only when I tell you to. These are dangerous weapons I hope you won't need."

He put the cap back over the end of the spear and handed it to Dr. Kincaid, who seemed perfectly happy to let Vincent take control of the situation.

"Each of you put your pack on and keep hold of these," he said, handing out the spears one by one. "What you carry on your back is all we have left of what Dr. Harding created. These notes and tools may well provide us with the clues we need to survive not only for a day but for a lifetime on Atherton. Care for them well."

Everyone did as they were told, though they all held their spears awkwardly.

"We're about to go someplace that will surprise most of you," said Vincent. "There are dangers in this place of a kind you've never seen. Follow close behind me, and use the spears as walking sticks to help you along."

He looked at each person slowly and steadily. Then he took a crossbow from where the spears had been stored, and he loaded it with an arrow from a container of a dozen arrows flung over his back. The loaded crossbow was a contraption Sir William,

Samuel, and Isabel had never seen before. Isabel felt inside her front pocket—three black figs and her sling—and she wondered if she would need them wherever they were going.

"Won't we need water and food?" asked Sir William.

Vincent turned to the group one last time before leaving. "There's plenty of water where we're going," he said. "Food will have to wait. Just stay close and walk in a line as best you can."

As they approached the far end of the laboratory, Samuel looked back at the columns of books that he wished he could have a chance to read. He couldn't stand the idea that they might be lost forever. He and Isabel were positioned in the line behind Dr. Kincaid and in front of Sir William, who took up the rear.

Vincent knelt down and peered beneath the last of the stone tables, and then he crawled underneath.

"Where do you think we're going?" asked Isabel, whispering to Samuel as she watched Vincent disappear into the darkness beneath the stone table.

"I wish I knew," said Samuel, crouching down as his turn came.

"Stay close to me, will you?" asked Isabel, following behind.

"I promise I will," said Samuel. "And I'm sorry for bringing you down here, Isabel."

She was about to tell him it was all right, that she felt afraid but safe within the group, when she came to a hole under the table and watched Samuel disappear into it. Cold air drifted lazily out of the hole, air that smelled like mud. She breathed in deep and stepped inside, touching the cool walls to guide her way.

As the pathway led downward and turned sharply to the left and to the right, the faint light from the laboratory quickly disappeared and was replaced by a new supply of light from somewhere around an unknown number of curves on the path. The group of five twisted and turned as the light increased before them. Looking back, Sir William saw only black, and he realized then that they would never go back.

"This place is changed," said Dr. Kincaid as they all stepped together into a wide, dimly lit cavern. Long shafts of stone shot down from a high rock ceiling and the stone walls dripped with water. Small pools lay here and there along the cavern, and crags of rock jutted out from the ground in every direction.

"I hope our way is not blocked," Dr. Kincaid continued.

"It well could be," said Vincent. "We should hurry before Atherton moves again."

Sir William came up alongside the two men and left Samuel and Isabel to marvel at the strange underground world they'd come into. Samuel poked his spear at the rocks and found them to be as hard as any others he'd encountered, though they were of a red and orange color he hadn't seen before.

"What is this place?" asked Sir William.

Vincent and Dr. Kincaid exchanged a knowing glance, and the two realized they'd need to tell.

"Make it quick," said Vincent. "I'm going ahead to choose a safe passage."

Vincent moved off and Dr. Kincaid stood before Sir William, Samuel, and Isabel.

"It used to be different," said Dr. Kincaid. "It used to be wider and there was better light, fewer stones strewn about."

He glanced at the walls of the cavern, trying to get his bearings. "Before, when the Highlands were up there"—he pointed toward the rock ceiling—"our way was very different. We could travel beneath the Flatlands and up through the inside of Tabletop, and then up through the inside of the Highlands. But the Highlands are below Tabletop now, so this cavern is new to me. It's not the same as it once was."

"So you've been to the laboratory before?" asked Samuel.

"Oh, yes, many times. I've even been to the Highlands, just not since the lock on the door was altered. The laboratory was *ours*, Dr. Harding's and mine, not his alone."

"This cavern leads home!" cried Isabel, realizing freedom might be possible after all. "It leads all the way to the Flatlands where we can find everyone!"

"If we're very lucky, yes," said Dr. Kincaid. "But our way is uncertain until we find the opening."

"The opening?" said Samuel.

"If we can make it to the inside, we can make it home."

"What do you mean, the *inside?*" asked Isabel.

"The laboratory, believe it or not, is located beneath Tabletop, so we're already free of the Highlands. It's disorienting, I realize, but the old passageways are changed or vanished. New ways are before us, but they still lead inside."

Isabel still didn't understand what he meant by inside, but

her mind was turning over the idea that she was beneath her home, maybe beneath the grove itself. She looked up half expecting to see the roots of the trees shooting down from the ceiling.

"My mind can't process where we are or how we got here," said Sir William. "This shifting world makes no sense."

Dr. Kincaid didn't know what he should say, because there was a part of him that felt just as Sir William did.

"Sometimes," he began, having struck on a way of explaining, "over the years as Dr. Harding and I worked beside each other, he would show me a page filled with calculations and drawings and he would say to me, *Don't you see? This is how we get from here to there,* but it was like a language I couldn't understand. His ways went beyond me, until I could no longer see where he was going. Atherton is like that. Our *way* is like that."

"That's not very helpful," said Sir William, smiling as he liked to do to brighten the spirits of those around him. Dr. Kincaid laughed and his mood improved. He was about to go on when Vincent came back into view through the shadows and light of the cavern.

"We should go," he said. "From what I can tell our way will be harder than before. It's flat, so we won't have to climb down as we used to, but much has caved in. I just hope there's still a way inside."

"How far?" said Sir William. He was aware that Samuel and Isabel hadn't slept for a long time. Vincent glanced at them, then back at Sir William.

"If our way isn't blocked, only an hour. We must get inside as fast as we can, then we can rest."

"What is this 'inside' you keep speaking of?" asked Sir William. "We don't understand."

"Please, just come along," said Vincent. "It will be easier to show you than to tell you."

Sir William knelt down in front of Samuel and Isabel, worried for them. "Can you do this?" he asked.

Isabel did not like being treated as a child. It was true she was afraid and unsure, but she didn't want anyone else to know. She scowled in Sir William's general direction, then marched right past him toward Vincent without a word.

"You found a tough one there," said Sir William, looking at the frail boy before him. Samuel had never been one to have a lot of energy, and his father remembered him as a reader, not an adventurer.

"If she can do it, so can I," said Samuel, and he, too, strode past his father in the direction Isabel had gone. In truth he was feeling tired and chilled, but he couldn't bear the idea of disappointing his father. If Isabel could be so brave and determined, so could he.

The group moved as one snaking line through the cavern, and a snake it truly was, for where a clear path had once been there was now something more treacherous. Many of the long stones that had hung down from the ceiling had broken off like great teeth, shattering on the ground and leaving a path filled with boulders. And while it seemed that Atherton was not moving, the sound of crashing and splintering rock echoed everywhere through the cavern. The light remained elusive, a light that was at once everywhere and nowhere at all. It was a light of yellow and orange caught in black shadows, full of mystery and depth.

After a trek that lasted more than an hour but less than two, Vincent came to a place where he held back his hand as if to tell everyone to stop and be still. Before them lay a pile of stones that blocked their way. Through the stones shone shards of light from a source that seemed brighter than what they'd encountered before.

"We have come to the place where Tabletop and the Flatlands meet," said Vincent, pointing to the pile of rocks pierced through with beams of light. "The inside is there."

It was a treacherous climb up the side of the pile of rubble that lay in front of them, and Vincent insisted on taking the old man up to the top first, where an opening remained. As he started back down to help Sir William, Samuel, and Isabel, there came a sound of cracking from high over their heads.

"Run!" screamed Vincent from his perch. A long stone shaped like a spear had broken free above the group of three and it was falling through the air. Sir William dropped his weapon and grabbed both children around the waist, then dove toward Vincent. When the narrow stone hit the cavern floor it burst into pieces, chunks sparking loose in every direction.

Vincent scrambled down the rock face and found that the three were bruised and scraped but otherwise unharmed.

"Let's get these two out of here," said Sir William, hauling Samuel and Isabel to their feet. They dusted themselves off and examined scraped elbows and knees, then the group of four began the climb to the top of the mountain of stones. Up they went, using their spears to balance and pulling one another up by the hand over the larger rocks. When they came to the very top Vincent went into the light and beckoned the rest to come inside.

When Isabel, Samuel, and Sir William were safely through to the other side, they climbed down the rubble without speaking, for they were overcome with surprise.

The five of them were inside Atherton, and a breathtaking new world lay hauntingly before them.

CHAPTER 22
INSIDE ATHERTON

"We must rest awhile," declared Vincent. "And this is a very good place to do it."

They had moved away from the pile of rocks and stood at the outer edge of a large alcove that looked out over the inside of Atherton. There was a large pool to one side, fed by a trickling but steady flow of water, and the alcove danced with liquid shadows shot through with the color of flames. Everyone removed their packs and stood together staring into the open expanse.

"Where does the light come from?" asked Isabel. She was mesmerized by beams of light radiating brilliantly from behind what could only be described as a range of mountains. It was as if they'd come inside on the peak of one of those mountains and found themselves looking down on formations of sharp spires rising up from a valley floor cast in the deep colors of night. The space seemed to go on forever, with cracks of dazzling light from the ground shining into the air.

"The light comes from outside," said Dr. Kincaid. He had looked forward to this moment as they'd made their way through the cavern. "The bottom of Atherton is shaped like half a circle. It's huge and heavy, and the very middle is filled with water and something heavier, something I don't claim to understand. But around the wide edge, where the Flatlands are above us, it's an open world, the world you see before you now."

"But how does the light get inside?" asked Samuel.

"The bottom of Atherton is not made entirely of stone. It's made also from something clear, or almost clear, something that light can penetrate."

Dr. Kincaid smiled and breathed deep the cool, wet air as if he had come to a place he remembered but had missed.

There came an unnerving sound inside Atherton that startled Dr. Kincaid out of his happy moment. Vincent whipped his crossbow into position quick as lightning, pointing the sharp arrow toward the sky.

"What was that?" asked Isabel. It had sounded like a scream, but an inhuman one. Through a beam of light far below, the shadowy figure of a flying beast moved across the cliffs. Isabel, Samuel, and Sir William had no memory of any such creature, a *flying* creature, and they were equal parts afraid and fascinated.

"Do you remember when Dr. Harding, or I should say Lord Phineus, called this place Pandemonium?" asked Vincent. The group nodded but didn't take their eyes off the moving shadow below. "He called it that for a reason, for it is here that he put some of the creatures he made that had no place on Atherton."

"Why did he put them here?" asked Samuel, feeling increasingly uneasy about this place despite its wild beauty.

"Because they were too dangerous to put anywhere else, and he couldn't bring himself to get rid of them."

"Now, Vincent," Dr. Kincaid broke in, "not everything inside Atherton is dangerous. And besides, everything that resides here is needed to make Atherton work. The Inferno, for one. Without it Atherton couldn't exist at all."

"The Inferno isn't what worries me right now," said Vincent. "It's the Nubian I'm concerned with."

"Dr. Harding sure did make a lot of things that do more harm than good," said Isabel, thinking of the Cleaners and the Crat and the Nubian, which she assumed was the thing flying around far below.

Dr. Kincaid didn't say anything. There was a part of him that agreed with the girl's assessment, though he had an unwavering love for everything Dr. Harding had created. He couldn't help himself. Creation was a glorious thing, to his mind, whether the creations were successful or not.

"We must get a few hours' rest," said Vincent. "The Nubian won't come this high up, and we're clear of the Highlands and Tabletop. Let's all get some water and lie down."

They moved back into the alcove, quenching their thirst and gathering in a tight group to keep warm. Very soon everyone but Dr. Kincaid and Vincent were asleep. They moved off, out of the alcove, and spoke in whispers.

“Do you think we can get them all through?” asked Vincent.

“I don’t know. It’s not an easy way.”

“Let’s allow them to rest for at least a few hours. They’re going to need their energy.”

“What about you?” asked Dr. Kincaid. “You need rest as well.”

Vincent gazed over the inside of Atherton, shot through with rays of yellow light, and heard the distant screeching of the Nubian.

“You go on, lie down,” said Vincent, concern rising in his voice. “I’ll sleep after I get everyone out of here.”

CHAPTER 23

NIGHT IN THE GROVE

There was a time when darkness in the grove had brought a feeling of calm stillness, when the work of the day was complete and tired but talkative people sat around the soft glow of evening fires. This was a feeling that still lingered unnaturally, even though everyone knew it was untrue. What had been tranquil about the grove was in the past. The true emotion, the deeper one as night came on, was fear.

"How is it you stay so still at times like this?" asked Horace. He had come to rely on Wallace's serene nature amid the calamity that surrounded them both. The two had been walking slowly and carefully through the largest of the third-year trees, searching for something they weren't sure they wanted to find. But now they had stopped and sat down to rest, talking quietly.

They carried no torch or light of any kind, but the grey hue of early night on Atherton softly covered the grove.

"There are two paths to peace," said Wallace. He had a stick in his hand and began carving lines into the dirt. "At least there are two that I'm aware of. One is to study the ideas and the ways of peace, to discuss them endlessly, to observe them and dissect them. The other is quite different."

The way Wallace had described the path sounded to Horace very much like the way any sane person would go about it. It seemed rather obvious that the study of a subject would naturally lead to understanding. That was certainly the way everyone approached things in the Highlands, where books were plentiful and study was common.

"The other path—the path I have taken—has nothing to do with any of that."

"You make no sense," said Horace. He was aware that he'd spoken a little louder than he wanted, and looking around he lowered his voice to a whisper. "You can't just become something without learning what it is you're trying to become."

"Can't you?" asked Wallace. There was an exasperating silence about him as he waited patiently for Horace's answer.

After a long pause, Horace said, "I'm unable to see the other path."

"That's because you're not on it."

"Are you *trying* to confuse me?"

Wallace lifted the stick from the dirt and, without cleaning the end off, began scratching his head with it.

“What if, instead of studying the thing you wanted to learn, you simply started performing the actions? The problem with most people is that they want to study subjects, but they don’t want to get anywhere near the discipline of truly learning.”

Horace thought this was a pretty interesting idea, though it was difficult for him to grasp.

“Tell me what you do that makes you this way,” said Horace. He hadn’t told anyone, not even Wallace, but the pressure of leading the people of Atherton was grinding away at his spirit. He missed his family—had barely seen them in days—and he was beginning to feel that the job was bigger than he was. The thought of a Cleaner hiding in the grove also weighed heavily on his mind.

“I take long walks all alone in the morning and in the evening,” began Wallace. “I look at the world around me. I think of what I want for Atherton—harmony between our peoples, food and water, understanding, patience. I spend a lot of time standing alone in a field surrounded by animals that don’t speak and are apt to wander off and get lost. The solitude sharpens my mind.”

Wallace stopped, but Horace wished he wouldn’t. He found that if Wallace kept talking, it took his mind off troubles of his own. “What else do you do?”

Wallace raised an eyebrow, surprised that Horace really cared about such things. He reasoned that the man must be struggling to keep up the fight, so he went on.

“Sometimes I eat nothing for an entire day, which I admit

sounds strange. But you'd be surprised what it does to a person to go without food even for a single day. Unexpected hungers rear their ugly head when basic needs are voluntarily given up. The things that are deep inside come looking for provisions — dark things that also want to be fed."

"What dark things come out when you don't eat?" asked Horace.

"Things like anger and deceit, fear and jealousy," said Wallace. "Although, with the Highlands beneath me now, I'm quite a lot less jealous than I used to be. I didn't see that coming."

Horace laughed quietly at Wallace's words and felt genuine surprise that this passive man before him was capable of feeling jealousy and anger.

"So you're telling me if I take walks all alone, tend sheep all day, and starve myself, I'll turn into a peaceful person?"

Wallace shrugged his shoulders. "My thoughts are often much darker than you might imagine when I'm starved for something to eat and standing alone on a hill for hours on end."

He looked thoughtfully at Horace, and then he spoke the last of what he would teach the man that night.

"You must know your enemies to overcome them. That is the path of peace for every person, and it comes only by doing, not by study of those who are already doing."

There was a rustling on the path behind them and they were both up in a flash, their backs to each other in the dim light of the grove. Everything was silent once more, and the two men turned and crept slowly toward the sound they'd heard, spears at the ready. All but a very few people had been ordered to huddle together behind ever-widening circular perimeters of men with weapons. At the heart of the inner circle were the children and mothers, the animals and the stores of water.

"This way," whispered Horace in his quietest voice. He was aware that Gill was scouting the perimeter of the grove on horseback, and the two parties might have unintentionally come close to one another in the dark.

Horace and Wallace crept closer to where the noise had come from, ducking under branches as they went. When the two had gone about ten paces down a hard dirt path between the trees they heard the sound again, only this time they saw what it was. A rabbit darted out from behind a tree and across the path, disappearing on the other side.

The two men breathed a sigh of relief and glanced at each other, then back at the path where the rabbit had crossed. A second rabbit hopped out into the same path, but this one was limping badly and moved slower than the other. It stopped and stood on its two back legs, looking curiously at Horace and Wallace.

"Looks like that one is having a bad night," said Horace. He leaned down and put a hand out toward the rabbit, and when he did, the Cleaner that lay hidden in the shadows leaped out with stunning force and speed. Its jaws slammed down over the injured rabbit, devouring it all at once.

Wallace remained perfectly still, several feet back from the monster, but Horace was unable to contain his voice in the shock of the moment and let out an almost inaudible bark that carried over Wallace's head and reached the tiny ears of the Cleaner. It turned ferociously, still grinding its teeth on the rabbit, and both men saw the hunger and wrath in its eyes as it reared up on its many legs, crashing through the limbs of the trees overhead.

The suction cups on the Cleaner's belly glowed and dripped slime in the grey night of Atherton. Its head came crashing down through the trees on top of Wallace. But Wallace was a smart man, good under pressure and aware of the importance of what he must do. He knelt down, as if in sacrifice, the bottom of his spear firm on the ground and its top well above his head. The Cleaner came down, mouth open and howling, and with incredible force it pounced on the spear and the man underneath it.

This was not an ordinary Cleaner, but the biggest of them all. Its mouth closed around the spear and it reared into the air, then it slammed back down toward the ground and crushed Wallace where he kneeled.

Horace stabbed at the creature's head as it flailed wildly in every direction, uprooting trees and batting Wallace on the ground as it swung its awful head. Finally, the beast lay on its side, wheezing and chomping at the spear caught in its brain, and then it laid silent and dead. Air and liquid escaped from all twelve feet of it in the wreckage of the grove.

Horace poked at its head to be sure there was no last gasp of life left in it. Then he searched the ground for Wallace and found that he had been batted off the path and lay motionless ten feet away.

He knelt beside Wallace, hearing the sound of approaching hooves through the trees. "Wallace?" he said, still whispering for no reason at all.

Without warning Gill galloped up on his horse and dismounted, standing next to his commander and surveying the scene of destruction. Four trees had been uprooted by the swinging head of the massive Cleaner. Roots were exposed everywhere, and the hulking body of the dead Cleaner covered the ground at the center of it all. Looking back at Horace, he saw that Wallace was not moving.

"You killed it," said Gill. "I didn't think that was possible. It was so big."

He walked closer still and gazed down at the two men, and Wallace opened his eyes.

"You're alive!" cried Horace, cradling Wallace's head. "You did it! You killed the beast."

Wallace's eyes were barely open. His neck was broken and his head had been dashed against a tree. There was almost no life left in him.

"You must follow your own path," said Wallace, struggling to breathe and force out the words. "You know the way."

"We'll follow it together," said Horace. He was crying, for he knew his friend was about to die.

Wallace smiled and gazed up into the limbs of the trees.

"Don't let Maude push you around," he said, and this made Horace smile.

Wallace's eyes slowly shut, and as they did he turned his gaze on Horace, mumbling his last. "You must lead the way."

And then the old shepherd was gone and the grove was bathed, if only for a moment, in the peaceful way of its past.

CHAPTER 24

THE KEEPER OF ATHERTON

"Edgar!" cried Dr. Harding. "Wake up! We've slept too long!"

Edgar leaped to his feet as he'd often done in the grove when Mr. Ratikan woke him unexpectedly with a whack from his walking stick. He had the distinct feeling that all was not right, that a new danger had arrived in the night. Edgar darted to the window and saw that there was only a trace of light coming from above. The floor of the Highlands was covered mostly in shadow, but the dim light revealed a quality to the land before him that Edgar didn't understand.

"The ground is moving," said Edgar, glancing back at Dr. Harding, who was struggling to stand up.

"Bring me to the window, won't you?"

Edgar returned to Dr. Harding's side and helped him up as

best he could. The two hobbled over to the window, where Dr. Harding leaned heavily on the stone sill draped in ivy. He looked down, breathing heavily and knowing his fate.

"We come to the second day, and the darkest hour of my existence."

"Stop talking like that!" said Edgar. He was tired of feeling the chill of insanity all around him.

Dr. Harding continued to speak in the bizarre, prophetic voice of a creator. "But it's true, Edgar. It's true because you will leave and I can't go with you. I didn't plan for this parting on the second day, but it comes to pass all the same." He was dying, there were no two ways about it, and Edgar knew it would be impossible to get him out of the Highlands.

"Why does the ground move?" asked Edgar.

Dr. Harding looked at the boy and then out the window, his breathing growing more steady.

"Water," he said.

Edgar looked down again and then he understood. The whole floor of the Highlands was covered in gently sloshing waves. The courtyard was gone, hidden beneath the water. There were no jagged shadows from trees or walls or anything else, only a dark glass surface that washed ominously across the world.

Dr. Harding slumped down along the edge of the sill and sobbed into the ivy. Edgar didn't know what to say and simply put his hand on Dr. Harding's shoulder. Dr. Harding put his hand on Edgar's and looked into his eyes.

"You have to leave this place before the water rises and covers the House of Power. When the tallest tower is no longer visible, Atherton will grow fiercer for a time."

"But I can't swim," said Edgar. "I don't know how." He was aware of the fact that while he could climb his way out of many dangerous circumstances, water was something he had very little experience with.

He leaned out the window once more. The light of morning was creeping in with the passing of time. The water, it seemed, was rising calmly but fast. Now there were waves but no whitecaps, a rolling sea that looked to Edgar as though it would swallow him up and never let him go.

"The water is rising quickly," said Edgar, coming back down to crouch next to Dr. Harding. "What should we do?"

With some effort, Dr. Harding pointed toward Mead's Head. "Go stand over there and do as I say."

Edgar did as he was told, and Dr. Harding instructed him to grasp the head and turn it one way and then another. It was different from the way it had been turned to open Mead's Hollow, snapping as it turned twice to the left and three times to the right.

"Now, push the head onto the floor," said Dr. Harding.

Edgar hesitated, feeling a certain unease about knocking the head off the pedestal.

"Push it off!" shouted Dr. Harding, and Edgar obeyed. Mead's Head tumbled heavily through the air, crashing at Edgar's feet and cracking into two halves. Out of the two halves there fell a silver key.

“Take the key,” said Dr. Harding. He coughed and wheezed, lifting his arm once more and pointing to the other side of the room where there sat a wardrobe. The wardrobe had walls of stone and a grave-looking wooden door that appeared as if it hadn’t been opened for a very long time. Now Edgar went to it, inserted the silver key into the lock, and opened the door.

There were only two things inside, neither of which Edgar had seen the likes of before. Or had he? His mind raced back to his second visit to the Highlands and the memory of a young boy pushing a toy between his hands as it had floated back and forth on the water. One of the things inside the wardrobe looked very much like a larger version of the toy Edgar had seen.

“It’s a boat,” said Dr. Harding. “You’d know that, if Dr. Kincaid hadn’t taken you away. You can get inside—it’s small, but it will hold you—and that long stick is a paddle. You can push yourself through the water with it.”

The wooden boat sat on its belly, ready to be boarded. It was indeed very small, unable to hold more than one person. Edgar glanced back and forth between the contents of the wardrobe and Dr. Harding.

“If you wait until the water comes through the window, you can make your escape in the boat. But you’ll need to be swift about it.”

Edgar placed the paddle in the boat and took the vessel by its pointed front end, dragging it out of the wardrobe until it sat in the middle of the room. It was dusty and dry, but very soon it would feel the power of water.

“We could both fit inside,” said Edgar, excited for a moment, but then realizing it would never work. Edgar kept his gaze on Dr. Harding and knew the truth. "You made this for me, didn't you? You knew it would come to this."

Dr. Harding smiled weakly. "If only we'd woken at dusk, you could have walked out in water up to your knees. Now you can only hope to paddle to the edge of the Highlands and climb out, for the waves will soon become violent."

"How violent?" Edgar was suddenly scared of riding on the water, and he darted to the window, hoping to find a calm sea. The water was nearly at the window, only a few feet below. It was coming for him.

"Get in the boat, Edgar," said Dr. Harding. With great effort he stood, gripping vines of ivy in one hand to stay up. "And don't be afraid. Just row to the cliffs as fast as you can and get out. When you reach the cliffs, climb like you've never climbed before!"

Water spilled into the room, sloshing over the edge of the sill on a silent wave. Edgar ran to the boat and got inside, shaking with fear, and the water began to fill the room. It covered Dr. Harding's feet and then rose up the lower part of his legs. As water poured through the window, Edgar could detect the boat begin to move under him. He unexpectedly felt a deep desire to embrace Dr. Harding, and he jumped from the boat and careered toward him.

"Edgar, no!" cried Dr. Harding. "Get back in the boat!"

But Edgar didn't listen. He splashed through the water that came to his waist until he was right next to Dr. Harding, and then he threw his arms around the man. Dr. Harding took his hand from the ivy, and gathering all of his remaining strength, he picked Edgar up as one would carry a child from a raging fire or a coming flood. The two locked eyes, and Edgar's fear was gone as Dr. Harding carried him back to the boat and set him gently inside.

"I have always loved you, Edgar," said Dr. Harding. "Take care of this place I've made for you."

Edgar nodded, feeling an odd sense of rightness at the command of his maker. He was transformed in that moment from an orphan of the grove into the keeper of Atherton, and he swelled with pride at the idea of protecting it, nurturing it, and making it whole once again.

The water was at Dr. Harding's chest as he pushed the boat in front of him toward the window. Edgar took the oar in his hands and saw that it would be close. If the water rose much higher it would fill the window entirely and then he could not get out. He would be trapped in the House of Power, pinned against the ceiling by the oncoming water. As the boat came near the opening, Edgar ducked down low and felt a great push from behind as Dr. Harding gave away the very last energy he had and sent Edgar out into the open water of the Highlands.

Edgar looked back. Dr. Harding held on to the ivy, looking dreamily out toward all that he had made. The water was at his chest now, but he seemed utterly at peace with the coming of the end. No more words were spoken between the two. Edgar could not watch the water overtake Dr. Harding. He turned instead to the sea and began to paddle away.

"Goodbye, Edgar," whispered Dr. Harding. He smiled and

his mind was as clear as it had been before Dr. Kincaid had found him, when he himself was only a boy. The fresh wonder of childhood washed over him. There were no more rooms in his mind, no more numbers, no Atherton. There was only the boy on the horizon, drifting out to sea as the water rose past the window and over the House of Power.

PART THREE

INVERSION

There is a tide in the affairs of men,
Which, taken at the flood, leads on to fortune;
Omitted, all the voyage of their life
Is bound in shallows and in miseries.

Julius Caesar
William Shakespeare

CHAPTER 25

A STORM IN THE HIGHLANDS

Edgar found himself tossed on the waves of a swiftly rising sea that was growing more aggressive as he made his way toward the cliffs. *How am I to get out of this boat without being dashed into the rocks?* Edgar thought. He felt quite sure that he was paddling directly into a catastrophe that would take his life.

But he kept paddling, remembering the words Dr. Harding had said the night before. *You must be free of the Highlands before the water reaches halfway to the top, or the power of the sea will destroy you. When you reach the cliffs, climb like you've never climbed before!* The water was well below halfway up the side of the cliffs, and already the waves were capped with white, slamming into the rocks and bouncing back toward Edgar on the small boat. It was as if some giant creature were shaking Atherton in its hands.

It was hard work keeping the boat moving out toward the edge. Uprooted trees and debris floated all around Edgar and threatened to careen into the side of the wooden boat. He was rowing with his back to the cliffs, his wounded shoulder burning with every stroke, and he could see that everything that was not connected to the cliffs or the floor of the Highlands was being sucked into the middle, a great jumble of wreckage crashing on the waves. If he were pulled back in it would be the end, and so he rowed feverishly, his wiry arms and legs fueled by a rush of energy to get free of the Highlands. He had to get free!

"*Heeeeeeelp!*"

Edgar heard the distant voice of Tyler calling from somewhere far off in the waves. He caught sight of him stranded on what looked like the detached side of a wooden house. He was holding on for dear life, careening between objects in the middle of the Highlands. Purely on instinct Edgar turned his vessel and began paddling frantically toward the stranded man. He worked the oar furiously, but as he struggled against the waves two harsh realities began to occur to him: Tyler couldn't climb out of the Highlands, and the boat was too small to hold them both. It was a futile effort that would end badly for both of them.

It was a terrible moment for a boy to endure—to leave a helpless man to die or try in vain to save him—but Edgar was mercifully spared the decision when the limbs of an uprooted tree crashed into Tyler and he disappeared from sight. The rising sea of Atherton had claimed him.

When Edgar came within a hundred feet of the cliffs he realized that the water was rising even faster than he could have imagined. It was nearing the halfway point, or so he thought by what he could see looking up at what remained of the stone walls surrounding him, and the waves were growing even fiercer. Edgar could feel that he was at the crest between waves that were pulling him inward and forcing him out to the very edge, and it scared him to think what would happen when he reached the rocks.

The waves crashed with a roar as he plunged the paddle into the water and rowed closer still. The waves began to take the little boat and move it quickly forward without warning. The hundred feet to the cliffs was cut to fifty and then ten as the boat was carried on the rising water with stunning speed.

Edgar stood on the boat, holding the edges with his hands as it swayed and spun in circles, and then he jumped into the air and hoped against all hope that he would find something to grab onto, that his head wouldn't be bashed against the rocks. He hit the cliff hard and began to slide, reaching wildly for anything he could hold. The boat was dashed against the rocks, pulled back on the waves, then smashed into pieces at Edgar's side.

He had found a slippery hold with one hand and without thinking of anything at all he had begun climbing. Like a spider he outpaced the rising water that slammed into the walls beneath him. He never looked down, only up, and he did just as Dr. Harding had told him. He climbed faster than he'd ever climbed before, losing and regaining his grip over and over again on the wet and muddy path upward. More than once his feet dangled free from slimy clumps of earth breaking off Atherton, but always he was able to regain control and keep moving higher.

Edgar had no idea how long he'd been climbing when his arms and legs and lungs started to burn so terribly from the effort that he had no choice but to slow down. It was then that he realized he'd overcome the storm in the Highlands. It was still raging beneath him, but it was not rising as it had been. It was, in fact, receding! The water had come to the halfway point and now it was moving down again, the waves every bit as violent as they had been before.

Edgar didn't take this monumental bit of good luck lightly and was soon off again at full speed. He climbed higher and higher along the slippery cliffs, feeling a sense of deep exhilaration as he went. There was a part of him that believed it was the last time he would climb like this, and he made the most of it. He and Atherton were one, both made by the one man, and he felt mysteriously linked to Atherton as he never had before.

When, finally, he came within minutes of his escape to the very top, he heard the waves below increase in intensity and looked down for the second time. The water was rising again, faster and with more force, and the very walls he hung on to shook in his hands. Dr. Harding had been right. If Edgar had been in the water and faced waves like the ones he saw now, he would not have lived.

Edgar scrambled the rest of the way out and tumbled over the edge into Tabletop, where something occurred to him that he hadn't thought of before. *How far is that water going to rise?*

Edgar leaned over the edge and had the harrowing thought that the waves might crest the Highlands and overtake Tabletop, the grove, *everything*. It would have been helpful if he'd stayed awake to hear what Dr. Harding had said about the water, but it was only a dreamy twinkle lodged deep in his mind and he could not get it out.

Edgar turned in the direction of the grove. He had come into Tabletop a good distance from his former home, and though he could see the trees it would take awhile to get there. He began walking, then running toward the grove, hoping to find people—rather than Cleaners—there.

In the distance he saw a horse and rider approaching, and soon the horse came near enough that Edgar could see the rider was someone he didn't know.

"Where have you come from?" asked Gill, surprised to see the wet and weary boy out in the open.

"There," said Edgar, pointing into the giant hole behind him that led into the Highlands. The sound of breaking waves far below could be heard. It was a haunting sound of echoes and booms, and Edgar could tell that Gill wondered what it was as he sniffed the air and looked toward the noise from the Highlands.

"You should go to the edge and look down. It won't take long on that thing," Edgar pointed to the horse.

"Who are you?" asked Gill, enormous curiosity in his voice.

"I'm Edgar."

Gill was aware of the boy from the stories that permeated

the grove, stories of a young boy who had climbed to every level of Atherton and then mysteriously disappeared.

"Everyone thinks you're dead," said Gill, excited at having found the missing boy. He reached his arm down and motioned for Edgar to take it, but Edgar was unsure.

"It's easy, honestly," said Gill, still holding out his hand. "We'll go to the edge and have a look, then we can ride back to the grove."

Edgar reached his arm up tentatively—the one with the missing pinky—and Gill snatched it, hauling the thin boy up into the air and onto the back of the horse.

"Hold on!" said Gill. He kicked the horse and they were off. Edgar was not prepared for the speed at which the horse could gallop and it took his breath away. He laughed out loud involuntarily despite all of the misery around him. He simply could not help himself. *This,* he thought in disbelief, *is almost as exhilarating as climbing!*

When they came to the edge the ground was shaking at their feet, and Gill gasped at the sight of crashing waves. The storm in the Highlands had the effect of drawing the blood from one's face, so stunning was the sight of raging water on the rise.

"How high will it come?" asked Gill, as if he expected Edgar to know.

"I'm not sure, but it doesn't look like it's going to stop anytime soon. It rises and falls, but mostly it seems to be rising."

Gill took one last look at the gargantuan hole filled with waves and thought for a brief moment about the house he had lived in, now covered and smashed by the deluge below. Everything the Highlands had been was gone, churned into rubble by the power of water. *Could it really be so?*

He kicked the horse and the two were off, speeding across open land, heading for the grove with news of a flooding world.

CHAPTER 26 THE NUBIAN

While Edgar and Gill raced toward the grove, a different group of weary travelers were quietly moving somewhere far beneath Tabletop. They had begun their journey at about the same time Edgar started his escape from the Highlands, working their way down the side of a rock mountain bathed in golden radiance. As they descended to the valley floor, yellow and orange beams of light cut through the darkness. The rising mountains twisted into unscalable precipices on every side.

The call of the Nubian pierced Samuel's ears. He sensed the flying creatures were near, waiting to attack. It felt as if he were trapped in a place of desolation that could not be overcome.

"How far do you think we have to go?" whispered Samuel. He and Isabel were walking side by side between the adults, using their spears as walking sticks as they came very near the bottom.

"I think it will be a while," Isabel answered. "How big do you think the Nubian are?"

Samuel held out his spear, examining it. He had read about the birds in books but had always assumed they were fantasy creatures invented by storytellers. "I wonder if their wings are wider than this spear."

"That they are," said Dr. Kincaid, bending down in order to whisper to the two children. "The Nubian is a marvelous creature, and highly necessary to the inner workings of Atherton. Without them—well, to be fair, without a *lot* of strange things down here—Atherton wouldn't work at all." He paused a moment, then added, "You know he hated birds and bugs."

"Who did?" asked Isabel.

"Dr. Harding. I think he feared them more than he hated them, but he needed them, so he put them down here where they couldn't get out. The Nubian move things around, sort of like when you move water through a grove of trees so that they can drink."

"Could they kill a Cleaner?" Samuel imagined a giant winged animal descending on the beasts outside. Dr. Harding seemed not to know what to make of the question. He pulled on his ear and looked off toward the sound of the Nubian.

"It doesn't matter," said Dr. Kincaid. "They can never leave the inside. It would be the end of Atherton."

"Why?" asked Isabel. "Why couldn't we let them go?"

ROCK-LIKE SKULL PLATE

RAZOR SHARP BEAK !!

HIGHLY ADVANCED MOVEMENTS

SCALES & FEATHERS

KEEP THEM INSIDE. THEY MUST NEVER GET OUT !!!

BLUE/RED SCALES WITH THE STRENGTH OF METAL.

DIFFICULT TO STOP THESE GIANT CREATURES

BE CARE

SCREECHING DIVE

THE NUBIAN

SMALL HORNS ABOVE THE EYES

DIFFICULT TO DESTROY, SHOULD THE NEED ARISE !

ALWAYS TRAVEL IN PAIRS - KEEP WATCH

“Because they’d kill a lot more than just Cleaners,” said Vincent, who had stopped and heard Isabel’s question. They had reached the valley floor within the inside of Atherton. Rock formations of red and yellow towered all around them, layered back like endless, rolling mountains. As in the cavern, sharp spires of stone pointed angrily down from the black ceiling far above, and everywhere the shadows of the Nubian were crossing like dark water through beams of light.

“At least the Cleaners are stupid,” continued Vincent, who had turned to look at everyone. With his crossbow in hand and broken nose he had the appearance of a warrior long at battle, unsure when he would return home. “And they were contained. The Cleaners weren’t supposed to leave the Flatlands.”

“That’s not what Dr. Harding said.” Dr. Kincaid was forever trying to defend the mad scientist.

Vincent sighed and shook his head, then returned to the matter at hand.

“If the Nubian were to leave the inside of Atherton that would make them”—Vincent searched for the right word—“*uncontained.*” A vague sort of concern rose in his voice. “They could fly anywhere they chose, and eat whatever they found.”

“How big are they?” asked Isabel, hearing the screeching move even nearer.

Vincent glanced up into shafts of light and shadow. “You’re about to see for yourselves.”

He told everyone to move back against the rocks where there were crevices in which to hide. It was possible to squeeze into the larger cracks, and they all began working toward this end.

"All but you, Isabel," said Vincent. She was startled to have been singled out at such a dangerous moment. "We need to show them they should stay away, and I understand you're even better than Edgar with a sling."

Isabel couldn't help smiling as she felt in her pockets for the sling and the black figs.

"Save the figs and use the rocks," said Vincent. "Aim for the first one you see. One shot, then come back into the rocks. Understood?"

Isabel nodded, searching the ground before her and finding a heavy stone the size of her fist. She set the stone in place and waited, watching the harrowing shadows of the Nubian above.

"How many are there?" asked Isabel. Everyone else had moved into the jagged rock openings.

"Only about fifty," said Vincent. He could tell that she expected all fifty to descend on them at any moment. "But the inside of Atherton is big and they're extremely territorial. They usually travel in pairs, so I suspect there will be two. You aim for the first, I'll aim for the second. Remember, *one* shot, no more."

It had been silent for a moment, but now the valley floor was alive with the sound of shrieking and the first of the Nubian dived for the ground. Isabel was instinctive with her sling in the same way that Edgar was when he climbed. She did not think. If she had, she would have run. Instead, the sling was spiraling around her head, fast and perfect, and then there was the familiar *snap!* The heavy rock was gone.

The Nubian came into full view, turning gracefully to the

side as the stone flew past. The creature had gigantic, powerful wings with scaly feathers that intertwined in a pattern of murky blue and bloodred. It moved as nothing Isabel had ever seen, fluid and smooth. She'd hit a man on a horse, but this was something entirely different.

"Get back into the rocks!" screamed Vincent, but Isabel was glued to the ground, mesmerized by the Nubian's shrieking descent. The flying beast, she saw, had a jet-black beak like a long spike that she could easily imagine ripping into her. Isabel's brain went cold. She could think of nothing but to hide, and so she ran away as fast as her legs would carry her down the path that led through the valley floor.

"Isabel!" cried Samuel. He couldn't bear the thought of seeing her stabbed and carried off by a giant flying creature with a monstrous black beak. Running into the open behind Vincent, he began waving his arms and yelling into the sky. "Leave her alone, you terrible beast!"

Samuel's father leaped out from the crack in the rocks and grabbed Samuel by the arm, dragging him back to safety. Samuel struggled and yelled, but Sir William refused to let him go.

A second Nubian came in behind the first, and both creatures dived toward the group. The first swooped low and fast behind Isabel, lowering its great claws as if to snatch her from the ground. Vincent fired the crossbow when the Nubian passed over. The arrow jammed into a wing and the Nubian howled in pain, flapping up and away unsteadily from the valley floor.

The second of the two Nubian was not deterred. It closed its wings entirely and flew like an arrow for the ground while Vincent bent down on one knee, trying desperately to reload. His hands fumbled with the arrow as the Nubian spread its wings and turned sharply, aiming straight for Vincent with its pointed black beak. Vincent looked up and knew without a doubt that he was finished. He wouldn't get the arrow loaded in time and the Nubian would overtake him.

But then he heard a sound he hadn't expected. It was the *snap!* of Isabel's sling, and this time she had used a fig as black as the Nubian's pointed beak. Unlike the stone she'd thrown before, the black fig flew fast and true, so fast that the Nubian could not react in time. The beast glanced sideways and was struck firmly in the neck. Screeching with rage, it darted up along the rocks, through a giant crevice, and out of sight.

Sir William let Samuel go and the boy darted out into the open. He stood before Isabel with some embarrassment for having tried to rescue her, only to be dragged back to safety by his father.

"Thank you for trying that," she said, surprised by how much it had meant to her.

Samuel nodded. "We need to find Edgar together, and we can't do it if you're dead."

The two smiled as Dr. Kincaid emerged from the rocks, staring at the whole lot of them with admiration.

"We may overcome this strange world yet," he said, smiling at the sound of the two Nubian trailing off. "The inside of Atherton is vast. Those two are the only ones we're likely to see for a while, and I don't think they'll be back."

Vincent nodded and winked at Isabel, and she winked right back at him.

"There's really only one thing the Nubian won't attack," Dr. Kincaid went on, still smiling in a jovial sort of way. "They won't even go near it."

And then Dr. Kincaid's cheerful moment came to an end, because he remembered they would all have to overcome the very thing of which he spoke. He'd done it before, but never with so many, and never with children.

"The Inferno," said Vincent.

Dr. Kincaid nodded, then deflected all of the questioning eyes with a wave of his arm.

"Vincent will get us through," he said. But there was a part of him that was sure they wouldn't all make it past the Inferno, and there was no other way to escape the inside of Atherton.

CHAPTER 27
ACROSS THE VALLEY FLOOR

"Is it day or night on Atherton?"

Isabel had been quiet for a while as they trudged along the valley floor. The shafts of light had grown dimmer, and it made her wonder why the light had changed.

"If I had to guess," said Dr. Kincaid, putting a hand on the young girl's shoulder, "I'd have to say it was morning on Atherton. But then I haven't been down here in a while, so I could be wrong. The way we're going is a darker way, so I'm not entirely sure it matters what time it is upstairs."

Despite all of their hardships, Isabel was amused by the thought of the outside as being upstairs.

"I wonder where my parents and Edgar are," she thought out loud.

Dr. Kincaid was naturally given to the qualities of a grandfather, and he tried to comfort Isabel.

"Dr. Harding can be very determined when he wants to be. I'm sure he found Edgar and managed to rid the world of Sir Emerik. And I have no doubt our climbing boy is already free of the Highlands."

Isabel laughed softly and Samuel slowed to join the two on the path. He was curious to know what they were talking about, but he was also looking for something to take his mind off the grim path they were traveling.

"And as for your parents," continued Dr. Kincaid, "I wouldn't worry too much about them. Changes are afoot! I believe you'll see them again soon."

Dr. Kincaid found that with Samuel on one side and Isabel on the other, guiding them through the shadows of the valley, he felt almost as if he *were* a grandfather to them both.

"I think the future of Atherton is in good hands," he said. "You two will do just fine."

Samuel seized the moment to ask Dr. Kincaid one of the many questions that had been brewing in his mind during the journey.

"Why did you take Edgar away from Dr. Harding?"

Dr. Kincaid looked straight ahead, and without much hesitation, he answered the boy so that everyone could hear. "He was more like Lord Phineus than Dr. Harding toward the end. Does that answer your question?"

Samuel nodded, feeling a little guilty for having asked at all.

But then Isabel asked just as difficult a question, and it made him feel better.

"Why did you work Dr. Harding so awfully hard? You must have known he was sick."

Dr. Kincaid looked at the children on either side of him with some surprise. "You two don't give an old man much benefit of the doubt, do you?"

Samuel and Isabel weren't even sure exactly what this meant, but they had a pretty good idea that Dr. Kincaid didn't enjoy any questions about his past.

Dr. Kincaid sighed deeply. "Are we close?" he asked Vincent. The sound of the Nubian cut through the air from a long way off, and Vincent looked up into the rocks.

Vincent said, "Not far to go, but plenty enough for you to answer the girl's question."

Dr. Kincaid scowled at Vincent, then looked back at Isabel and saw that he hadn't distracted her one bit. The girl wanted an answer, and he would have to provide one.

"If you must know, it was mostly out of my control. I told them time and time again not to push so hard. There is nothing so fragile as a brilliant young mind. It's a delicate thing, easily traumatized by demands it cannot achieve. But then, I have to admit, even I was too demanding of him. Not at first—at first I was always the one to make them leave him alone—but after a while, well, as a man of science, I couldn't help it. He knew so many things I didn't, and I wanted desperately to understand."

Silence fell over the group and the Nubian screeched again, closer but still far off.

“He wanted to please everyone,” said Dr. Kincaid. “But when it was all over, he pleased no one. There’s a lesson in that, don’t you think?”

Isabel and Samuel nodded, and then Samuel remarked, “The Dark Planet must be in terrible shape if Atherton was so important to them.”

“You have no idea,” said Dr. Kincaid. “And yet, they have always found a way to survive. It would not surprise me if they’ve already cooked up some other way of making do. It’s a dirty place and getting dirtier, but who are we to say they can’t solve their own problems? We’ve certainly got enough of our own.”

He was about to tell them other ideas that had been in the works to save the planet of his origin, but he was cut off by Vincent. They were now approaching the Inferno.

They had come to a place where tunnels led off in many directions and red stone reached into the sky all around them. They were trapped but for the tunnels as a way out, and all the tunnels were dark.

“You must each listen carefully,” started Vincent. “And know before we begin that this is a hard way that cannot be avoided.”

As he spoke, a small, fluorescent light that looked like a dancing blue dot in the air crept noiselessly out from between two rocks. It hovered silently behind Vincent in such a way that he could not see it, but the others could, even though it was no bigger than the tip of a spear.

The dot came around to the side of Vincent closest to Isabel, and she reached out toward it, drawn by the pulsing blue light. Vincent glanced behind and saw what Isabel was after.

"Don't touch it!" he cried. She was the most curious among them, and he should have known to warn her sooner. But Isabel had already extended her arm and the blue dot moved toward her, as if it wanted to be caught.

The glowing light was a bug that was part of the Inferno, and Isabel could hear its microscopic wings beating ever so softly as she touched it. The result was not what she'd expected. Her hand felt a shock of electricity that then flowed down her arm all the way into her toes. It seemed to paralyze her momentarily, and she could not move her muscles to flick the glowing blue bug away from her skin. She was being electrocuted, though not enough to kill her.

Vincent carefully swished the bug away with his sleeve. It hung in the air once more, turning from blue to green to red. Then Vincent blew softly and the bug bounced on the air back into the dark opening from where it came.

"They turn red when they're angry," said Vincent.

"What was that thing?" howled Isabel. From her shoulder all the way to the tips of her fingers there was a painful tingling that made her itch frantically. She shook her hand but it was no use.

"Hold your hand over your head," said Dr. Kincaid. "It will go away in a few seconds."

Isabel held her arm up and tried not to scratch. She'd never felt anything so powerful. It was like her arm had fallen asleep and woken up all at once, little needles poking up and down her skin.

Sir William came over, held her arm up, and looked at Vincent. "Why did you bring us this way?" he asked with dismay. Things were getting more perilous by the moment—first the Nubian, and now this new threat. He truly wondered if he could trust the men in which he'd placed so much hope. How well did he really know them?

"Because it's the only way out," said Vincent. "If there were any other options, believe me, we wouldn't be going in there." He pointed into the Inferno.

"You should have told us it would be like this," said Sir William. "It wasn't fair to drag us down here without telling us how dangerous it would be."

"Would you have come with us if we'd told you?" asked Dr. Kincaid.

Sir William didn't answer and Dr. Kincaid went on.

"The Highlands were already filling with water, crashing into the middle of Atherton. This was the *only* way. If we'd said you'd have to do battle with flying beasts and tiny winged zappers, would you have come? Of course not!"

Sir William seemed, for the moment, to concede. "I have to get them back home," said Sir William, glancing down at Isabel and Samuel. "Just be honest with us."

Dr. Kincaid faltered a moment. Sensing there was no other option he decided it was, indeed, time for honesty in all matters. "Things are going to get worse before they get better," he said.

"What do you mean, *worse?*" asked Samuel. "How could they get any worse?"

"The Inferno is . . . w-w-well, it's complicated," stammered Dr. Kincaid. "But I've done it many times before, and I'm old! If I can make it, so can you."

"There are things in the Inferno that you'll want to lay a hand on," Vincent told them, thinking about the task ahead more carefully. The fire bugs were mesmerizing, he knew; they *wanted* to be touched. It was hard not to obey. "But all of them are dangerous, and most of them can kill you."

Vincent looked at Dr. Kincaid as if to say, *This is your department, don't you think?*

The sound of the Nubian grew nearer and angrier, and Samuel imagined the one injured by the arrow now looking for revenge.

"How's your arm feeling, Isabel?" asked Dr. Kincaid. Sir William let go of her hand and she shook her arm hard, scratching at her elbow.

"It's better," she said. "It still itches, but the pain is gone."

"Wonderful!" said Dr. Kincaid. "Now listen, all of you. Vincent is absolutely right. There's no point in explaining every little thing to you, but nothing that's in there is meant for humans to go near. Unfortunately, it's also the only way out from beneath Tabletop. Where we're about to go is under the Flatlands, and once we get past the Inferno, the rest of our way is easy." Dr. Kincaid marveled in his own mind at the outrageous imagination of Dr. Harding. The way down from Tabletop had been erased by the changing world, and yet the way across—the way into the Flatlands—was still there.

"The Nubian are circling," said Vincent. The group looked up and saw familiar, eerie shadows moving high on the red rocks above.

"There's time for just a little instruction," said Dr. Kincaid. "For one thing, we don't have to be quiet. Nothing inside there can hear us so it won't matter if you want to talk as we go. There will be a lot of fire bugs—more than you can imagine—but if you go slowly and blow on them, you'll be able to avoid them. Don't let them touch your skin. Your hair should be all right."

He looked at everyone, and seeing that all but Vincent had a healthy head of thick hair, he nodded.

"Cover up as much as you can, but remain watchful. There is another creature inside that eats the fire bugs."

"What sort of creature? How big is it?" asked Samuel. He had already wanted to turn back at the thought of being electrocuted by thousands of tiny glowing bugs. What could possibly want to eat them?

The shadows of the Nubian came lower on the wall and their screeching filled the air.

"Follow Vincent," said Dr. Kincaid. "He'll try to clear the way. We have to go!"

The Nubian were diving together, one after the other, as Vincent crept into the Inferno. Dr. Kincaid followed, then came the children, and finally Sir William. The moment the five of them were inside the dark opening, the Nubian turned back, shrieking with anger.

"We come now to the last of our difficult passage," Dr. Kincaid mumbled. And then, wanting to make sure everyone understood the seriousness of the situation, he said one more thing. "I'm sorry to say we saved the most dangerous part for the end."

CHAPTER 28
FLIGHT FROM THE GROVE

While Edgar sat with Maude and Horace on the steps of Mr. Ratikan's house, the ground rumbled oddly at their feet, accompanied by the eerie sound of water rising in a storm over the Highlands—a new threat they didn't have the first idea how to manage.

Horace, Maude, and Isabel's father, Charles, had welcomed Edgar, but there was precious little time and so the questions had begun almost immediately. As he sat on the steps he had once approached every day for food, Edgar hurriedly explained about Dr. Harding and Dr. Kincaid, about Vincent and Sir William, and of course, Samuel and Isabel.

"They've gone underground, into a secret place that's safe from the rising water," said Edgar. He couldn't imagine how they'd ever escape Dr. Harding's laboratory, but he also wanted to provide a little hope. "The two from the Flatlands—Dr. Kincaid and Vincent—they knew where they were going. There must be a passage out."

"At least they're safe from the Cleaners down there," said Maude. Charles nodded earnestly, but in truth, though no one was willing to say it, survival inside the violent heart of Atherton seemed impossible.

As Charles hurried off toward the village to tell Isabel's mother what he'd learned, Horace began questioning Edgar again. "How high will the water come?"

"Dr. Harding said it would rise all the way to the top."

"Will it reach higher than the edge of the Highlands?" asked Maude, grave concern in her voice.

Edgar hesitated. It was a point that Dr. Harding had come to as Edgar lay half asleep, a fact he was embarrassed to reveal.

"He said everyone must leave for the Flatlands," said Edgar, rubbing the pain out of his shoulder. "He wouldn't tell me why. But you should know he was a little crazy. He'd been bitten by this terrible animal, and his mind wasn't quite right to begin with. I'm not sure he could be trusted in the end."

Edgar hated saying these things, but the truth was he really couldn't be sure Dr. Harding had been altogether sane. Edgar remembered that they should go to the Flatlands, but why? There was nothing out there but Cleaners. No food, no water, just barren, open land where an exodus of humanity would make for easy prey.

"I have thought of the Flatlands as well," said Horace. "I

can't say exactly why, but it has felt to me as if Atherton itself were calling us to go to there."

Horace had a new resolve, his plans bolstered by the news from Edgar. Maude wasn't so sure.

"It's open space out there," she said. "And there's nothing. No water, no food. It's desolate. At least here, in the grove, we have trees to protect us and we can set our backs against the cliffs leading down to the Highlands. The Cleaners can't come up from behind us there. What possible reason could there be to venture out into the wide open nothingness of the Flatlands?"

She had made a great many indisputable points. And yet, Horace was unmoved. "If there is an ounce of truth in what this man has told Edgar, then we have no choice but to go. This man, Dr. Harding, *made* Atherton."

"And then he lost his mind," said Maude, anger rising in her voice. "Don't forget we knew him as Lord Phineus, who would love nothing more than to send us to our death and laugh all the way to his grave."

"We can't stay here," said Horace. "It was never the plan, you know that."

Maude looked away toward the grove, aware that the situation was hopeless.

"Why can't we stay?" asked Edgar. "Maybe she's right. Maybe we could manage it."

Horace didn't feel he had the time or the patience to explain, but he felt he somehow owed it to Edgar. "The Cleaners are coming," he began. "We have scouts on horses, and I tell you it's only a matter of time. They went first to the two villages, but when they've finished destroying those places, it's here they will come. From both sides they'll attack the grove until nothing remains. The grove will draw them in, but we must be gone when they get here."

"Why did you do this?" asked Edgar. "I don't understand your plan and where it leads."

"He had a hunch," said Maude in a critical tone.

"A hunch that Wallace agreed with," said Horace, hesitating before continuing. He wished that Maude would be more agreeable.

But then he heard the sound of hooves tearing through the grove. Gill rode up hard and fast through the trees. The horse nearly collapsed from lack of water and food as Gill dismounted and bolted for the steps to Mr. Ratikan's house.

"They're on the move," said Gill. "All of them, from both sides. All of the Cleaners are coming!"

"How many?" asked Maude, standing as though she were ready to fight.

Gill looked at Edgar and wondered if he should answer with a young boy within earshot.

"I've eaten Cleaners for breakfast," said Edgar, sensing the man's concern. "There's nothing you can say that will surprise me."

Gill looked out into the grove and pointed in the direction of the Village of Rabbits. "Five hundred from there." Then he pointed toward the Village of Sheep. "Five hundred more."

A thousand Cleaners heading for the grove—one for every man, woman, and child of Atherton. It was an insurmountable number.

Horace looked in a different direction through the clearing, toward the barren path that led to the Flatlands. "Something awaits us there," he said. "I *feel* it. And Wallace felt it, too."

The mood in the grove was one of grumbling and dissent as Horace, Maude, and Edgar approached. There had been precious little food and water to give out and provisions were running lower by the hour. Soon there would be nothing, only the approaching Cleaners and an army too tired and hungry to fight. Many from the village had witnessed the water rising in the Highlands and had returned with something well past fear in their eyes. Everyone who stood before Horace looked dazed, as though finally the world had crushed their spirits entirely.

The time had come for Horace to set what remained of his plan into motion, and he stood before hundreds of people speaking in the loudest and most authoritative voice he could muster.

"We must leave this place," he shouted. "Together, as one people, we have overcome a maddening world that threatens to destroy us."

No one made an attempt to disagree. Horace found the eyes of his wife and child, huddling close together in the middle of the crowd, and his heart nearly broke. He wished this duty could fall to another, that he could go and comfort them. And yet his wife smiled up at him, nodded encouragement and understanding, and he was able to accept his circumstances for what they were. He alone could lead them.

"I have tried to show you the way at a time when no clear path revealed itself," continued Horace, his words a solemn reminder of a lost friend. "The water comes to flood us from behind. The Cleaners come from the sides to devour us. There is but one path that remains, though it may seem the least agreeable of them all."

Horace looked away from the group and toward the Flatlands, which no one could see. "We must leave for the Flatlands. No other hope remains."

There was a ripple of shocked exclamations from the group as they realized they would have to leave the safety of the grove. The trees had felt so protective, shielding them from having to look outside at the failing world around them. It had almost seemed peaceful, as if it had all been a bad dream.

The voices of dissent began, but they were stopped by the sound of one boy, a boy who had spent most of his life in the grove.

"He's right," Edgar spoke up with confidence. The boy who'd climbed to every part of Atherton had taken on a sort of mythical status among the living. Everyone quieted.

"I've spoken to the one who made this place," said Edgar, his voice booming louder than he thought possible. Everyone gasped at once, trying to grasp what this meant. "And he told me we would find peace in the Flatlands."

A wave of mumbling came over the crowd and the children began to shout that Edgar was right. Soon the children's voices were louder than the swell of skepticism behind them. They *wanted* to go, to follow the person who they deemed *their* commander.

The grove would have to be abandoned, along with everything else, and they would have to face whatever awaited them in the unknown world of the Flatlands.

CHAPTER 29
THE INFERNO

Sir William had been feeling a growing unease as he and the others made their way through the inside of Atherton. There was a part of him that wanted to take Samuel and Isabel and leave these two men he'd never met before. It seemed to him with each passing step that he and the two children were being led deeper into disaster.

He stood in the dark opening to the Inferno and looked back where the Nubian had been, listening as they trailed off. "Wait a minute," he said, peering into the darkness where he could barely discern the outline of the two men. He held Samuel and Isabel on either side, one under each arm. "I'm *responsible* for these two, even if you aren't."

"There's no place for you out there," Vincent called, gesturing with his chin. "Only death awaits if you take them out of the Inferno. Even if you get past the Nubian on your own, then where will you go? This place was not meant for humans, and *that* way" — he pointed forcefully to the outside — "leads only to the laboratory. In case you've forgotten, the laboratory is in the Highlands, which is under water."

Sir William took his hand off Isabel's shoulder, scratching the beard that had grown fallow beneath his chin.

"It's the only way," said Samuel, looking up at his father. "I know you feel bad for leaving me — for leaving Mother — but there was nothing you could do. No one blames you, least of all me, and Vincent knows the way. We have to learn to trust him."

At that moment Sir William realized just how deep his guilt for being trapped in Mead's Hollow had weighed on him. Until then he hadn't really seen the connection between his protectiveness of the children and his guilt for having left his own son fatherless for so long.

"You're right, Samuel. I do feel terrible I haven't been there to protect you. But you're also right that there was nothing I could do about it." He looked up at Vincent and Dr. Kincaid who stood impatiently waiting. "But I still don't know how to trust either of you. This way you're taking us better not be some sort of trap."

Dr. Kincaid spoke before Vincent had the chance to. "Vincent has one duty, to protect the four of us at all cost. If anyone comes to great harm it will be him, of that you can be assured."

Sir William remained unsure, but he resigned himself to the path he would have to take.

"Let's not assume my demise already," said Vincent. "I've made it through here with an old man in tow several times before. I believe we'll be fine, if you'll only listen and pay attention."

There were tentative nods from everyone as Vincent turned and disappeared into the darkness. "It's a small space, so use the walls to guide you and follow my voice," he called out loudly and with great authority. "There's only one way to go for a while. The first thing you're going to see are more fire bugs. You'll want to touch them because the way they drift and sway makes them look so drunk with happiness, so harmless. Don't give in—*don't touch*—but also, don't turn away. If you take your eyes off them you're likely to feel a shock you won't like."

Isabel breathed in shallow fits and starts because she knew what it would feel like if one of the fire bugs touched her. Though she wasn't crying, by the sounds she was making in the dark it seemed to Samuel that she was nearly hysterical.

"Stay right next to me," he said, holding her hand. She gripped his fingers so tightly it began to hurt, but he didn't say anything. The two followed Vincent's voice through the dark.

"Here's one now," he said, and sure enough, out of the dark came a tiny glowing blue light, swaying softly in the air. It seemed not to be aware of them as it came very near Vincent's face. The small creature created enough light that everyone could see Vincent's eyes and nose and lips. "You can be touched three times by a fire bug in an hour. Any more contact than that and your body will start to shut down."

"How do you know that?" asked Isabel, realizing that this

meant she could only be electrocuted twice more and she might have to be carried out of the Inferno — or maybe even die.

"Because I touched three of them on my first journey through here," said Vincent. "And it took me an entire day to recover. I felt then as I do now that if I'd touched another, it might have killed me."

Vincent blew softly into the air and the fire bug drifted off.

"You don't have to blow very hard to make them change course," said Vincent, moving again. "Just be careful you don't blow one into someone standing next to you."

"I wish I hadn't touched one," said Isabel. If Vincent could have seen her thick dark brows set low over her eyes he would have known just how upset she was with herself.

"You're the curious type, but maybe that's a mixed blessing. My guess is you're going to be *very* careful, aren't you, Isabel?"

Isabel had to admit to herself in the silence of her own fuming that Vincent was right. There was nothing that could make her voluntarily touch a fire bug ever again.

They walked on and soon blue fire bugs became more frequent, until somewhere along their journey they realized that they were no longer touching the walls for guidance. The light from the fire bugs was enough to illuminate the walls, the floor, the low ceiling. They were in what felt like an underground tube about the width of Vincent's outstretched arms. The ceiling was taller than the tallest among them — that being Sir William, at six feet — and the space had an unfamiliar feeling of being warm in a place that seemed as if it should be cold.

"Why is it warm in here?" asked Samuel. Isabel had let go

of his hand and was now blowing fire bugs to the side. They were everywhere, hundreds of them swinging slowly back and forth in the darkness.

"We're getting closer," said Vincent. "It will get even warmer." He blew fire bugs to the left and to the right, clearing a path for the rest as best he could.

"Get used to moving the fire bugs aside," he said. "Soon there will be thousands in the air all around you. It's only your skin you need to worry about, so stay covered up but for your face."

Isabel let her hair fall down in front of her eyes so that only her nose stuck out from her hair.

The bugs grew thicker and the way was bathed in fluorescent blue light. Samuel smiled at Isabel and she gasped at how white his teeth and eyes were. "You look weird," she said.

"So do you," said Samuel. If it weren't for Isabel's nose, he might have thought he was looking at the back of her head.

"You're going to want to touch the Rivers of Fire," said Vincent. "Don't touch them."

Samuel turned more quickly than he should have, and when he did there was a fire bug directly in his path. It landed on his cheek and the electricity shot through his face, down his neck, through his chest, and down his legs. He could not move and felt as if his insides were being torn apart until Isabel, cool-headed in the moment, took a section of her long hair and batted the fire bug away.

"Ohhhhhhh! That itches SO badly!" he howled. Isabel continued to blow a wide path of bugs away from Samuel as he jumped up and down, itching furiously. It looked like he might scratch right though his skin as Sir William held him steady and tried to calm him. A full minute passed before Samuel seemed to be able to continue on.

"Only four more fire bugs can land on the two of us," said Isabel. Secretly, she felt a little better that she was no longer the only one who had been touched.

"Like I said," said Vincent, seeing that the excitement had died down, "you're going to want to touch the Rivers of Fire you're about to see. Don't."

Everyone seemed to catch their breath at the same time as they rounded a jagged corner. Trails of an orange substance ran leisurely along the floor of the tunnel. They were the width of a child's outstretched hand, and they moved like they were made of something a thousand times thicker than water.

"It's something very much like molten glass," said Dr. Kincaid. "If you touch it, it will set your finger on fire."

He looked back at Sir William, who wore a robe dangling to the floor. Everyone else wore trousers and long shirts, but the robe would be a problem. "Do you have anything on under that?" asked Dr. Kincaid. "You're going to drag it into the Rivers of Fire and set yourself aflame."

Sir William was nervous about disrobing, not so much because he didn't have very much on underneath but because it would expose him to the fire bugs. Still, he saw the folly of walking along a path cut through with streams of molten glass—whatever that was—and so he took the robe off. Beneath it he wore a shirt with no sleeves, boots, and something that looked like a towel wrapped around his waist. He was about to toss the robe behind him when Dr. Kincaid suggested otherwise.

"You'll never make it past the bugs like that," he said, and he was right. As they stood, dozens of fire bugs sat on everyone's clothing or hair. Sir William would never make it without the robe.

"Hike up the bottom and hold on tight," said Dr. Kincaid. "You must now watch the floor as well as the air. Don't step in the Rivers of Fire."

The three who had never been through the Inferno now became fully aware of an odd, new sound that repeated all around them: *fffffzzzzzziiiip! fffffzzzzzziiiip! fffffzzzzzziiiip!* Samuel and Isabel asked what it was.

"Watch the floor," said Vincent. "And you'll see."

They watched as fire bugs dropped into the orange liquid and the *fffffzzzzzziiiip!* sound burst into the air. The Rivers of Fire were alive with electricity and heat, fed by the falling bugs.

"Follow my lead," Vincent said. "The fire bugs will thin out some, but don't take this as a sign that we should let down our guard. There are fewer fire bugs for a reason." He didn't know how else to prepare them for what would come next without scaring them. He walked on, knowing that at any moment it would happen. And so it did.

They had come upon a place where numerous holes—about as wide across as Samuel's head—pierced the floor between the flowing streams of orange glass. In a flash, something long and skinny, about the width of a man's leg, shot furiously out of the hole. With a hissing sound, it opened its mouth and flicked a glowing blue tongue into the open air. There was a *pop* as a fire bug touched the tongue and disappeared.

The beastly creature stood erect for a moment, then began slowly moving down again, turning its slick head from side to side. Despite its eerie blue eyes, there was no sign that it had noticed the people who had entered its domain.

"Cave eel," mumbled Dr. Kincaid. He had never gotten used to seeing them and his voice was ghostly.

"What's a cave eel?" asked Samuel.

"It eats fire bugs by the thousands," said Vincent. "You only get to touch a cave eel once. It's a quick death."

"This place makes no sense," said Sir William, flabbergasted by the bizarre and seemingly useless nature of his surroundings.

"Oh, but it does make sense!" said Dr. Kincaid. "Every living thing needs energy, especially in Atherton. The union of fire bugs and cave eels creates untold energy in the form of electricity and heat. This power made Atherton grow and evolve. The eels and the fire bugs are like a perpetual engine, don't you see? Together they *make* the Rivers of Fire. And these molten rivers run through the inside of Atherton, just as blood runs through the inside of *you*."

"Doctor!" cried Vincent. Dr. Kincaid could become talkative at the most inopportune moments. "This is no time for a scientific conversation."

Another cave eel erupted into the open air, then another.

They popped up about every ten seconds, then slowly crept back down again between the flowing orange liquid on the floor.

"You have to be kidding me," said Sir William. As if the horrific sight of cave eels weren't enough, Sir William was finally touched by a fire bug on an exposed ankle. Samuel brushed the robe along his legs and the bug was gone, but not until after Sir William let out a scream that nearly sounded like the Nubian. "I hate these bugs," he grumbled after the initial shock, trying desperately to remain calm for the sake of Samuel and Isabel.

"I know it seems impassable," said Vincent, trying to keep everyone's attention even as they were being electrocuted. "But you're wrong."

Vincent stepped out among the cave eel holes and waited. At the moment one shot up into the air next to him, Vincent moved along its side, careful not to touch it. "As long as you stay away from the holes and don't lose your nerve, everything will be fine."

With fire bugs in the air, Rivers of Fire at his feet, and holes that contained monsters with glowing blue tongues, Samuel thought it looked near impossible. "Dr. Harding was mad," he said. "Truly, truly mad."

Dr. Kincaid had the urge to explain how brilliant the Inferno was—that it really wasn't meant for people but that it had a marvelous purpose—but he held his tongue and followed Vincent's steps carefully. Vincent would guide Dr. Kincaid through the cavern first, then come back for the others.

The cave eel bay, as it was called, was only a hundred feet long. It was very well lit from all the glowing tongues, fire bugs, and radiant glass running along the floor in channels. He followed Vincent across the bay and felt the swish of a cave eel only once, very near to his arm. Soon Dr. Kincaid was at the other side and Vincent came back through for the others.

"I think it would be best to carry them," he said to Sir William. Isabel and Samuel exchanged a look that said this was a very bad idea.

"We'll be fine," said Samuel. "Isabel, you go with Vincent, and we'll follow closely."

Sir William felt this was probably the only way, so he nodded his agreement. Vincent took Isabel's hand and they began moving across the bay. There were dozens of holes, and all around her the cave eels were shooting up in search of fire bugs. The heads were dark grey and formless, like balled-up fists with luminous eyes and gaping mouths. Isabel wondered what a cave eel would think if she stepped over the top of one of the black holes.

They had come very near the other side when one of the cave eels—one that had already darted out of its hole and slid halfway down—shot back up into the air. When it flicked out its tongue, it missed the fire bug it was aiming for. The bug zipped toward Isabel's ear without her notice, and when it landed the shock went through her head, down into her arm, and into Vincent's hand. The two were being electrocuted by one tiny bug, and neither of them could bat the bug away.

Samuel saw what was happening and sprang forward, over the top of a black hole, and slapped Isabel in the side of the head before falling to the ground.

"Samuel, no!" cried Sir William. The bug was dislodged from Isabel's ear and danced off merrily as if nothing had happened. The cave eel from the hole that Samuel had just passed over shot up, barely missing him, but where Samuel lay on the floor of the tunnel left him in a very dangerous position. Samuel was snaked like an *S* around three of the holes, and his head was perilously close to one of the Rivers of Fire popping with electricity.

Dr. Kincaid hastened out into the bay and retrieved Isabel, carrying her to safety. But something about the way Samuel had moved over the hole had set off a reaction in the cave eel bay. All of the creatures came out at once, their tongues darting overhead madly and filling the space with what looked like a night sky full of blue candles, rising and falling in spasms of anger.

Vincent and Sir William carefully helped Samuel to his feet, blowing fire bugs to the side, and the three zigzagged their way the final few steps out of the cave eel bay.

"Is she all right?" asked Samuel. Sir William was on his knees hugging his boy mercilessly, telling him to please be more careful.

"I'm fine," said Isabel, though she was scratching her ear almost comically hard, her hair dancing around over her head with static electricity. They stood as a group looking back over the frenetic lights of the Inferno, wondering how they'd ever made it across.

"We made it!" cried Dr. Kincaid. "We're no longer under Tabletop. We're under the Flatlands now. The rest of the way is quick and easy. Soon we'll be outside once again!"

Everyone smiled, elated at the prospect of escaping the inside of Atherton. Even Sir William finally seemed convinced that these two men could be trusted.

Vincent had moved ahead of the rest to scout their way. And it was this fact that made what happened next possible, for Vincent would have been watching the group carefully.

While no one was paying much attention, a fire bug danced out of the bay all alone and landed softly on Isabel's hand, and she felt something deep inside that made her think she was about to die. This time she did not convulse at the touch of the fire bug. She only went limp, barely breathing at the edge of the Inferno.

CHAPTER 30
A THOUSAND CLEANERS

Within the throng of a thousand people living on Tabletop there were three who could not bring themselves to leave the grove. Nobody knew they had decided to stay, and with so much commotion it was easy to ignore the fact that these three were making preparations of their own.

Charles and Eliza, Isabel's parents, were two of the three. The other was Samuel's mother, Adele. The three of them had formed a tight bond over their common loss. None of the three had any interest in leaving the grove, because it was the only place where they felt Isabel and Samuel might return to, if they were to return at all.

It was Maude's husband, Briney, who was first to discover their plans. He came upon them fortifying one of the abandoned houses in the village.

"Charles?" interrupted Briney. Briney had come to like all three of them very much in the preceding days, and he felt terrible for their loss. "What are you doing out here all alone? We're about to leave."

"We're staying here," said Charles, lashing some boards together with twine made from the thin bark of the trees. "For when Isabel and Samuel come back."

Briney was fairly certain that neither of the children would return, that they'd been lost in the Highlands and could not have escaped the rising water. He felt he needed to speak the truth, but he didn't want to further discourage them.

Eliza could tell Briney was struggling with what to say. "It's all right, Briney," she said. "We know Isabel and Samuel might not come back. But they're all we have, and if there's even the smallest chance, we have to stay."

"But the Cleaners . . . ," protested Briney, yet knowing they would never listen.

"We appreciate your concern," said Charles. "But we're staying."

Briney couldn't help embracing all three of them, wishing them well, and telling them he didn't want to leave them behind.

"When they come back," said Briney, trying with all his might to encourage them, "race as fast as you can to the Flatlands. I'll be looking for you."

Adele, the quietest of the group, spoke up. "Go take care of Maude. She's going to need you."

"Maude is the stronger of us two," said Briney. "But you're

right, Adele. She does need me. I don't think she can keep going if we're not together to the end."

As Briney made his way back into the swarm of people preparing to leave, he felt they were like an army readying for a march into battle. There was an electricity about their movements, not desperate but purposeful, brought on primarily by Horace's leadership. It was true there was every reason to believe the day would hold death and destruction, but Horace led them straight and true and this made all the difference.

Before leaving, they lined the children and mothers up the very middle of the grove. In the paths between the trees next to the children, rows of men and women with supplies were positioned. After that came two long lines of men between the next row of trees, each with wooden spears. Through a final row of trees on both sides rode the remaining men from the Highlands on horses, ten on each side.

At the front of the procession were Horace, Maude, and Edgar, and at the back were a cap of twenty men prepared to fight off as many Cleaners as they could. Soon the party was moving, like a long arrow of humanity, steadfast on the outside, but delicate at its center.

Edgar was the first to sense something larger than a rumble from the Highlands and from the ground beneath their feet. "Something's changed," he said, walking alongside Horace and Maude. But then the feeling went away and he shrugged, though certain he'd felt a kind of swaying that he hadn't before.

Briney came alongside the group of three and told of Charles, Eliza, and Adele's decision to stay.

"I suppose we should have expected that," said Maude. "There's not much optimism for where we're going. At least if they stay, there's a chance Isabel and Samuel will come back."

"They're not coming back," said Edgar. "They're underneath the Highlands, just like the rest. None of them are coming back."

Secretly, Edgar felt terrible for not staying in Tabletop himself. Losing Samuel and Isabel was devastating in a way he'd never experienced before, and he didn't think he would ever make another friend. Even though something told him they weren't dead yet, in his mind he could only envision them trapped in the laboratory, waiting for the water to find its way in. The waves had been so powerful that he couldn't see any other outcome but that the water would crush them in the end, if it hadn't already.

"Don't be so glum," said Horace. "You said they weren't dead when you last saw them. Maybe they found some other way out. Best not to think terrible thoughts based on what you don't know."

Edgar didn't respond. His mind was distracted as they came to the edge of the grove, for the soft swaying had returned under his feet. He put his arms out in order to keep his balance, while rows of men on horses stumbled back and forth and others began to scream. The ground was soon moving like an earthquake, uprooting the larger trees in the grove and sending people scattering in every direction.

And then there came the sound of crashing waves, so loud it made them all turn back. They couldn't see anything through the trees, but if they could have, they'd have been aware that the water had suddenly risen the last hundred yards without warning. The waves had crested Tabletop, a thin film of water making its way into the grove.

The ground stopped moving, and with it the sound of crashing waves subsided. But in its place there came a new sound in the stillness of the air. It was the sound of breaking bones, coming from both sides of the grove, through the fallen trees that lay in tangled heaps along the ground. The thousand Cleaners had arrived.

"Go!" cried Horace. "We must run!"

It was harder going than it would have been before the trees were knocked down. About half of the grove was still standing, but the other half lay in disarray. Most people had to maneuver around countless obstacles, with the sound of breaking bones growing ever closer.

Gill was waiting on his horse as the people reached the edge of the grove and burst into the open. "Stay in formation!" he howled. "And follow those in front of you!"

The lines of people stayed together as best they could, following Gill's orders as he moved back and forth along the line. When half of the people had emerged from the grove, the sounds of war welled up and overtook the world of Atherton.

The Cleaners had come in from both sides, crawling hideously over one another in a rampage to reach the fresh food that lay hidden in the grove. They attacked as one powerful wave over the first line of defense—the riders on horses—and the men of the Highlands stabbed with spears, holding the beasts back. The Cleaners were momentarily surprised and reared back on one another, slashing for position, their anger flaring up into a violent rage of swarming for the front of the line.

It was a chaotic battle in which horses and men alike were felled. But miraculously, the line held as everyone within the arrow of humanity exploded up through the middle toward the end of the grove, charging with all their might. Yet the walls grew ever weakened by the violence outside.

Soon the second line of defense—the row of horseless men with spears—began to engage among the many who fought the Cleaners. A group of men, Horace among them, fell into position at the very back of the line to help the twenty who were already positioned there. Meanwhile, Maude had been ordered to take Edgar and escape the grove.

Soon all but the tail end of the line was free of the grove, moving quickly toward the Flatlands. Only Horace and thirty or so men remained, trying desperately to hold back the relentless tide of Cleaners.

And then, without warning, the ground began to shake once more as it had only moments before. More trees toppled over, pinning man and beast, and the Cleaners were thrown into confusion. They attacked one another, clamped down on the trunks of trees, rolled uncontrollably along the shaking floor of the grove.

When the quake subsided, the sound of crashing waves returned, louder than before. Something about the sound sent the Cleaners scattering in every direction. No longer were they interested in fighting and destroying. It looked as if they seemed not to know where to go and could only clang their terrible legs and teeth together senselessly.

"What's happening?" cried one of the men.

Horace didn't respond. Instead he roused the men, yelling for them to charge with everything they had left in them and to leave the grove with the rest of the group. And so they did.

When they emerged from the fallen trees they looked back and saw that nearly all of the trees in the grove had fallen over. Within the knotted roots and trunks the Cleaners that remained could be seen returning to the felled animals and people. They were, for the moment, satisfied with the bounty before them, uninterested in the idea of chasing after more that would take work to destroy. One of the horses, free of a rider, came bounding out of the trees and galloped at full speed toward the Flatlands, the only one lucky enough to emerge unharmed.

Looking past the Cleaners, Horace could see that the water was like a great lake of blue, frothing with whitecaps and spilling over into the far end of the grove. He worried about Charles, Eliza, and Adele, then turned and fled with the remaining men toward the Flatlands. Gill drew up alongside them on his horse in a state of panic. He had the additional horse that had escaped the grove attached to a rope.

"Hurry! Our time may be running out!" cried Gill.

"What do you mean?" said Horace. He'd run out of the trees so fast that he could barely breathe.

"We're sinking," Gill explained frantically. "Tabletop is sinking!"

Horace couldn't believe what he was hearing. He'd imagined it, but it came as a shock to find that it was actually true. He and Wallace had agreed—if the Highlands had fallen, why not Tabletop? "Are you sure?" he asked.

"I've ridden ahead and seen it with my own eyes!" said Gill. "It's already come down five feet or more. If we get another quake like that last one I'm afraid it will be too late. We'll be trapped."

This was the sort of motivation Horace and the men needed. In an instant they were charging for the edge of the Flatlands, glancing back as they went. Some of the Cleaners had moved away from the carnage and began pursuit. They were fast, maybe fast enough to catch them before they could get out, and Horace could not help thinking he'd made a mistake staying in the grove so long.

CHAPTER 31 THE FLOOD

While the people of Atherton raced for the edge of the Flatlands, chased by a growing number of Cleaners, another race was underway inside of Atherton. Isabel was barely breathing and Vincent had never felt so awful in all his life. He kept hearing a dreadful voice over and over in his head: *If she dies, it will be your fault. You will have failed her.*

He carried her as fast as possible, even running when he could catch his breath, along the path that led under the Flatlands. It was the most open and expansive part of the inside of Atherton, and very soon it would be the only place inside that could ever be reached again. As Tabletop sank, so went the way in which to find the Inferno, the Nubian, all of it. Those things would remain, but it was uncertain if humans would ever see them again.

The light remained, shooting up in fiery beams from the ground, and the mountains within Atherton rose all around them on every side. It was a stunning but desolate place, dry and lifeless, and yet it had an indescribable, haunted beauty.

Dr. Kincaid had tried to explain, to pass the time, that it was the Inferno that made light possible inside Atherton. The fire bugs, the cave eel, the flowing electric glass, all of it had something to do with how Atherton's underbelly was formed, how the sun could find its way through. He didn't claim to understand it, only that it was a delicate balance, and that all these things that were happening inside were important to what happened outside.

"How much farther?" interrupted Sir William. He and Samuel were keeping up better than Dr. Kincaid was, but Vincent was a remarkably fit leader. He had far more energy than all the rest, even while carrying a sixty-pound girl.

"If we go quickly and don't stop, only an hour. We have to get back to the rocks where Dr. Kincaid can help her before it's too late."

Sir William had already asked what Dr. Kincaid could do there that he couldn't do inside Atherton. He'd been told that there were certain medicines they should have brought along for just such an occasion, but that in their haste they'd left them behind. Dr. Kincaid had grave doubts, as did Vincent, that the medicine would do any good. Isabel was barely breathing and was cold to the touch. She might die at any moment.

When the first of the people from the grove arrived at the place where the Flatlands began, Horace knew the time had come to stop and face the oncoming massacre. He knew that if he didn't stop and convince the men who were with him to do the same, many more would be lost.

He beckoned the thirty or so men around him to stop, and to his great surprise they made no effort to dispute his idea. They knew, as Horace did, that the only way to get everyone out was to stay and fight, to create a diversion.

"You have done a great service to the living in Atherton," said Horace. "Generations will recall this moment. They will remember how you stood and fought a terrible enemy so that others could live!"

The men gathered around him and called out a great cheer. They had been chosen for reasons they did not know to stand between the forces of destruction and a peaceful people. They formed groups of four or five each, turned to the sound of breaking bones, and dived headlong into a sea of Cleaners, beating them back with ferocious resolve.

As fate would have it, Horace was one of the last to fall, and he was given the gift of seeing with his own eyes the children and sheep and rabbits being hoisted out of Tabletop and into the Flatlands, their little feet dangling in the air as they were yanked hard and fast into a new life he would never know. He knew as he passed that his family and the others would make it out of Tabletop.

Horace's eyes closed and he was at peace, a leader among

men, sleeping at last and searching on the other side for his good friend Wallace.

A small number of Cleaners bolted for the Flatlands, hearing the sounds of voices and seeing the immense quantity of food that lay in wait for them there. But they were greatly outnumbered and no match for the men and women who remained. The Cleaners were beaten back with flying rocks and spears by a great horde of humanity from above in the Flatlands. The few who remained in Tabletop were soon lifted out, and the whole race of men in Atherton pelted the Cleaners with weapons until they retreated out of reach.

A huge shout rang out as had never been heard in Atherton. It seemed that everyone who lived was shouting at once, raising their voices with anger at all that had been taken from them, and with joy at all they'd overcome.

And then, as if to show them who really was in charge, Atherton began to quake as it never had before. It rumbled so hard and fast that many next to the very edge almost fell back into Tabletop as it careened spectacularly downward beneath them. In moments, Tabletop went from being five feet below them to thirty.

With a falling Tabletop the water came over the edge of the Highlands. Like a monster it charged, washing over the grove and pushing all the trees and homes from the ground. The Cleaners could hear the water rushing for them, and they reacted by trampling over one another in search of the Flatlands. But finding the edge leading thirty feet up meant finding a wall they could not scale. They attacked one another and leaped into the air, snapping their teeth.

And the water kept rolling through, covering Tabletop in a thin layer that glistened in the sun.

When the quake quieted to a mere tremor, Maude searched through the throng of people, trying to find the one person who had been put in her charge. She had lost her grip on him at the edge of the grove and hoped he was near, in the swarm of children. But she was wasting her time. She was in a place that had once been the lowest place in Atherton but had been transformed into the highest. Looking down, she wondered where the boy had gone. And she was right to wonder, for Edgar had gone back to the grove.

The first wave came into the grove without warning, toppling over a few of the trees that were left standing and barreling through the doorways of the very few houses that hadn't fallen over. This came as a surprise to Charles, Eliza, and Adele. They'd been spared the coming of the Cleaners, who were drawn into battle with the departing horde of people, but the wave was only the first of many that were about to overtake them. They had not prepared for the eventuality of a flooded grove.

And so it was a very good thing that Edgar had been the first to realize what was happening and to turn back. Something deep inside him had taken over when the ground shook so violently that second time. He was the firstborn of Atherton, and maybe this gave him certain powers of perception about the place of his birth. He began to remember his dream of the night before, of the words Dr. Harding had said in the House of Power. Suddenly, he was sure that Tabletop would sink, that the water would come, and that Samuel and Isabel's parents would perish if he did not go back for them.

And there was another part of the dream that made him feel a peculiar certainty that Isabel and Samuel were in danger but still alive, that he would see them again. They, too, were children of Atherton. They were born here, and Edgar sensed them moving inside, as if trying to be reborn as Atherton was being reborn. He felt Atherton had brought him by this way for a purpose bigger than himself—to bring Samuel and Isabel's parents to the safety of the Flatlands or to die trying.

Edgar now had a little experience on the water and had an idea of what might keep them afloat if the water reached as high as he thought it might. The space of Tabletop was an enormous area to fill, but the water was already flowing so fast over the edges of the Highlands, Edgar thought all of Tabletop would have a layer of water upon it within minutes. After that, it was just a matter of how fast and how high the water would rise.

He jumped down out of one of the only trees that remained standing and landed in a foot of water at his feet. He lapped up handful after handful. Even in the face of escalating danger he could not help but quench his thirst. The water was pushing hard against his legs and another wave was rising out of the Highlands, threatening to bowl him over.

“Charles! Where are you?” he screamed as he made his way into what little remained of the village.

“We’re here!” cried Charles, stepping out of a door and onto a porch just as a five-foot-high wave slammed into the house. The wave knocked Charles and Edgar off their feet. Edgar had taken hold of a fallen tree with roots that were still lodged in the ground and he was sucked under the hanging branches. When he emerged, gasping for air, chunks of tree and house were floating all around him, threatening to hammer him unconscious.

Charles had recovered from the blast of water and retrieved Eliza and Adele from inside the house. When they came out, Edgar had made his way to the porch, and the four stood together as the water receded. Another wave out of the Highlands was building as the four braced themselves.

“After this one comes through, we need to run for it!” said Edgar.

“I’m not leaving here,” said Eliza. “Not without Isabel.” The wave struck the porch and the four held on tightly.

“I was wrong!” said Edgar. “She’s still alive, and so is Samuel! I’m sure of it. But we must go to the Flatlands! There’s no other way out for them or for us.”

Eliza and Adele were struck by the courage of this boy—how he had come back to get them—and as the water receded once more, they relented.

“How do we get out?” asked Adele, looking at Edgar and Charles, her wet hair hanging in strands before her face. “We have to find them!”

Edgar moved to the door of the house where water was standing two or three feet high. "We need a rope. A long one," he said.

"I have it!" hollered Charles. He had made a stash of provisions in the house and waded through the door looking for the rope he'd saved. "Here! Here it is!"

It was still wound tight and he threw it over his shoulder. When he came out the door he saw Edgar, Adele, and Eliza staring with horror at two Cleaners swimming through the water, their jaws chomping at the surface as they were propelled on flapping tails. They could swim surprisingly well. It appeared to come naturally to them.

The two Cleaners approached the porch, snapping their teeth as if laughing with glee.

"Hold on!" commanded Charles, and a moment later, the biggest wave yet smashed into the house and blew it over. The Cleaners were swept away, past Edgar and through the trees. Charles, Eliza, Adele, and Edgar screamed for one another as they were all pulled under and through the grove. None of them knew how to swim.

When the wave was gone, its power taken by the vast open space of Tabletop, three feet of water remained, a shifting lake that spread all through the trees. Edgar and Charles popped out of the water first, quite near each other, and to their left Eliza emerged drenched and coughing. Adele was nowhere to be found and they called out for her.

Edgar had quickly grown used to the feeling of water

around him, as if he were made for water in the same way he was made for climbing. He dived under, searching the fallen trees for any sign of Adele. He came up for air, went back down, and this time he saw her, trapped within the tangled roots of a third-year fig tree. She was not moving.

"Here!" cried Edgar, calling for Charles. He followed Edgar to the tree and the two dived under, releasing Adele's legs and hauling her to the surface. Her face had turned a shade of blue and she was cold all over. They didn't know how to help her.

"Put her over your shoulder," said Edgar. "We have to get out of this grove before it kills us."

Charles hoisted Adele up and her chest slammed into his shoulder, shooting water out of her lungs and mouth. Adele was a small woman, and as Charles moved, she bounced up and down, her chest pumping with air and pushing out water. Then, miraculously, she began to cough.

Charles placed her down in water that came to the tops of her legs and he lifted up her back. Soon, she was able to stand on her own and the group of four was moving fast out of the grove. The waves had stopped and the farther they went the lower the water became until it was splashing at their ankles and they were able to run once more.

At the edge of the grove, where the water was shallow, they encountered a Cleaner, staring them down. Its jaws were snapping wildly, but it was unable to move.

"What's happened to it?" asked Eliza.

"It must be the water," said Edgar. It seemed right to him

that Dr. Harding would plan it this way. Before them lay a Cleaner thrashing with rage and might, but its legs were gone and only the wild teeth and tail remained. The legs had retracted, leaving only small stumps that were too short to carry the Cleaner anywhere. It also appeared that the Cleaner was having some trouble breathing, as if being submerged in water had changed it into something entirely different. A sea monster lay before them, only it had been pushed out of the water and here it was, hopelessly stranded.

The group of four walked past the Cleaner as it snapped and tried to attack them, but it could not move to sink its awful teeth into a leg or an arm. It struggled to breathe as they made their way past, its middle heaving in and out.

"Can you keep running?" Edgar asked Adele.

"I think so," she answered. They began moving faster toward the Flatlands, looking in every direction for Cleaners as they went. At a dead run it would take them twenty minutes or more to get across, but even from where Edgar was he could see in the distance that Tabletop had moved down. How far, he couldn't say.

They saw no Cleaners as they went, but soon Edgar spotted them in a writhing pile at the edge of the Flatlands. He could make out the shapes of people above, hurling rocks down at hundreds of Cleaners. The Cleaners seemed intent on leaping and scratching at the wall, trying to get out, totally immersed in the effort of trying to exit Tabletop.

"They want out," said Charles. The group had come to a stop out in the open.

“They must know the water will change them,” said Edgar. “Maybe the change hurts.”

Eliza thought the whole messy business of Cleaners was sickening, and she made a sour face at the thought of these monsters transforming.

“We need to change course, stay wide of them,” said Charles. He had been able to keep the tightly wound rope over his neck and shoulder, and Edgar wondered aloud how long it was.

“I don’t know, maybe fifty feet,” said Charles.

“That will be plenty,” said Edgar, though he secretly knew that if Atherton began moving again the Flatlands might well rise quickly out of reach of a fifty-foot rope.

They set off at a run once more, taking a diagonal path to the Flatlands that led away from the thrashing pile of Cleaners. When they were but a few minutes from reaching the rising, jagged cliffs leading to the Flatlands, the ground began to sway beneath them.

“Don’t stop!” yelled Edgar. All of them were out of breath, but Edgar the least. He was a boy who had spent his life climbing to heights no one could imagine. He had boundless energy, and raced ahead of the rest at full speed.

“I’ll start up,” he hollered back at Charles, who struggled to go on. “You’ll need to throw me the rope.”

Edgar charged on as Atherton shook with the pains of birth—a new world being formed and shaped just as Dr. Harding had planned—and the Flatlands rose higher. When Edgar reached the wall, he climbed without delay, the stones rumbling in his hands as he went. Looking back, he saw waves ten times higher than the ones he'd endured in the grove. It was enough water to cover all of Tabletop, and Edgar knew he and the others must hurry.

The Cleaners became aware of the coming wave as Edgar had, and they scattered in every direction, searching for a way out. Some of them spotted Charles, Eliza, and Adele as the three darted for the wall. Charles removed the rope, seeing that the wall had risen to forty feet above, and he threw it to Edgar who hung high on the shaking wall.

It took two more tries, but Edgar finally caught the rope and began moving up at an astounding pace. From behind came the giant wave, and from the side came the menacing Cleaners looking for one last meal to devour.

"Throw the rope!" cried a voice from above. It was Gill, and others were with him. Edgar had come within five feet of the top as Atherton began to settle into a gentle quake. Edgar was unwilling to take a chance that they might miss the catch, so instead he kept the rope gripped firmly between his teeth and scaled the last of the wall in a matter of seconds.

Gill took the rope from the boy's mouth and hollered down. "All of you! Take hold!"

They had thought of going one at a time, but there was no way for that now. They would all have to take the rope at once and be hauled up. The wave was growing in speed and size as it came, cresting at twenty feet tall. The Cleaners were very nearly on top of them as Charles wrapped the end of the rope around himself, tying it tightly, then took one woman under each arm, holding fast and screaming into the air.

"Pull us up!"

Gill and ten other men were at the ready when Edgar gave the signal to pull on the rope. The boy couldn't help joining in the effort, all eleven people moving farther and farther from the edge, bringing with them a growing length of the rope. When they had most of the rope pulled up, everyone who had stood at the edge backed away, for the wave was about to strike the wall.

Edgar watched as the powerful wave slammed into the wall and white water shot high and fierce into the air. Then he ran for the edge, hoping against all hope that Charles, Eliza, and Adele had been able to hold on.

CHAPTER 32
EDGAR'S DEPARTURE

When Edgar arrived at the edge and looked down, he saw three battered and bruised people hanging soaked and gasping for air against the rocks. Charles had held on, but he was quickly losing his grip.

"I can't hold them, Edgar!" he screamed.

And there was more trouble than that. A second wave was forming that threatened to suck them out to the quickly forming sea below, and worse, the Cleaners were leaping out of the water all around them, snapping their jaws very near Charles's feet.

Edgar sprang into action, climbing down the side of the cliff without hesitation. When he arrived beside them, Adele put an arm around his shoulder and he winced in pain. But she was light, almost as light as he was, and he was able to take most of the weight from Charles.

"Gill! Pull us up!" cried Edgar. The rope began to move again, bringing the group of four within a few feet of the top, where they were grabbed and pulled into the Flatlands just before the second wave hit.

"Away from the edge!" said Gill. "This one's going to come all the way over!"

Charles helped Eliza, and Edgar tried his best to run with Adele as the wave crashed, sending a wall of water over the edge where it pounded into the Flatlands with a roar.

The water receded, leaving behind a half-dozen Cleaners that had been tossed over the edge, their legs already beginning to shrink inside them so far that they could hardly move. As they flailed on the ground, men with spears finished them off without difficulty.

It was then that Atherton began what would be its last quake. It was the longest of them all, though not as violent, and when it was over, everyone who remained walked to the new edge of the world and looked over in wonder. Tabletop was far below them, two hundred feet or more, and it was filling rapidly with water. Cleaners were jumping along the edge, getting accustomed to the fact that they were no longer land animals, but instead creatures of a great lake.

"I think the transformation of Atherton is very nearly finished," said Edgar. There was a ring of authority in his voice that even he didn't expect, but he was beginning to recognize his intuition about such things and to understand that somehow, some way, Dr. Harding had inexplicably connected Edgar to Atherton. Edgar now knew that the water would rise, but only as far as the edge, and then Atherton would be the way it was meant to be from the start.

Maude and Briney came up alongside Gill, looking beaten and tired. Briney had a bunny sack over his shoulder, filled with the very last of the rabbits.

"He's gone," said Maude.

Her words reminded everyone within earshot of Horace, their fallen leader, and a deep silence ensued. There was much to be celebrated, but a terrible price had been paid and it was beginning to sink in.

Edgar had endured tremendous hardship and loss along with everyone else, but it was he who was the first to begin thinking of a calmer future. "When you get your inn going again and there are rabbits running everywhere, will you cook me one that's crispy with fig dust?"

"I would if there were any figs to be had," said Maude. "But I'm afraid the grove was lost, and in all the chaos, no one thought to bring a fresh fig along for the journey."

Edgar dug down inside his shirt pocket and removed the chunk of Cleaner he'd been carrying around for the past two days. He unfolded wet leaves surrounding a clump of meaty green slime and, digging his fingers inside, he produced three soft but shiny figs. They were perfectly preserved as he'd known they would be. Dr. Harding had told him so in his dreams on that last night in the House of Power, and so it was.

"We can start a new grove," said Edgar. Gill was very pleased at the sight of the round figs covered in slime, and he took them from Edgar. A worker from the grove was called over and came near, retrieving the figs. Edgar watched as the man disappeared into a crowd of ogling people, and then he glanced to his right where he heard sheep. He counted five, along with a shepherdess who watched over them. And there were the two horses, held by one of the few men who remained from the Highlands.

"A male and a female?" asked Edgar.

Gill nodded with a smile. "A good bit of luck, don't you think?"

There was a group of men standing around one of the fallen Cleaners that had been thrown by the wave into the Flatlands. Edgar went to it and asked the people to step back.

"May I use your spear?" asked Edgar, gazing up at a man standing beside him. The man handed it over, and Edgar thrust it into the Cleaner's side four or five times in a small circle, then he handed the spear back again.

"Thank you," he said.

The man nodded and looked at Edgar as if he'd lost his mind, but Edgar knew what he was doing. He reached down and tore a chunk of the Cleaner free where he'd made the circle, and then he ate it. Everyone gasped in horror at the sight of the boy with green slime running down his chin.

"It tastes best if you cover the black with the green," said Edgar, recalling how Dr. Kincaid had showed him the best way to enjoy the remains of a Cleaner. He wiped his mouth and went for another chunk, holding it out to Gill who stood near.

Gill sniffed it warily for a long time, but his nose was the smartest part of him, and it was telling him that this revolting clump was something his nose wanted him to eat. And so he did, smiling at the sweet and salty taste in his mouth.

Edgar felt certain he'd made his point—that there was plenty of food to be had while they waited for more rabbits and sheep and figs—if only they could find a way to retrieve the Cleaners from the rising sea of freshwater. He surveyed everything before him, thinking of the long journey across the Flatlands that he was about to take.

"I think we've got all we need to start again," said Edgar. "It will be nice to have so much water for a change."

Charles, Eliza, and Adele were sitting down, sorely beaten by the events of the day, and in no shape to make a long trek across a deserted land.

"There's someplace I need to go," said Edgar. "I'll be gone for at least a day, maybe longer, but I need to go alone. I'm not sure what I'll find there."

"I'll go with you," said Gill. He was not as accustomed to Edgar's secret ways as some of the others had become, and he didn't want to let the boy go wandering around without protection.

"You're needed here," said Edgar, reaching out for the spear that Gill held in his hand.

"What if you find Cleaners out there or some other terrible enemy?" said Gill, sniffing the air in search of something unexpected.

“All the Cleaners are gone,” said Edgar. “There’s nothing left to harm us except ourselves.”

Gill understood the meaning of what Edgar was saying. There were four groups of people together that would need to work together as one to survive, and without Horace to lead them it might not take long for them to begin fighting over supplies and territory. He handed Edgar the spear and started back toward the others to begin the hard work of making a new home. Only Maude and Briney remained.

“You sure about this, Edgar?” asked Briney.

“He’s sure,” said Maude. “Come on. Let’s go find a good spot to build an inn for you to run.” She looked off toward the shepherdess and said something to Briney she’d been thinking for a while. “I wonder if she would teach me how to tend sheep.”

“I bet she would if you showed her how to cook a rabbit,” said Briney. He was happy to see Maude’s interests leaning toward quieter things. The two moved off, and for a moment Edgar stood alone, trying to get his bearings. A much younger boy of five or six ran up and handed him a piece of Cleaner and a jug of water.

“This *is* good!” said the boy, stuffing another piece of the slimy meat into his mouth.

“I’m glad you like it,” said Edgar, taking the meat and the jug.

“The water is rising fast,” said the boy. He was afraid of being washed away or of being eaten by a Cleaner. “Are you sure it won’t come any higher than the edge?”

Edgar's gaze shifted to the giant hole leading down into Tabletop. It was outrageous, the idea that the grove was under water and he would never see it again. His old home had vanished.

"I met the man who made this place," said Edgar. "And he told me the water would never reach the Flatlands. You're safe here."

The child beamed and this made Edgar very happy. He watched the little boy run back into the sea of people, and then without any more hesitation he started on his way toward Dr. Kincaid's home.

CHAPTER 33
REUNITED

It was a long walk across the vast Flatlands, even longer than Edgar remembered, and the day was nearing its end when he arrived at the towering rocks that surrounded Dr. Kincaid's home. He found his way to the pile of boulders that blocked the path, climbing over and down the other side. When he rounded the last turn of the old trail and came to the table where he'd first eaten black and green, he expected to see the old man sitting there. But the chairs were empty and the place had a desolate feeling of having been left behind.

Edgar crossed to the opening of the cave and peered inside. It was dark, but not pitch-black, and this made him think that maybe Dr. Kincaid's home wasn't entirely empty after all. He went inside, calling Dr. Kincaid's name.

"Edgar?" It wasn't Dr. Kincaid, but another voice that Edgar knew. It was a voice that made him dash into the cave to the familiar place where he had once laid with an injured shoulder and a severed finger. Around the very same bed stood Vincent, Sir William, Dr. Kincaid, and the boy who had spoken Edgar's name. Samuel cried out Edgar's name again and bolted from the group, embracing his friend.

There were hoots and hollers from both boys at the sight of each other. Vincent, Dr. Kincaid, and Sir William came over to the two excited boys and joined in the celebration, laughing and patting them on the back.

"Where's Isabel?" asked Edgar. "I want to see her!"

The laughter died down faster than it had begun and Edgar knew something was wrong. He didn't wait for the men to stand aside. Instead, he burst right through them toward the bed.

There, cold and unmoving, was Isabel. Her face was white and her eyes were closed.

"She's not gone," said Dr. Kincaid, coming up beside Edgar. "She's still alive."

"What's happened to her?" he asked. "Will she wake up?"

Dr. Kincaid was worried she might not, but he wasn't going to tell Edgar, at least not yet. "She's been through an awful trauma, but there's a chance she'll recover."

The men and boys stayed at Isabel's side and talked in whispers of what had happened to them. Edgar had to tell them that Dr. Harding was dead, and Horace, too, but that he'd managed to save Samuel's mother and Isabel's parents. Sir William and Samuel explained how they'd been reunited, their excitement over hearing of Adele's safety overshadowing the losses of the day.

"Did the water rise as he said it would?" asked Dr. Kincaid. He was very curious about the things Dr. Harding had told them in Edgar's absence.

"Why, yes, it did," said Edgar. "How did you know from way out here?"

"I have my ways," said Dr. Kincaid, and then Vincent hit him in the arm.

"He's an old fool," said Vincent, then he asked Edgar a question of his own. "And the Cleaners? What happened to them?"

Edgar took great joy in telling them all that they would never have to worry about Cleaners again. They talked for a long while, and Edgar was able to hear about how they had escaped the Nubian and the Inferno, how they'd come all the way under the Flatlands and through a yellow door hidden in the cave. After a long while everyone but Vincent went out to the table for a moment of fresh air.

"How big are the mountains inside?" asked Edgar, thinking they might be the last place on Atherton where he might find good climbing.

"*Very* big," said Dr. Kincaid. "But you'll have to kill me to get the letters that will open the yellow door." He was determined to keep Edgar safely away from the inside of Atherton.

A brief moment of silence was broken as a steady noise emerged from far away, faint at first, but growing louder until it was unmistakable. It was the sound of horses' hooves, from more than one horse.

"Who could that be?" said Dr. Kincaid. The group ran down the path to the pile of rocks and Edgar quickly climbed to the top. On the other side, in the grey light of early evening, stood two horses. Gill was riding one, with Adele on the back. On the other were Charles and Eliza.

"Give a horse a little Cleaner meat and they perk right up," said Gill, smiling broadly.

"How did you find me?" said Edgar.

Gill tapped his enormous nose on one side. "Never underestimate the power of my snout."

Charles rolled his eyes. "We watched you leave. You were heading like an arrow in one direction, and it wasn't hard to pick up your trail. Why did you come here?"

Before Edgar could open his mouth, Samuel and Sir William joined him on top of the pile of rocks. The resulting celebration was one that Edgar would never forget. After everyone briskly dismounted, Gill and Charles hoisted Adele up to the rocks where she threw her arms around Sir William and Samuel. Adele was so unexpectedly overcome by seeing Sir William again that she danced and cried and laughed all at once.

Soon enough, Charles, Eliza, and Gill had climbed up as well. They didn't want to disturb the festive atmosphere, but they had come for another reason.

"Where's Isabel?" asked Charles.

It was Dr. Kincaid, waiting below, who answered. "Let's see if we can't get everyone down from there and over to this side," he said. "Edgar, you could be of some help, couldn't you?"

After Edgar had shown everyone the easiest way down from on top of a big pile of rocks, Eliza asked again, "Have you seen my daughter? Do you know where she is?"

Dr. Kincaid came alongside the two parents and guided them around the path toward the table and chairs. He was pulling on his droopy earlobe, trying to figure out how to explain that Isabel was there but might not make it through the night. When he was just opening his mouth, the two parents bolted from his side and ran toward the table without warning. For sitting there, along with Vincent, was Isabel.

"You're all very, very loud," she said. "You woke me up."

Everyone gathered around her — first her parents and then Edgar, Samuel, and the others. She was alive! And the color was already returning to her face.

The whole group talked about all that had happened, and after a while they laid under the stars, whispering to one another about the inside and the outside of Atherton, about Dr. Harding, about water and Cleaners. Until all at once they felt the end of a great adventure come upon them, and they were tired beyond words. Everyone fell asleep, and they slept well, knowing they'd made their peace with Atherton and its maker.

CHAPTER 34
ONE YEAR LATER

Anyone who might have arrived a year after the brief but catastrophic period of changes on Atherton would have assumed it had always been this way. The idea of three towering lands, each one reaching higher in the air, would have been absurd.

There would come a time, much later, when the children of Atherton would debate whether or not any of it had ever happened.

Such is the way of civilization in any form, and Atherton's small footprint in the universe would be no different. There would be talk of the Dark Planet and the strange shape of Atherton in the past, of great battles and heroes. But much of it would not be believed, and the daily movements of life would wash away all memory in the same way that places like the grove and the House of Power were lost forever.

But for now, everyone remembered. There were those who wrote things down in journals and drew pictures of lost places they could only visit in their minds. And yet so much of what had been lost had come back in almost exactly the same way. Thousands of fragments of uprooted fig trees had been pushed to the edge of the great lake in the middle, where they were harvested, dried out, and used to build anew.

There were three new villages, though they were much closer together now, within an easy walk of each other. There was a new inn at the Village of Rabbits, cobbled together from debris washed ashore. It was known not only for exceptional, fire-roasted "hoppers," as Briney had come to call them, but also grilled Cleaner, a specialty that made for long lines in the evening hours. Maude walked every morning to the Village of Sheep nearby, and she tended the lambs. Horace had not been given the chance to take Wallace's advice, but somehow, without hearing it firsthand, Maude had learned the shepherds' ways by watching. All her anger and frustration was gone, and in its place a quiet and increasingly wise woman remained.

The Flatlands were fertile with the addition of water, and a large grove that had been planted with seeds from Edgar's three figs was thriving. There were rows and rows of new saplings, and every day Edgar and Isabel tended to them with great care. The two were increasingly close to each other, and there were certain expectations on Atherton about them that neither Edgar nor Isabel minded very much. Samuel was their constant companion, learning about the grove and in turn teaching both of them to read and write.

Very few men of the Highlands survived the two exoduses, first from their home in the sinking Highlands and then from the coming of the Cleaners. In the end, it was they who saved everyone else, led by one of their own on horses only they knew how to control well enough to fight with. They had ruled over everyone for a long time, but in the end, Atherton had taken them.

Some would say Atherton had punished them for their earlier misdeeds; others would say this was an idea born out of a long-simmering jealousy of the luxuries those in the Highlands had enjoyed for so long. But the truth could not be denied—the biggest loss of life had come from those in the Highlands, and the survivors were safe because of what they'd done. There were few who could look at the wives and children of those men who were lost and not feel the weight of the price that had been paid.

The water had stopped rising at the edge of the Flatlands as Edgar said it would. At night it looked as if the lake was lit by a deep and hidden inferno blazing somewhere beneath the surface. And so it was that it came to be known as the Lake of Fire, a place of darkness fused with light. No one could look at the Lake of Fire and not think of what lay beneath, but only the diving Cleaners could see those things now—the House of Power, the grove, the other villages.

It was on just such a night that Vincent and Dr. Kincaid stood on a wide and sturdy pier built from parts of houses that had come ashore. They stood together, Vincent with a spear tied to a rope and Dr. Kincaid watching intently.

“Here comes one now,” said Dr. Kincaid. “Don’t miss this time.”

“Why don’t you go back home and read a book,” said Vincent. “You’re making me nervous.”

Dr. Kincaid laughed. He didn’t want to go read a book. He wanted to bother his closest friend while the man tried to catch a fish.

“You’re going to miss it,” said Dr. Kincaid.

“No, I’m not,” said Vincent.

The swimming Cleaners were not the smartest of creatures, and so they really weren’t that difficult to kill. A well-thrown spear attached to a rope was the easiest way to land one. After that all you had to do was haul it in and club it over the head a few times and you could feed a great many people for several days.

Vincent threw the spear fast and hard toward the shadow beneath the surface and the shadow moved off. He had missed.

“Told you,” said Dr. Kincaid.

Vincent sighed and reeled in the line, searching the water for another try.

“There was a time I thought Dr. Harding was mad to bring people here before it was finished,” said Dr. Kincaid, turning to deep thoughts as he often did when the two fished together at night. “But that time has passed. I think we were needed, just as the Inferno and the Nubian and everything else was needed. He knew. The birth of Atherton had to include people, or it wouldn’t have worked. I’m sure of that now.”

“Why do you say such ridiculous things?” said Vincent.

"Because that's what men of science are best at," said Dr. Kincaid. "It's not ridiculous to me, only to people who lack the intellect to understand. I feel sorry for you."

Vincent rolled his eyes. "All right, if you're so smart, you catch a fish," he said, holding the spear out to Dr. Kincaid. The old man looked at the weapon and then at the glowing blue water filled with shadows.

"If I were to catch one, it might do irreparable damage to your self-worth. I can't risk that."

Vincent laughed and went back to his work of watching for a shadow close enough to hit.

Gill and Sir William walked up behind them and onto the pier, where Gill sniffed the air and knew without looking that Vincent had yet to catch a Cleaner.

"Slow going tonight?" he asked.

Vincent scowled. "We only started a few moments ago. Give me a little more time."

Sir William smiled, then turned to Dr. Kincaid. "Have you seen Edgar?" he asked. "He didn't show up for his riding lesson today."

Sir William had taken to watching over the boy in the absence of a father, and Dr. Kincaid had very much appreciated it. Dr. Kincaid fancied himself more the grandfatherly sort and liked having Sir William there to help with the boy.

"Come to think of it," Sir William added, "have you seen Samuel or Isabel? All three of them have been mysteriously absent all day."

"Vincent?" said Dr. Kincaid. "You don't suppose . . ."

Vincent nodded knowingly, and then went back to his fishing.

"Those three have overcome the inside and the outside of Atherton. I think they'll be fine."

Dr. Kincaid pulled on his earlobe and gazed thoughtfully over the glowing water. Then he turned back to Sir William.

"You can trust Edgar," he said. "He knows how to take care of them."

Sir William nodded and felt reassured. He had finally come to trust the old man of Atherton.

Edgar was the first to go right up to the edge. He had done it once before and knew that gravity had a powerful effect this close to the rim of Atherton. Samuel and Isabel weren't sure. It felt strange, the way Atherton pulled on their feet and almost dragged them to the very end. Edgar had crawled over, but now he swung around and dropped his legs over the side of the world, feeling them pull in as if his feet were tied to strings and someone was gently drawing them near the bottom of Atherton.

"Come on, you two," said Edgar. "Just crawl over like I did. You won't fall off."

Isabel's thick black brows moved lower over her eyes and Edgar thought, as he often did recently, that she was a pretty girl. He especially liked that her skin was darker than his and that her hair was pitch-black. And he liked her nervous smile when she was afraid but excited to try something new. She had just such a smile on her face as she began crawling toward Edgar with Samuel close behind.

When she arrived and hung her legs over the edge it took her breath away. The fear of sitting on the very edge of Atherton gripped her, but Edgar held one of her hands firmly and she felt better. It was exhilarating to lean slowly out and look at the stars and the Dark Planet below.

Samuel came up next to Isabel and let his legs dangle over. He was nervous and scared but also thrilled to have finally come to a place they'd spoken of often.

"I've thought of climbing down there," said Edgar. "To see what it looks like."

"That would be a terrible idea," said Isabel, sure that it was only a matter of time before he tried.

"I know a place where the climbing is quite good," said Samuel.

"I know it, too," said Isabel.

"The inside," said Edgar. "I know all about it. Why must you torture me?"

Dr. Kincaid and Vincent were the only ones who knew the eight letters that would open the yellow door into Atherton, and they were unwilling to let the secret out.

"One of these days he'll tell us," said Edgar. "He has to."

For now it was good enough to sit at the edge of the world and look out with two friends. He thought back to a time before he'd come to know them, and there was a pang inside him as he remembered how truly lonely he had been.

"We should be getting back," said Edgar.

“Just one more minute,” said Isabel, those piercing dark eyes locked on Edgar.

“All right, a little longer.”

The three friends sat close, laughing and talking quietly, their legs swinging happily over the edge of the world as they talked of all that had happened and all that was to come on the world of Atherton.

Edgar turned quiet and thought about how he’d been *made*, not born like his friends. He didn’t really understand this, but he thought of it often. Edgar and Atherton had both been made by the same creator. He felt more than ever that Atherton really was made for him alone, at least at the beginning, and that Dr. Harding had loved him enough to build a world for him, to shield him from life on the Dark Planet. He had made the place, then the boy, but in Dr. Harding’s mind Edgar had always been first and foremost.

Edgar’s thoughts turned to a place he didn’t often let himself go. Had the making of Atherton driven Dr. Harding mad, or was it something else, something more painful? It didn’t seem to Edgar that making a place could cause such trauma, but that making a person might. It was sad for a boy to think such thoughts, but Edgar couldn’t help it. He felt more and more certain that what had driven Dr. Harding crazy wasn’t losing Atherton but losing the son he’d made to inhabit Atherton.

“We’d better go,” said Samuel, stirring Edgar from his thoughts. “It’s a long walk.”

Isabel looked at Edgar and saw that he was feeling a little

sad, so she did the kind of thing she always did, the kind of thing that made Edgar like her so much.

"I bet I can sling a fig farther out into space than you can."

Edgar gazed out into the stars. "No, you can't. I'm stronger than you."

The two crawled away from the edge with Samuel, who was given the task of determining the winner. Slings were produced along with one black fig each, and the empty space of the Flatlands filled with a whirling sound made by two children of Atherton.

And then they let the figs go—*snap! snap!*—and they watched as the black figs flew straight and true. When the figs were a little way out over the edge, they turned down sharply, pulled toward the Dark Planet by the force of gravity.

"It's a tie," said Samuel. He began walking toward the villages, knowing his judgment would not stand.

"That was no tie," said Isabel. "Mine went farther."

"Mine's on its way to the Dark Planet," said Edgar. "It was definitely the faster of the two."

The three children argued as they went, and Isabel was pleased that she'd turned Edgar's mind away from the quiet thoughts he wouldn't tell her about. She wondered if Edgar would ever share what had really happened to him during his time alone with Dr. Harding. Isabel could only say for sure that the spirit of the boy who held her hand was deeper than all the rest. She somehow felt, as all the other children born on Atherton did, that without Edgar, Atherton itself would grow lonely and die.

These were strange thoughts, but walking together with her friends and feeling the calm of Atherton all around her, Isabel was at peace. They walked on, staring up into a sky that used to hold their home and the homes of others, and the three of them were happy.